# London Calling

# Books by Deborah Grabien

## The JP Kinkaid Chronicles

Rock and Roll Never Forgets
While My Guitar Gently Weeps
London Calling
Graceland *
Book of Days *
Uncle John's Band *
Dead Flowers *

## The Haunted Ballads

The Weaver and the Factory Maid
The Famous Flower of Serving Men
Matty Groves
Cruel Sister
New-Slain Knight

## Other Novels

Woman of Fire
Fire Queen
Plainsong
Dark's Tale

* *forthcoming*

# London

# Calling

Book #3 of the JP Kinkaid Chronicles

## Deborah Grabien

**Plus One Press**

*San Francisco*

This is a work of fiction. All of the characters, organizations and events portrayed in this novel are either the products of the author's imagination or are used fictitiously.

Plus One Press

www.plusonepress.com

Book Design by Plus One Press

Cover Photograph by Michael Klenetsky
www.MK.FotoTime.com

Publisher's Cataloging-in-Publication Data

Grabien, Deborah.
    London calling : book #3 of the JP Kinkaid chronicles / Deborah Grabien.—1st. Plus One Press ed.
        p. cm.
    ISBN: 978-0-9844362-0-0
    1. Rock Musicians—Fiction. 2. Musical Fiction. 3. Murder—Fiction.
4. Film Festivals. 5. France—Fiction. 6. Racism—France. I. Title.
II. Title: London calling
    PS3557.R1145 L66 2010
    813'.54—dc22
                                                        2010905026

First Edition: August, 2010

10 9 8 7 6 5 4 3 2 1

*For every musician who's ever rocked*
*against racism, stupidity and intolerance*

# Acknowledgements

A special thanks to Jay Thomson, Gene Clark, Mark Jacobs, Craig Juan, Mike Urbon, Rudi, Bob Minkin, and you know who else, for providing me with the soundtrack by which I was able to write this series.

Also thanks to Amelia Davis and Bonita Pasarelli of MSFriends / Rock for MS, and to the memory of the extraordinary Godfather of Rock Photography, Jim Marshall.

# London
# Calling

# *Prologue*

## May, 2006

*"(beep) You have reached the voicemail of Patrick Ormand, San Francisco Police Department, Homicide."*

"Oh, bloody hell!" He couldn't be away from his desk—not possible. It was a cop shop; wasn't there always someone there? Shit, shit, shit. Where the hell was everyone? "Come on, mate, pick up the damned phone, come on...."

*"If you need immediate assistance, or wish to report a crime in progress, please hang up and dial 911."*

"I don't need 911, you berk!" Christ, I was losing my mind, shouting at a recorded voicemail message to a mailbox nine hours away. Where the hell was Patrick? Typical of him; when all I wanted was a bit of privacy and some peace, he was all over the place, digging in the dirt, and giving me nightmares. When I actually did want a word with him, he'd gone walkabout. "Why the fuck aren't you at your desk, you useless git? Just pick up the phone!"

*"To leave a message on this machine, please press one."*

I shifted the phone from one hand to the other. My hands were sweaty and shaky, and it wasn't all because of the weather. Not that the South of France wasn't nice and warm in May, but this was nerves, and worry, and fear for my wife's safety. It was also the first ominous twinges of my multiple sclerosis, threatening to stage its own little meltdown. Bad timing.

Not to mention frustration. I mean, it wasn't as if I'd wanted to call Patrick Ormand in the first place, you know?

*"To have this call forwarded to my cell phone, please press seven three six, followed by the pound key. (beep)"*

Thank Christ. I fumbled the number in, pressed the pound key, and waited. One ring, two rings....

He picked it up on the third ring, and I let my breath out. I hadn't even realised how tense I'd gone, until I actually did relax, and my knees went out from under me. Luckily, there were chairs and chaises scattered about, next to the pool. Our hired villa wasn't short on places for people to park their bums.

"Patrick Ormand speaking." He sounded peculiar, rather groggy. "Hello?"

"Christ, there you are. Finally. This is JP Kinkaid. I need help." There was a glass of orange juice on the little iron table next to Bree's usual chair. She'd left it there when the local cops had come and taken her off. My throat was tight. "You all right, mate? You sound strange."

"Well, I was asleep." He was sounding more like himself, right down to that slightly amused note that always made me want to bash him, the smug bastard. "It's ten past four in the morning. What kind of help? And where are you calling from?"

I'd forgot all about the time difference—that is, I'd remembered it, but hadn't connected it to him not being awake, or at his desk. I probably ought to have felt guilty about waking him, but sod that; he'd been awake at four in the morning often enough when we'd first had to deal with him, and he could bloody well be awake now. It wasn't as if he hadn't cost me some serious kip in his time.

"Sorry." I shifted the phone from hand to hand. "I'm calling from the South of France—our villa in St. Raphael. Look, I'll keep this short, yeah? We're here—the whole band, I mean, Blacklight—because we're supposed to be playing a sold-out show at Frejus tonight. The Cannes festival begins tomorrow. We came to promote a film we were in, made back in the late seventies, by a bloke called Sir Cedric Parmeley. Got it so far?"

"Blacklight, gig, film, legendary director who must be about a hundred years old by now. Yes, I've got it so far." He was taking notes, maybe just in his head, but there was no way he wasn't getting this down somewhere. He never missed a detail. "Go on, JP. What's the problem?"

"The problem is that someone firebombed Parmeley's villa early this morning. It was unbelievable—you could see it all over the south coast. No idea what they used, but whatever it was, the place went up like a Guy Fawkes display—sorry, right, make that a July Fourth fireworks thing, or whatever works for you. They found two bodies in the rubble, badly burnt. It looks to be Parmeley and one of his bodyguards."

I stopped, and swallowed hard. The picture was too fresh in my head: the local cop in charge, Mac ringing up to tell me Dom had been taken off in handcuffs, and Bree....

"JP?"

"Yeah, still here. There was a dustup at a private party Parmeley gave for the band, a few nights ago. I don't really want to go into it, not right now, but his bodyguards went up against Dom— Domitra Calley, you remember her, Mac's bodyguard? Two to one, not a fair fight, and Bree got involved."

"Well, that's not too surprising, is it?" There was something in Ormand's voice besides attention; it sounded like admiration. Bloody wanker. "I mean, your wife doesn't make any secret of the fact that she thinks loyalty is a good thing."

"Trust me, I'm aware of that. I damned well ought to be." My voice was starting to get ragged. The fucking clock was ticking away, and my wife…. "That firebombing. They found a third victim—the bodyguard Bree nailed—on the grounds of the villa, half dragged under a bush. The cops say he was knocked out with a kick to the jaw, and then his throat was cut."

I stopped. My voice was all over the place, up and down, edge of complete flipping out. I tried to steady it, breathing the way I'd breathe if something had triggered my heart, with its prolapsed valve, into arrhythmia. After a few deep breaths, I'd got it under better control.

"The cop, the local Inspector in charge, he's a Corsican called Santini—total wanker, speaks perfect English, but won't. It's pure spite. He came by about half an hour ago, with a little sidekick of his. Mac rang me up, just before Santini got here—he was down at the Les Sirènes sur Mer cop shop, because they'd taken Dom off in handcuffs. They said they were charging her with collusion, or conspiracy, or something."

I stopped for breath. I was panicking, or trying not to. My heart rate was all over the place. "Patrick, they've taken Bree off. No cuffs, possibly because she's my wife, rather than an employee, or maybe because Bree's white. It's bullshit, and Santini knows it. The fucker's in on it. He wasn't even bothering to put up a front, you know? No real reason given."

"Not good." No amusement, not anymore. "This is really not good. It sounds like a mess. Anything else?"

"I think they're trying to make a case that Blacklight's involved somehow, the whole band. I've got no clue what they're on about. I can't get any answers. They're insane."

4

Right. It was about to get tricky. The worst he could do was to say no. Of course, if he did, I was personally going to fucking kill him. I took a good long breath.

"Bottom line is, they've arrested Dom and Bree on murder charges. The cops are claiming they did it together—collusion. They won't say collusion in what, though. They took Bree off about twenty minutes ago. Patrick, there's something going on here, something huge, and I don't speak the language. I need help. We need help."

He was wide awake now. "Jesus. All right. What is it you think I can do for you?"

I'd known that was coming. Somewhere at the back of my mind, I'd been hoping he might offer on his own, but of course, being Patrick Ormand, he had to make me beg. Bastard.

But I had a card to play, one card, and I played it. If I'm being honest, here, I'll admit that I'd rather have rolled around naked in broken glass.

"Take a week off work. Bree needs help. Dom needs help. They're in the Les Sirènes sur Mer lockup on murder charges. We've got our corporate lawyers on it, but I want someone with legal cred in our corner."

I could hear myself, the control slipping just enough, urgency and panic beginning to take over. Mac was down screaming at the cops, ringing up the British consulate, and I was up here, about to completely flip my shit. "Take a week off and come out here, next available flight. We'll book you, everything first-class—I'll ring up Carla Fanucci. You've met her a few times, at gigs. She'll handle everything, the plane, whatever it takes. We'll pay you for any lost time from your job, double, triple, whatever it takes. You used to work drugs, and we're ten minutes from Marseilles. You still work murder. We don't know what might be involved, but we need someone on our side, someone with a badge, someone who can work it. I need my wife."

5

I swallowed, hard. He wasn't saying a word, not a single bloody word. He was going to make me ask him, formally, officially. And of course, there wasn't a damned thing I could do, else. I couldn't have done it, not for anyone but Bree, but I asked him.

"Will you help us?"

Not a good moment, really. This wasn't going to stand out as one of the picture-postcard moments of this trip. And he was taking too long to answer. I remembered that sadistic streak of his, all too well. Smug bloody bastard.

"Call Carla." He sounded completely himself now, a touch of predator in his voice. This time, I was damned glad to hear it; there was no way it was aimed at us. "Tell her any time after about eleven this morning should be fine. I'll need to hand off two cases I'm working on, but they're both in the bag, it's just a matter of getting my assistant into the loop. I need to let the commissioner know, and I have to call a friend of mine at Interpol. Things are a lot more complicated than they were back before 9/11, but I've still got buddies there and I can arrange for official credentials. Tell Carla eleven. I can get on the first flight out after that."

"Right."

I closed my eyes for a second, because they were stinging. When I opened them again, there was Bree's abandoned glass of orange juice, and the sun was warm, and her chair was empty. And suddenly, there were tears on my face and I let them come, let the pain and the panic into my voice, and I stopped caring whether Patrick Ormand heard it or not. "Thanks, mate. Bree'll be glad to know you're on the way."

# Chapter One

## February, 2006

*"(beep) Thank you for calling. You have four unheard messages. First message, sent today at eight fourteen a.m. To listen to your messages, press star...."*

Some days, you just don't get to hear what you want to hear, or do what you want to do.

It was pouring outside, absolutely pissing down rain. That's normal for San Francisco in early February; we get these endless El Nino winters, day after day of steady miserable downpours, where hillsides wash away and posh homes slide into huge sinkholes and people start thinking right, maybe the Druids were wrong and the sun's not coming back after all.

By the time winter hits February, the days seem about two hours long and it's dreary as hell. These are the days when anyone in their right mind stays indoors, doing whatever makes them happy.

Actually, the two things that make me happiest are music and my wife, but doing either of them before breakfast isn't really an option these days. Multiple sclerosis has a habit of kicking in hardest first thing in the morning, or at least mine does. And I'm not really functional before coffee and a look at the newspaper anyway, you know?

"Crap." Bree was sitting opposite, doing two of the things that make her unhappiest: paying bills and balancing the chequebook. She wasn't actually talking to me, just muttering. She does that when she's coping with money. "What's wrong with these people? Why hasn't the damned thing cleared? I sent it a week before Christmas—it was supposed to buy food over the holidays. What kind of idiot sits on a charitable donation instead of cashing it?"

"(beep) JP? It's Ian Hendry. Listen, I've got sad news—Chris Fallow died last night. Meg rang up, says she was with him, he just went out nice and peaceful in his sleep. The funeral's on for next Monday; we're hoping you can make it. (beep) To save the message, press one…."

"Oh, damn it!"

"What's up?" Bree looked up at me, saw my face, and closed the chequebook in a hurry. "John, what's wrong?"

"Chris Fallow's gone." Damn. This was going to hit Mac and Luke really hard; they'd known him back when they were still a sort of blues-folk duo called Blackpool Southern, well over thirty years ago, now. "He died in his sleep last night. I don't think you ever met Chris—he never came to America with the band. He was a really good bloke. Best manager a band ever had."

"Oh, John. I'm sorry, baby." She came around behind me, and draped her arms over my shoulders, her cheek against my hair. "I know the whole band really loved him. That sucks."

2

"Yeah, it really does."

Chris Fallow's death wasn't unexpected—he was in his late seventies and he'd had things going wrong with him since I'd met him, thirty years ago. He'd been Blacklight's manager since basically the beginning of time, and he'd been in hospital for the past seven months or so: two bouts with cancer, pneumonia, emphysema, the lot. Mostly, we'd all been amazed at how long he'd hung in.

So yeah, it wasn't a shock. But it was another cold moment in a world that seemed, more and more, to be full of them: end of an era, another one gone. I reached up and got hold of Bree's hands. There are moments when I just want the human touch, you know? Moments like that, no one but Bree will do me.

"Ian says the funeral's Monday. I need to ring Carla and get a flight—she's probably going herself. Did you want to come along for this, love?"

"I can't." She sounded stricken. "Oh, crap. I've got that reunion party I'm catering—it's next Friday. I can't cancel, I've already banked the deposit and anyway, it would leave them in the lurch. Damn! I suppose I could do it, the funeral I mean, but I have the kitchen booked from Wednesday on, and cooking for ninety people with jet lag, I don't think I can, but I don't want to leave you to have to deal with it, *shit*—"

"Oi! Bree, stop, slow down, will you? Don't get your knickers in a twist, okay? No need. Just relax."

She was already getting panicky. The idea of me going off to deal with something stressful at a distance, and her being out of helping range in case my health got stroppy, always made her nuts, but unless I was imagining things, she seemed a lot edgier these days, more easily shaken off her balance. I couldn't sort it out; you'd think, with us finally safely married, she'd be able to relax, but no. "I'll fly out Sunday and come back Wednesday or so; no need for you to drag yourself along for this. It'll be lots of standing about in a churchyard, and people you've never met, and everyone remembering the good old days, and quite a few of the bad old days, as well."

There were probably going to be a lot of people there who'd known Cilla, as well, but I wasn't about to mention that. The last thing Bree needed was reminders of my first wife. She was likely to get plenty of that when we left for London on our official honeymoon, in April.

I patted her hands. "Honestly, Bree, not a problem, all right? You'd be bored blind. And anyway, I want your first look at London to be a happy one, not a funeral. So let's save your first trip for the honeymoon, yeah?"

"Okay. Thank you, John. I really couldn't see any way of getting out of the reunion thing." She bit the top of my ear, just a nice light nip. "Mmmm, yummy yummy husband. It's what's for dinner. Wait, what time is it? Make that, what's for lunch."

I grinned at her. "The other white meat, you mean. Right. I'd best get the rest of these messages; they're probably from the band."

*"(beep) JP? Hi, it's Carla. I didn't know if Ian was going to call you, so I figured I'd better. Chris Fallow died in his sleep last night. The funeral's Monday and I'm holding two seats for you, Virgin Airlines, first class, Saturday out of SFO. Can you let me know if Bree's going? If yes, I'll confirm both seats and if not, I'll knock it back to one—or if you want me to keep it so you can have the seat empty, or for one of the guitars, I can do that too. Let me know which day you'd prefer the return flight—call me at the office or on my cell. (beep) To save the message…."*

Of course Carla'd got me a flight; if it had been a bit later in the day, my brain would have already known that. Carla Fanucci runs our band's American operations out of her office in Los Angeles. Her business cards say she's Blacklight's US liaison and PR person, but she does a hell of a lot more than that. Hell, she'd

4

arranged our wedding, back at Halloween. The day Carla leaves something undone, or even done imperfectly or with a single detail missed, she'll probably go off looking for a sword to fall on. Not that we'd know anything about it, because the rest of us would have already died from the shock.

I hit the "return call" option, and got the travel details sorted out. Bree'd given up coping with the chequebook, and was loading the dishwasher. The reunion party she was doing the catering for in just over a week was the first job she'd taken on in nearly a year; between Blacklight's tour, my first wife's suicide, my health issues and our getting married, she'd basically set a complete moratorium on work. That was fine with me, mind you, what with me being a selfish ponce who wants my old lady there to look after me and cater to my every whim, but the truth is, I knew it was getting to her, the not working.

Bree cooks—it's what she does, and she loves it. And I may be spoiled, but I want her to do what makes her the happiest, especially since she's spent well over half her life making sure that I get to do what makes me the happiest.

Also, she's slightly nuts on the subject of money. She's spent the last twenty five years convinced, against all sense or reason, that her money and my money had to be kept separate. Even though we were now one person in the eyes of the State of California, it was going to take her some time to sort out that the millions of dollars growing mould in my accounts were legally hers to buy anything she wanted with. And since she hadn't earned anything to juice up her own private accounts with for a good long time, she was feeling twitchy over it.

I knew why she was so scrupulous about the separate accounting, of course, or at least I know now. Somewhere, probably in the middle drawer of her psyche between her clean knickers and her ridiculous Joan of Arc complex, she'd got the idea that my money was also Cilla's money, and that she herself had no right to it. Which was noble, I know that. But it was also insane and infuriating and created potential problems where there really weren't any.

I love my old lady. I love her more than life, but there's no denying she's got a few quirks of conscience that might have been specially designed to drive me round the fucking twist. It was especially infuriating since she's the one who handles all my money, anyway, and always has. There's nothing I wouldn't trust Bree with; she's kept me sane, sober, unaddicted and alive since the day we met. You'd think she'd get that the last thing she needed to worry about was the ethics of spending my money, but that's Bree for you.

She'd finished the clearing up, and headed into the alcove with her computer. I heard her singing to herself, under her breath; it sounded like the Rolling Stones, "Live With Me". I bit back a grin and turned back to my messages.

"(beep) Johnny? Good morning, mate, it's Mac. Look, can you ring me back? Ian said he was letting you know about Chris, so I'm guessing you've already got a flight by the time you get this, but I need a word about something else. We saw a rough cut DVD of that Parmeley film, 'Playing in the Dark,' down at Ian's office. The film's a lot better than it was, but there's a lot of Cilla in this thing, and I don't know if Bree can cope. And Parmeley wants to get it in for consideration at Cannes—the damned thing has to reach the festival people by 17 March. So let's talk after the funeral, yeah? Snog your old lady for me, and I'll see you Sunday. (beep)"

Oh, bloody hell. This was something I'd thought might happen, and I wasn't looking forward to coping with it.

Back in late 1978 and into 1979, Blacklight had agreed to let the band be followed about with a camera by a famous director called Cedric Parmeley, who wanted to do a documentary film about rock and roll. The idea was that Blacklight would be filmed in the studio, and then on the road for the recording sessions and American tour for our album, *Pick Up the Slack*. He was also covering two other bands, a London legend from the early sixties who were just beginning to disintegrate, and the darlings of the then-current East London punk/New Wave scene. The idea struck Chris Fallow as a damned good one, free PR, exposure, the lot, and he convinced us that, so long as we had final approval over our part of the content, we ought to do it.

The film was a mess. We'd taken one look at the damned thing and brought out lawyers, money and all the noise we could make. The funny thing was, we weren't the ones making the biggest fuss; both the other bands involved completely lost it, with even more noise and fuss. Parmeley might have been able to get round the other two bands, but he wasn't getting round Blacklight Corporate, not with the money we were prepared to throw at keeping that train wreck of a film off screens. And he absolutely wasn't getting round Chris Fallow.

So *Playing in the Dark* had been sitting in a can in Parmeley's villa in the South of France for donkeys years, but now he'd fixed it and wanted to release it. And I was going to need a better reason than my first wife sitting in my lap for half the film to be obstructive about it, if everyone else involved wanted to greenlight it.

I snuck a quick look at Bree. She was making notes about something, the menu for the reunion gig she was doing most likely, and comparing her notes with whatever she was looking at onscreen. She had a pair of drugstore readers on. The glasses were a recent thing, and they scared me. Because, you know, Bree is supposed to be invincible. I need her to be invincible, and of course she isn't, never has been, and it was still taking me far too long to cop to it. Of course, the glasses were also endearing as hell, because they made her look like a cross between a cranky old librarian lady and a really pretty schoolgirl....

She looked up right about then, and caught my eye, and gave

me one of those smiles. I don't know that she actually can read my mind—I sincerely hope not—but there are moments, after so long together, that she just seems to know when I'm watching her, or thinking about her, and then the big green eyes come up and find me and, well, yeah, there you go. I blew her a kiss, and went back for my last message.

"*(beep) Yes, good morning, Mr. Kinkaid. This is Susan at Dr. Majewski's office. We have the results of your echocardiogram, and Dr. Majewski would like to know when you can come in to discuss it. (beep)*"

It's like I said before: some days, you just don't get to hear what you want to hear, or do what you want to do.

If I'd thought the weather at home in San Francisco was miserable, I'd forgotten how nasty the UK gets in February.

Chris's memorial actually turned out to be quite nice in a sentimental way. He'd opted for cremation, with his ashes scattered over Meg's garden at their house in Hertfordshire. Meg told us he'd put a line in his will, saying she could make CDs out of as much of the ash she liked, just so long as the band autographed them and sold them for at least twenty quid each. That was pure Chris, you know? The ring of genuine gold, and it put him right back among us for a minute, in the best possible way; we'd all burst out laughing, so the tone was set early on.

But I'd been right about the levels of nostalgia. There was a lot of talk about the early days of Blacklight, and a few people, old acquaintances I barely remembered, came up to offer me condolences on what had happened to Cilla. I was glad Bree had stayed home. She'd have hated this.

Chris's widow Meg, who looks rather like a skinny Queen Victoria with soft white curls, was supported on all sides; rockers to the left of her, rockers to the right. She was calm about everything, and it probably didn't hurt that she had to spend a good deal of time on Luke Hedley's eighteen-year-old daughter Solange, who was trembly and tearful.

Meg and Solange were old news. God bless Meg, she'd been there when she was needed most. When Luke's wife Viv died of ovarian cancer in 1989, Luke had been left a widower with a toddler to raise on his own. And Meg had been right there, going down to Kent and staying at Luke's farm, Draycote, being there for Solange, while Mac had been there to keep Luke from falling into tiny broken pieces.

If I look at it, I do get that we're all probably too protective of Solange. She's actually quite tough and sensible, and not even too spoiled. But she's the only child in the entire extended band family, you know? Plus, we'd all of us loved her mum, and Solange looks so much like her, it's scary.

Besides, she'd been through some tabloid hell last year. Not her doing; it happened when an American paper had done a dirt piece on Blacklight and written her up as some sort of trashy brat. The piece had skated the edge of being actionable, but never quite crossed over; they'd covered up the smell of libel, or whatever that sort of smear is in legal terms, by dripping a sort of fake syrupy tone all over it.

Back in 1989, I hadn't been there. During the not quite month between Viv feeling a sharp pain in her abdomen and her dying in her bed at home while holding Luke's hand, I'd been in hospital in San Francisco, sick as a dog with what the doctors thought was some sort of bizarre virus. A long time down the road, my neurologist let it slip that she thought it might have been the first visible touch of my MS.

But all I knew at that point was that everything hurt. They couldn't seem to pin it down, and they couldn't make it stop. And Bree, twenty-seven years old, had stayed at my bedside at San Francisco General Hospital and visibly aged, sleeping there, having friends feed the cats and bring her clean clothes, holding my hand during the lucid moments, holding back the news about Viv, knowing I couldn't do a damned thing to help, afraid I would drag myself out of bed and try. I might have, too. I may be lazy, but I'm not disloyal.

Anyway, that had been a damned bad month for Blacklight. But now, eating canapés and drinking tea and remembering Chris, I felt again that we'd been damned lucky to have Chris and Meg Fallow running things, keeping our shit together for us. As good a dad as Luke had been, Solange would be very different without Meg's having been there. Also, we'd likely have been skint, instead of indecently wealthy—one of Chris's big things had been making sure that the business end of Blacklight was clean, visible and stone solid.

We fetched up at Mac's London house after hugging Meg goodbye, and shaking hands all around. There were limos to spare, since Blacklight was paying all the funeral costs. I was staying at the Dorchester, in Central London, but we were heading to Mac's place first. Sir Cedric Parmeley's distributor had sent a DVD of the current cut of *Playing in the Dark* along to the Blacklight management offices off Kensington High Street, and Mac had got hold of it. We were off to give it a look.

There was also some band business to discuss. Ian Hendry, our brilliant road manager, had basically been doing the full management thing as well as his own job since Chris had ended up in hospital, this last time. It was obvious that Ian was going to get promoted to full manager, with a nice extra share of Blacklight's bonus revenue. What needed discussion were the finances, plus sorting out who else was getting promoted or moved around. And I had a question of my own to ask, advice I was hoping to get about money I'd been paying every month for something that no longer existed: Cilla's upkeep, and the maintenance on my London house.

There was filthy sleet coming down, and the limo driver was

taking it nice and slow. Good. I wasn't used to weather like this, with ice on the roads, and I was missing Bree behind the wheel of our Jaguar. And even though we had Mac's bodyguard, Domitra Calley, in the car with us, protecting Mac from the weather wasn't part of her job description.

Mac's house is one of my favourite places in London. He's got a place near the river, off Knightsbridge and near Sloan Square. The house is a nice Edwardian thing, eight rooms plus a completely silly little glass conservatory in the garden. He always says he bought the place for the garden, and if I'd ever seen the slightest evidence that he knew or cared about gardens, I might even believe him. Personally, I've always thought he bought the place because it had room for a very large bed, and enough walls with unbroken surfaces for him to hang his art collection on.

Actually, in decent weather, Mac's garden is a brilliant place to relax, and I found myself wanting to show it to Bree. We've got a superb garden ourselves, back in Pacific Heights, and they're not all that different, really. Mac's garden is huge, especially by London standards. It's got an enormous twisted oak tree right in the middle of it, with mellow brick paths and roses climbing up weathered old wooden trellises and, of course, there's that little chichi knockoff of Alexandra Palace by the south fence. But Mac's a London boy, same as the rest of the band, even if he started out with rather more dosh and privilege than the rest of us. So far as I know, the only thing he does with plant life is smear it all over one of his groupies and lick it off.

Since the last time I'd visited, he'd knocked out a wall, to make a sort of media room. He had a big flat-screen monitor on one wall, and ten seats that looked as if he'd nicked them from the Hammersmith Odeon, or something. They even had cup holders, which was lucky, since there was a small fridge in one corner. And of course, there was a state of the art sound system.

Mac was rummaging in the fridge. "Dom, angel, would you like

11

a nosh? Drink? Oh, right, I forgot, you're off to visit your gorgeous baby sister. Not to worry, I'm indoors until tomorrow, so off you go, and mind you smooch the luscious Savannah for me. Johnny, what's yours? I've got cider, juice, and of course masses of spring water."

We settled in eventually, and Mac got the DVD going. "Right," he said, "here we go, then. *Playing in the Dark,* new and improved."

I hadn't seen the film, in any shape or form, since early spring of 1982. My memory of that particular viewing was tricky—there had been a puddle jumper from London to the South of France, where Cedric Parmeley had a villa, and a hazy memory of a film that seemed to make no sense at all.

Problem was, I wasn't sure just then if it was the film's fault, or mine. Everything in my memory from that period is pretty thoroughly off, you know? I'd been in London in autumn of 1980— Blacklight had been in the middle of recording our *Partly Possible* album—and I'd been drinking pretty much all day and most of the night. It's one of those things, you don't admit it to yourself, or you tell yourself *right, no problem, it's under control,* all the usual rubbish, but of course it was a problem and it wasn't under any sort of control. I was basically sozzled all the time.

I chilled out when I got back to San Francisco, at least enough to where Bree didn't realise what state I was in with the boozing. But when I ended up back in London in spring of 1981, acting as the world's least qualified caregiver for my estranged heroin-addicted wife after she had cancer surgery, I was a bloody wreck, and toward the end of that mess, the boozing went red-line on me.

I remember the overdub sessions for *Partly Possible*; we did them at Abbey Road, in London, so I wouldn't have to leave the city. I remember some scattered moments from that time in London when the album was being mixed and mastered, but the only thing that's really clear in my memory was the nonstop jones to go home to California, to get the hell away from the house in Camden Town, away from Cilla, away from feeling dislocated.

Toward the end, I dealt with it by stumbling about in an alcoholic haze. I'd got off heroin with not too much fuss, but looking back, I was never half the junkie that I was boozer. I had just enough awareness left to dread Bree finding out.

It was nearly a year before I did something about it. Back in London for the European leg of the *Partly Possible* tour in spring of 1982, two things had happened. I'd taken that puddle jumper to France and watched a movie and remembered damned near nothing about it. And then, one morning, I'd woken up with a sore neck and a screaming hangover, in a Northern Line tube station, where I'd passed out after the pubs closed.

Luck must have been looking out for me that time, because I hadn't been picked up for vagrancy or public drunkenness; that would have been all anyone around me needed, you know? But the fates cut me a break. That was the last click of the gears, telling me *right, it's time to get this done.*

So I'd gone home to San Francisco and Bree. I'd lost weight, I had the shakes, and the shakes were affecting my ability to play. That was it, the part that pushed me into stopping, into confessing to Bree, who'd literally just turned twenty, that I was still drinking, that I needed to stop because it was killing me. That's a memory I don't suppose will ever cloud over: me, crying with my head in her lap, begging her to help me.

And bloody hell, she'd done it for me.

Our house, at 2828 Clay Street in Pacific Heights, is one of those Queen Anne Grand Victorians, the sort you see in posh magazines about architecture. It has eleven rooms, all of them oversized, and that doesn't include the garage, where I have my studio. It's got nooks and crannies and edges and rafters and beams. Point is, it's got maybe a thousand perfectly good places to hide bottles of bourbon, of brandy, of whatever you happen to be drinking and don't want your old lady—who nearly went to jail when she was a kid of seventeen because she tried to help you with a little problem you were having with a nasty mixture of heroin and cocaine—to find them.

So mostly what I remember about that summer was a miserable grinding haze of no booze at all, period, full stop. Bree took the tough love road, that time; she found every bottle I'd stashed away, poured them all out, made me tell her whether she'd missed any, and then smashed every damned bottle but one. She kept the last one, and told me that if she found me boozing, or lying to her about it, she'd beat me over the head with it. She meant it, too.

But none of that would have done any good at all, not a damned thing, if I hadn't wanted to stop. The thing about quitting, about stopping? You've got to really want it, want that result. And I did, but it took me a long time, too long, to understand that yeah, right, so I'd be letting the band down if I didn't stop. And yeah, okay, so I was barely thirty years old and the booze was making me old long before I ought to be. But at the bottom of it, then and now, was a bad feeling that I was somehow betraying Bree's trust, and she didn't deserve that.

When I think about it now, I mostly wish I'd realised it, back then, at the time. That's the part I'd like a time machine for, so that I could go back and fix it. The fact that she was rescheduling her final classes at the culinary academy without telling me, so that she could slip out when I wasn't expecting it, and come home to make sure I wasn't fucking up? I know all that now, but I didn't know it then. I wish I'd got it, understood how deeply I was invested in her being that invested in me. I would have let her know. But I didn't.

There was music and a narrator's voice, coming out of Mac's speakers. I pulled my attention out of the past and back to

Cedric Parmeley's film, took a mouthful of apple juice, and settled in to watch.

Blacklight was the middle segment in this thing. The idea had been a sort of "past, present, future" scenario: Benno Marling's band, The Isle of Dogs, with a brief near-Beatles level of fame in the mid to late sixties and then a slow slide to middle tier status, were supposed to represent the past. Blacklight, at the top of our game and doing stadiums at that point, were the present. And Typhoid Harry, all Doc Martens and shaved heads and piercings and tats, were supposed to be the future of rock and roll. Funny, that was, because as it turned out, Blacklight was still here and still one of the world's top touring bands, and the other two had long since died off as functional musical acts. Benno and his guitar player, Jimmy Wonderley, still gigged occasionally, but it was all small clubs and whatnot. As the Isle of Dogs, they were long gone.

"I'll just skip to our segment." Mac reached for the remote. "Unless, of course, you've got a yen to see Benno and that lot in full Isle of Dogs teddy boy velvet drag, sucking on cigs and trying to look dangerous? Because Parmeley's got historical archive footage in there, from about 1965."

"Ta, mate, I'll pass." I was grinning. "I remember the teds and the sideburns. And bloody hell, the Slim Jim ties! No, just hit me with what I get to vote on."

"Right. Take a deep breath and strap yourself in, Johnny. It's going to be a bumpy ride."

He clicked the fast forward, and there we were, sitting in the studio at Abbey Road.

My first thought was how damned young we all looked. Luke's ponytail was still gold. Mac's whipcord length of muscle and bone looked as if he didn't have to work to maintain it, and never would. Cal and Stu looked about twenty—Stu, who wears a grizzled little beard these days, was clean-shaven. I could hardly

15

stand looking at myself, casual and lounging and healthy, as if I might live forever without having to think twice about it, with my Les Paul Deluxe balancing on my knee and a lot more brown hair than I have now falling over my eyes.

And there was Chris Fallow, just one quick shot of him talking to our chief engineer. I felt my heart turn over. He'd been ill so long, and I lived half a world away, but damn it, we'd lost something, and it suddenly hurt.

The first section, the studio sessions for *Picking Up the Slack*, was fascinating, in a weird way. Through a glass darkly, and all that rubbish, but really, it was spooky. What I was watching made sense, though, which I didn't remember anything at all about the film doing the first time around I'd seen it.

And then the session shoot was over, conversation, some technical natter, and the entire band was heading out of the studio and out of nowhere, there was Cilla.

Spiky blonde hair, black lace gloves, skin-tight trousers, perfect makeup, leaning over to kiss me, sliding her arm through mine. Rick Hilliard, our road manager at the time, was right behind her. Knowing what I knew now, I felt something acidic and nasty moving around in my stomach.

"Sorry," Mac said. He meant it, too, and I suddenly had to swallow the urge to ask him if he'd guessed about Cilla and Rick, even back then. It made me cringe inside, because the answer to that was almost certainly yes; Mac has a sort of sixth sense for bedroom issues. "But you should really see the whole thing, Johnny. See if you think Bree can cope. Because honestly, the film's quite good, as these things go."

"Yeah, okay. Let's see the rest of it, then."

The film went on. There was a moment when I had to stop my hands from knotting together hard: Luke and Viv, Viv alive and gorgeous and just old enough to drink, looking so much like her daughter did today that I wondered, how in hell was Luke supposed to cope with watching this? Hell, how did he cope with looking at Solange, day in and day out?

I shot a sidelong look at Mac, Luke's oldest friend, his writing partner, Solange's godfather. He had his profile to me, just watching. His face was hard and smooth, impossible to tell what he was thinking, but something was jumping high up on his cheekbone, a nervous little muscle flutter, and I knew he was feeling it, as well. Bloody memory.

And for the rest of our segment, wherever I was that wasn't actually onstage, there was Cilla, at my shoulder, holding my hand, staring at the camera, at one point sitting on my lap and kissing me, chattering for the camera bloke, while I laughed and leaned over, nibbling her ear, my hands resting light and easy against her, whispering something, smiling, happy, together.

I felt my shoulders wanting to twitch. Who in hell was she, and who in hell was that bloke who looked like me? Where in hell had we gone, all of us?

"Nearly done," Mac told me. "But there's a short thing right near the end of our segment—it ends at the Hurricane Felina show, remember? Concert footage, and damned good."

"Oh, bloody hell!"

It was uncanny, just frozen there in time: the moment that had completely changed the way my life had gone. The Cow Palace, San Francisco, part of a benefit for a few thousand Category Five hurricane victims. There it was, right there: a commotion at the front of the stage, a girl falling off her boyfriend's shoulders, hitting the floor hard. Me, edging toward the wings, jerking my head, talking to someone. Me shaking my head, moving back out into the spotlight….

That had been Bree, sixteen years old and standing in the wings, working as a volunteer for the medical clinic her mother basically ran for the benefit of the City's low-income families and street people. That was the first moment I'd seen Bree, changing everything in my world, my life, my future. That was Bree I was talking to, jerking my head toward the crowd, looking into a pair of muddy fierce green eyes and knowing, all the way down where that stuff lives, that I'd just seen my future, kismet, karma, the rest of my life.

There was no physical clue to her presence. I might have been signaling to the curtains, for all there was of her; Parmeley's camera had missed her entirely. Invisible, once again.

There was the show ending, us leaving, me looking preoccupied and Cilla holding on to my hand, smiling into the camera, the glint of her wedding ring showing through the black lace glove. I had a lump at the back of my throat.

"Right—that's it. After that, we move on to Typhoid Harry and the Clash Wannabes." Mac clicked the remote, and the screen went dark. There was a dry amusement in his voice; he'd never been a fan of skinheads. "So, have we got a problem? Both the other bands are okay with it as is. Parmeley apparently wants to do a few more tweaks, and then send it in for the Cannes judges. And look, Johnny, I don't want to nark Bree—the girl's been through quite enough shit, what with one thing and another. But do you think Bree being upset is a valid reason to refuse permission? Because personally, I don't."

"No, no more do I." It was true; I didn't. What's more, I didn't imagine for one moment that Bree would, either. "She won't like it. Hell, I don't like it. But we can avoid a lot of the grief, Mac. There's no need for her to watch it, except maybe the premiere, and after that, we don't ever have to deal with it again, right? So yeah, as far as I'm concerned, you can tell Parmeley to go ahead and submit."

"Good morning, John. Bree, are you coming in? Good. Susan, can you hold any calls, please?"

I'm damned if I know why my doctors always ask Bree that.

18

She's never once consented to sit out in the waiting room unless they were doing something to me that she couldn't legally be there for, things like the annual nightmare MRI my neurologist makes me get for my MS, or the echocardiogram I'd had a few weeks earlier at the demand of the cardiologist who had just asked my wife the same stupid question he always asks her.

"John, don't look so nervous."

The cardiologist's name was Bill Majewski. Nice enough bloke, but he seemed to have graduated from the sort of medical school that specialises in teaching future doctors how to ooze a cheerful genial vibe to their patients, whether that was appropriate or not. Personally, I suspect he'd be cheerful and genial even if he was telling his patients they needed their heads cut off. I put up with it because he's damned good at his job; he'd long suspected that the odd little clicks he'd picked up the first time I'd gone to see him back in 1998 were something he ought to keep an eye on. Thing is, it wasn't until recently that there'd been anything solid, and of course, it had to be a noisy headline-grabbing heart attack, right at the end of Blacklight's gig at a sold-out Boston show. Sod's Law, and all that, never fails.

"Right," I told him. "I'm not nervous, I'm jet-lagged, is what I am. I've only just got back from a funeral in London."

Actually, what I said about not being nervous was true. I wasn't nervous, not about whatever he wanted to tell me. I was edgy because if it sounded remotely bad, Bree would flip her shit; she always does, if the news means my life is going to be less than perfect. And I was edgy because after heroin addiction and alcoholism and multiple sclerosis and the heart attack, after the yearly routine of being shot full of orange dye and slid into an MRI machine, I've got a thing about doctors. Just because I need them doesn't mean I have to like them.

"So." I kept my voice as casual as I could. "What's going on, then?"

"Well, I've got the results of that echocardiogram back. Sorry it took awhile; I wanted to talk to the cardiologist at Mass General, the doctor who saw you the night you had the heart attack. But the results look fairly straightforward."

"Good." The procedure been straightforward as well, especially compared it to the MRI. Of course, the echocardiogram had a head start, because a lot of the little indignities that go along with the MRI were missing from this one. There was no stripping you naked and stuffing you into one of those bloody little open-backed cotton gowns that leave you wondering if your bum's showing, for one thing; it was just shirt off, and that was it. And there was no dye shot into your veins. All they wanted was for you to stretch out on the table so that they could attach sensors to your chest with sticky tape; it's a good thing I'm not a particularly hairy bloke. "Glad to hear it. So, what have we got, then?"

"We've got a mitral valve prolapse, for one thing." He sounded casual, but shit, my neurologist had sounded exactly that casual while she'd pointed out the white lesions on my brain that meant I had a potentially crippling, potentially fatal disease. I never trust a doctor to admit something's serious. The sods probably all think they might get sued if they aren't either patronising or perky. "MVP, for short. Which is pretty much what I'd suspected it would be. All the indicators pointed that way. There's a little scarring, too."

"Right. Ta. MVP." Another bloody medical condition with an M-initial to remember. Bree wasn't melting down, so that much was all right, you know? She's a doctor's daughter, and she usually knows when shit's serious enough to melt for.

On the other hand, she wasn't relaxing, either. When Bree hedges her bets about anything to do with my various medical issues, it means things have a shot at going either way. "Good to know," I told him. "Care to tell me what that is? And in English, please, mate."

Majewski explained it. He even picked up this bizarre little plastic model of the human heart he keeps in a drawer, fully chambered and perfectly coloured, right down to the aorta and whatnot, and demonstrated what he was talking about. Made me feel like I was back in Clapham Comprehensive: Heart Health class 1.0, except they hadn't taught us about hearts.

Basically, if I was following this properly, we've all got something called a mitral valve in the heart. Its gig is connecting the left atrium of the heart with the left ventricle. Sometimes—apparently, this is quite common—the flaps on the valve bulge up into the atrium, instead of doing what they're supposed to do, which is to close nice and smooth when the heart contracts. They call the flap malfunction a prolapse, and that's what had caused that ticky little echo Majewski'd been hearing all these years.

Mine had done the prolapse boogie with an encore—a sort of backspit of heart blood, which he called mitral valve regurgitation. Lovely, yeah? I got the immediate mental picture of a sort of Edgar Allen Poe thing, a beating heart puking all over the place, and then, of course, I couldn't get the picture out of my head. All I needed was the Masque of the Red Death and a raven, or something....

"...the heart attack you had in Boston was possibly triggered by an episode of mitral valve regurgitation. We're going with that for the moment and I'll be straight with you, John, we aren't sure about it—for one thing, I want to keep an eye on that scar tissue we picked up. But I'm willing to bet you've had other regurgitative episodes—that would go hand in hand with the irregular heartbeat you get sometimes. There may be a complication from the MS, as well, but I should really talk to your neurologist about that, so I'll get you to sign a HIPPA waiver on your way out...."

Majewski was rabbiting on. My attention had wandered off, but since Bree was getting every word, and understanding it a lot better than I ever would, I wasn't worried. She'd know if I needed to do anything about something I might have missed....

"So far as I can tell, there was no noticeable extra damage to the heart. But you're fifty-four—almost fifty-five, right? In a few weeks?"

"March third." Bree spoke up, finally. "Have I got this wrong, or isn't there something about MVP and antibiotics?"

"I always forget, you're Miranda Godwin's daughter." He nodded at her; of course, he knew her mum. Miranda's one of the city's top surgeons. "You have it right. If John's going in for anything that requires surgery—especially things like dental work— the usual thing is to make sure the MVP patient takes a dose of antibiotics beforehand. Emergency surgery, they should be told about it, so that they can get some into his IV. Other than that, we'll keep an eye on it, and I want to schedule a follow-up echocardiogram for you in six months. We want to be cautious. Mostly, just use common sense, and for Christ's sake, John, if you have another heart attack and don't bother letting me know...."

"Another heart attack? Not going to happen."

Bree sounded quite fierce. I grinned at her, and raised one eyebrow; she can't do that. She went pale, which was silly, really. She ought to have sussed out by this time that I not only loved the idea of her taking on the doctors on my behalf, I actively wanted her to do it. She bit her lip, but went on. "Is there anything we ought to avoid?"

I opened my mouth, and shut it again. Majewski shot me a grin. I knew damned well she'd meant things like plane travel, long trips, stress, things like that. And of course, the cheeky bugger thought she'd meant sex.

"Nope. And lucky for you both—did I congratulate you on the wedding? Anyway, we're done. Assuming nothing out of the way happens, I'll see you in six months. Off to Europe, are you? Have a nice honeymoon."

# Chapter Two

*"(beep) JP? Hey, it's Carla. Just calling to confirm your travel plans. I've got you and Bree booked for Thursday night on Virgin—the flight's scheduled to get into Heathrow at just about three in the afternoon, local time. There are three first-class seats reserved, one for the two guitars—I've cleared it with the airlines, so there shouldn't be any security issues, once they check that the guitars are really guitars and not bombs. You have the honeymoon suite at Claridge's for the first week, and then you move over to the mews house in Chelsea for the rest of the trip—the keys are at the London office, with Susan Alexander. Oh, and that question you had, about the monthly payouts for the London house account? I passed that on to Maureen Bennett, in Finance, so call her when you get a chance, okay? And I left a message for Bree—she's going to download your boarding passes and print them out. We have your interferon already shipped over, two months*

*supply—we can get more if you need it, so let me know if the trip looks to go long. Call me if you need anything else, and if I don't talk to you before you go, have a fantastic time. (beep)"*

I've been flying all over the planet for so many years now that I just don't even think about it anymore, beyond the occasional *oh shit* moment of realising I've been overbooked, too many events and not enough time left before and after flights. A touring band travels. You learn to adjust to the realities of that, and there have been some serious adjustments, especially after 9/11. Even though we generally find a central base of operations during a tour, two floors of the Ritz in Paris for ten days so we can turn the gigs around the Continent into day trips and that kind of thing, there's still a lot of flying involved.

So it took me a while to sort out why Bree was so bouncy and nervous. Of course, she hadn't done much touring during our first two decades together; Cilla had been alive then, and even though we were long separated and long estranged, Bree had perfected that damned trick she has, of disappearing into the ozone somewhere. She'd come along on fairly local tours—hell, she'd jumped at it when Tony and I took the Fog City Geezers on a ten-day West Coast run of club gigs, from Seattle down to San Diego—but the full-scale Blacklight tours, she'd avoided when possible. Twenty five years of living with an Englishman and a touring musician, and this was her first trip to Europe.

So, yeah, part of the nerves were probably coming from those particular realities. But it wasn't until I finally got around to the sticky question of *Playing in the Dark* that I finally twigged. Right, I know, I'm occasionally dim.

I suppose I'd been subconsciously avoiding it. The whole subject was likely to make her prickly; hell, it made me prickly. But I had to let her know what I'd told Mac. Somehow, though, like a lot of subjects you don't really want to deal with, I just couldn't seem to find the right moment to bring it up.

I was actually helping her do the washing up after dinner, about a week after her catering gig was done, when she brought it up herself. She was in a really mellow mood; the cheque for the gig had cleared, and having a few thousand dollars sitting in her personal account, money she'd earned herself, seemed to have taken a load off. And then, of course, she dropped the question on me.

"By the way, I keep forgetting to ask—what ever happened with Cedric Parmeley's movie? I know you said Mac had a copy of the rough cut, or something. Did you ever get the chance to see it? Was it as bad as you remembered?"

She'd just handed me a very heavy piece of cookware—she's got a lot of stainless steel pots and pans, All-Clad mostly, and this one weighed a metric fuckload. I'd just been giving it a good rub with the dishcloth when she dropped the question, nice and casual, and I nearly dropped the pan. That would have damaged either the pan or the floor; either way, she'd not have been happy. So I was glad I held on.

"Yeah, I saw it." Damn the girl, she knows me too well. I thought I sounded perfectly normal, but apparently not; the fading red hair swung and her eyes turned my way. *Shit.* So much for not dealing. "Actually, Bree, we need to talk about it. I'm afraid I made a sort of executive decision, because Mac needed one, and I don't think you're going to like it. I don't much like it myself. But...."

I'd been rubbing the pan without thinking. I suppose it must have been dry, because she reached out and took it away from me. I kept a wary eye on it, and on her.

"Oi," I told her. "I'm not saying a word until you put that damned thing back where it belongs. Last thing I need is you going upside my skull with that. Your cookware's so heavy, we ought to have roadies for it. Put it down, love, all right?"

"Have you been watching old American sitcoms when I wasn't

25

looking? Hang on while I plug the kettle in—I think I want tea."
She had a grin for me, but it was a small grin and it was gone a
moment later. Something in my voice had given it away, that
whatever it was, was major enough to make me dread telling her
about it.

The kettle whistled, and she poured out two cups. "Okay.
Now. What is it I'm not going to like?"

I told her about the film. Once I started talking about it, of
course it just came straight out, no fuss at all. She's not the
world's best listener with most people—she gets impatient and
interrupts a lot—but not with me. When I've got something serious I need to tell her, she gives every ounce of attention she's
got.

This time, I ended up telling more than I thought I even knew.
While she was sitting there, watching me over the rim of her tea-
cup, listening to me talk about it and not saying a word herself, a
few things came up in me that I hadn't known were there. How
unnerved I'd been, watching it; how I'd looked so bloody young,
so healthy, indestructible really, but Jesus, there was Viv, and
Chris Fallow, and Rick Hilliard, and they'd all looked young and
healthy and indestructible, as well, and they were gone.

And of course, there was the big thing, the one that came
jumping out of nowhere and hit me, right in the heart: Cilla, just
beginning her long crippling love affair with heroin, with her
spiky blonde do and her gorgeous cheeky grin and the little shine
of her wedding band through her lace gloves, the band that
matched the one I'd worn.

In my luggage, already packed, was a really nice wooden box,
with a tight seal designed to last and an oil finish to protect it for
awhile. The box had been made for us by Bruno Baines, the brilliant luthier who'd made Little Queenie, my favourite guitar.

But it was more than a box, it was a coffin. It had Cilla's wedding ring in it, the ring Bree herself had suggested we take back

to London with us, and bury in Cilla's garden in the Camden house she and I had bought together....

"Hey." Bree was up, and around next to me, kneeling on the floor next to my chair, looking up into my face. She got hold of one of my hands, and wrapped it up between her own. "Hey. It's okay, John, stop biting it back. Just—let it out."

I must be really disconnected from my own shit, because I'd been talking and talking, remembering and then talking a bit more, and I hadn't realised that I'd started shaking. It took Bree coming round the table and letting me know, to clue me that I'd started crying, as well.

I hadn't done any grieving for Cilla. I hadn't believed I missed her at all. And really, I didn't, you know? The Cilla I was grieving for, the girl I'd married, who'd pushed me and teased me and wanted me to be the best in the world, the girl I'd snorted coke with and shot smack with and drunk bourbon with and pinned to the bed in room after room of the best hotels in the world, the girl who'd never missed a single gig of mine? That girl had stopped existing a long time ago. She'd basically died when she walked out of a Seattle hotel room and left me there, chosen the dope over me. She only existed up there on the screen of Parmeley's movie.

But up there, she was alive, and young, and vital. And more to the point, so was I, and we were still up there, the two of us still in love, flies in amber, like the amber necklace she'd stolen from Harrods because Rick Hilliard, who'd been pulling her behind my back, had dared her to boost it....

"It's okay, baby. It's okay."

Bree was rubbing my hands, crooning, consoling me the way you might croon to a child who'd broken something he'd treasured. She's not the most maternal woman on the planet, but right now, this was just what I needed.

It eased up after awhile, and I stopped, and wiped my eyes. She got up, and I heard a small exhale of discomfort; she'd been kneeling like that for a good ten minutes. But I couldn't see her face because she'd got behind me, leaning her cheek against my hair, rubbing my neck and shoulders. Another moment of invisibility, that was, hiding herself away; no way for me to tell how hard those few minutes, of me mourning the first woman I'd loved and married, had hit Bree.

Simon, the youngest of our cats, seemed to be having a rare moment of paying attention, because he wandered into the kitchen and jumped into my lap. Between the purring cat and Bree leaning up against me, I calmed down.

There was still something I needed to get clear with her, though, whether I could see her face or not. I swallowed some tea, and cleared my throat.

"Bree. Look, love, I just wanted to say I'm sorry about being high-handed. But us not liking the reminders, that doesn't really justify us telling him he can't do his movie, does it?"

"No, it doesn't, and you weren't high-handed." I still couldn't see her face. "Honestly, that would be inexcusable. Movies are Parmeley's life, the way music's yours. Or the way you're mine. And anyway, you said there was a time issue, right? I trust your judgment, John—if you don't think it's a bad film, then it's not a bad film. I'm fine with it."

I got a hand up, found one of hers, and gave a squeeze. She was quiet a moment, and then spoke into my hair. "Don't think I don't love you for asking me. It's amazing that you would. But you're the one really affected by it. I'm assuming Parmeley did some serious clean-up on it, because from what you told me about the original, he must have been out of his mind."

"Yeah, he got rid of a lot of the stuff that was ringing everyone's buzzers. The dope use is down to the occasional joint being smoked. That first version had shots of me chugging off a bottle of Jim Beam, and some of Rick Hilliard snorting coke—it was a fucking mess."

28

"Horrible." She'd let go of me, finally, and gone back to her own chair. I could see her, making a face. "What do you suppose he was after, filming all that stuff? Artistic verisimilitude or whatever it's called? Cinema veritè? No, wait, cinema veritè is something else, isn't it?"

"God knows. Whatever it was, we weren't having any of it. And our stuff wasn't even the worst of it. There was a really ugly thing in the original, one of the Isle of Dogs roadies beating the shit out some kid in the alley behind one of their gigs, and Parmeley actually showed the drummer for Typhoid Harry, I've forgotten the bloke's name, cooking up some smack and shooting up, backstage before one of their gigs in Paris."

"Jesus."

She shivered suddenly, and one hand moved up to her face, in that old masking gesture she'd used for so many years. It was unconscious, and really, she'd been using it less and less since the summer, but I knew what it meant, now. It was instinctive, the reaction of a woman in her forties to a situation a girl just seventeen had faced, watching the bloke she'd unluckily fallen in love with at first sight, who'd rung her for help because he was deep into heroin withdrawal, slice his finger as he tried to cut the drugs she'd stolen for him....

"It's okay."

I jerked my head up. She was watching me, her face cupped in her hands; I'd been so far off there that I hadn't seen Bree's Siamese, Farrowen, jump into her lap. I wondered how much of that memory had shown in my own face, how much she'd guessed.

Of course, it really wasn't a memory, not for me; it was the absence of one. That entire episode was a complete blank in my memory. I'd rung her begging for help, she'd provided it, I'd overdosed, been deported, got clean. And Bree, a week or so after her seventeenth birthday, had only escaped a good long jail term because her mother had taken the blame.

"Damn, Bree. I really love you. You know that, right?"

"Yep." She smiled at me suddenly, across the table, across the teacups, across both cats, across the endless expanse of years and memory. "Right this moment, I do know."

I don't really know what I was expecting, about Bree and how she'd like London. And I don't think, now, that I really had the first clue about what was supposed to be going on during a honeymoon, either.

This was the second time I'd got married. The first time, I'd been booked for three recording sessions, and we'd gone round the council and got married between the second and third sessions. I'd been recording a total of five weeks, with a lot of work at night. Mostly, Cilla would come round the studio and meet me afterward and we'd go catch some local gigs, go see a flick down at the Odeon, get some kebabs at the local takeaway, score some blow, and go home and shag. In those days, we had a nice little flat in a subdivided Edwardian house in Bayswater, not far from the Lancaster Gate tube station, and the City seemed very compact, some days. Small, you know? It was me and Cilla going all over the place, up High Holborn and down the Kings Road, me sitting in at the clubs. God, we were young.

So I hadn't had a real honeymoon the first time, not the sort of proper scheduled ceremonial thing the word seems to mean to most people. I'm really not clear on that, anyway. I mean, it seems to date back to a time when the groom was supposed to deflower the bride, or something, and I'd performed that little ritual for the bride about twenty-seven years ago. But even if I wasn't really sure what it was supposed to be in aid of, I was going to make damned sure that Bree was going to get to do, well, whatever the hell this was supposed to be about.

We got off on the right track, champagne for her on the plane and a very smooth flight, especially for early spring. I've found the airspace over the North Atlantic can get really bumpy in April, but on this flight, we ran into no turbulence at all. Seemed like a good omen, you know? We'd even both managed a decent few hours of kip, or at least Bree said she'd done. I've got no trouble sleeping on long distance flights.

I woke up once during the flight, opened one eye for a moment, and found her with her eyes wide open, bright green, fixed on me. With Bree, that bright clear colour is her "Turned on and ready to go" signal, but somehow, the idea of joining the old mile-high club didn't really appeal, so I lifted an eyebrow at her and grinned, and she'd grinned back, and closed her eyes again.

I hadn't really given any thought to getting to Claridge's from the airport, beyond getting a taxi and showing Bree just how comfortable a big London cab can be. So I was surprised to see a bloke wearing livery just outside Immigration, holding up a sign that said *Kinkaid.*

"A limo into town?" Bree, pushing one of our two luggage carts, stopped and kissed me. It was a real kiss, hard and fast, tongue tip to tongue tip. "John, you're brilliant! Where did this sudden organising streak come from?"

I opened my mouth, about to confess that whoever had put this together, it hadn't been me. Right then, a tiny voice at the back of my head popped in to tell me, *right, you berk, shut up and take the praise,* and okay, so, probably bad karma, not owning up. Sod that. There was no damned way I was telling her I hadn't arranged it.

I kissed her right back and made a mental note to quietly find out who to send flowers to. My money was on Carla; one reason she's so good at the operations part of her job is that she's got an unbelievable eye for just this kind of detail. If I had to arrange half the rubbish she manages to do without ever breaking a sweat, I'd fuck it up completely. The woman's a bloody wonder.

The weather cooperated as well, which was a surprise. It was

31

clear and actually verging on warm. I'd half expected it to be chilly and wet, basic London weather, the kind everyone associates with every cliché in every movie ever made, but no. You'd think it knew I wanted a perfect welcome for Bree.

I got the chauffeur to take us once around Hyde Park. Bree rolled down the window and I pressed up close to her, pointing out Rotten Row and the Round Pond and taking mock swipes at her head when she laughed at me for not being able to identify individual buildings in the distance. Every bush seemed to have fresh new green growing on it, and every flower seemed to be showing buds.

If my wife had been pleased with the limo at the airport, the first look at the Brook Penthouse up top of Claridge's Hotel took things up to a whole new level.

We were taken up by some bloke in a pricey Jermyn Street suit. He had the vibe I've come to associate over the years with the concierges at really stellar hotels, information retrievable out of thin air, no demand or requirement he couldn't meet, that whole thing. Before the limo had actually slid to a stop, he'd basically snapped his fingers and a small army of blokes in matching jackets had our luggage loaded onto carts that looked to be fitted out with fucking 24-gold trim, and had disappeared into the hotel with it. I managed to hang on to both my guitars; I'd brought Little Queenie and the Paul Deluxe along, knowing I was likely to be doing some work down at Draycote with the band at some point. Anyway, I never travel without at least one axe.

The Suit Bloke—I didn't hang on to his name—gave us a nice understated welcome, bowing over Bree's hand but not kissing it. Her eyes got very wide, and very green, and I had a moment of wondering just how much sex I'd be getting and providing once we got to Paris, where the concierges kiss the pretty lady's hand as a matter of course, and where every lady is pretty, the pretty ones are beautiful, and the beautiful ones are goddesses.

Right. I know this probably sounds dim, but I think I was as stunned by the Brook Penthouse as Bree was. I mean, you don't usually stay in hotels in the same city you've got a nice house in, or at least I don't. I've never stayed at the Mark Hopkins or the Fairmont, back in San Francisco. I was born and raised in South London, lower middle class family; the only thing that kept us eating on a regular basis was me being an only child, after my baby brother died. Even if I had wanted to sneak off to a hotel for a night, just to see what that whole thing was all about, it wouldn't have been Claridge's. That was for the nobs.

The Brook Penthouse—it had a private rooftop terrace that opened out over Brook Street—was mind-blowing. The beds were big enough to stage military manoeuvres on, never mind basic sex. The windows were taller than either of us. There was a full dining room. The bath was marble and sunken and thoroughly decadent. We apparently also got our own private butler service with the price of the penthouse, which probably was going to cost me enough dosh to wipe out the national debt of a few small countries....

"Gordon *bleedin'* Bennett!"

That popped out before I could swallow it. If I'd wanted to make certain the locals knew they were dealing with a Londoner, and what class of Londoner, I'd made a damned good job of it. Bree loves the phrase, though, and she was grinning. Took me a few seconds of being mortified to realise that Suit Bloke was grinning, as well, even if he was doing a decent job of covering it. Sod it—I was paying for it, right? "Nice digs, mate."

At that point, I decided not to even think about what this was costing. After all, Bree'd had a twelve thousand dollar guitar designed and built for me as a wedding prezzie, and I'd got her fuck-all. If I was going to fetch up in bankruptcy court, we might as well have the coolest accommodations in town on the way there.

We had a sensational dinner, just the two of us, in the hotel that first night. I don't get jetlag much, not going earlier to later, anyway, but Bree hadn't done this before, and I didn't want to drag her out across London and have her fall asleep before she could swallow her pâté. Luckily, Claridge's has a brilliant restaurant, Gordon Ramsey; I'm unfortunately rather challenged in the area of cookery and *haute cuisine,* but it tasted fantastic to me, and Bree, trained chef, was practically crooning to her pricey fish.

We came in for some nice personal attention, as well, and Bree got to talk shop for a couple of minutes with the bloke whose name is over the door. She was given champagne and I got them to bring her some fresh raspberries, and then it was a quick walk around Bond Street to burn off dinner and then back up to the posh penthouse, to try out the battlefield-sized bed in the way we both assumed it was meant to be used on honeymoon, and to show my wife what I personally meant when I looked down at her face against the pillow and told her, "Welcome to London", tasting her sweet and salty, sweat on her collarbones, making our own music out of breath and friction, and the lights of London giving us our very own mirror ball.

Looking back at it, that week was what I suppose poets and whatnot mean when they use the word "idyllic." Everything that could go right, did. It had been a long time since I'd felt that healthy, or that young.

We got the staff at Claridge's to get us a hired car and a driver, and we were driven all around London, the driver stopping wherever I told him to stop and adding some suggestions of his own. We went to places I'd never bothered to visit, playing tourist with my American wife, and the truth was, I had a blast.

We went to the Tower of London, and Bree fell in love with the ravens; we also met a purebred Siamese cat who looked exactly like Farrowen, stealing a half-eaten ham and cress sandwich someone had dropped, near the steps up to the White Tower.

Turned out the cat was called Simon, just like one of ours, and belonged to the Beefeaters who guard the grounds. We saw the Houses of Parliament and Westminster Abbey and Big Ben; we saw the Millennium Dome and the *Cutty Sark*.

There's something quite cool, in a silly sort of way, about playing tourist in your own town. Halfway through the day, we sent the driver off to get himself some lunch, and had ourselves a nice cuddle and snog in the back seat of the hire car. I don't know if anyone saw us back there, but sod it, it was our honeymoon, yeah? And I gave the driver a huge tip afterwards.

Toward the end of the week, we took the tube over to Knightsbridge, and Bree discovered Harrods and Harvey Nichols and the rest of the shops. That wasn't the reason we'd gone; we wanted a look at the house we'd hired, actually quite close to Mac's place. We were due to leave Claridge's and move into the mews house momentarily, and we hadn't even seen it yet.

But Bree saw a coat in the window of Harvey Nichols, a kind of Edwardian coachman's thing, or maybe it was supposed to be sort of vaguely military, in a deep jade colour. It turned out to be made of pure cashmere, but looking at it through the fancy windows, all I knew was that it looked really soft. It had about twenty small buttons up the front, and some on the big folded-back cuffs, as well. Bree loves buttons.

She stopped, and made a noise.

"Right." I slid my arm round her waist. "Do you fancy that, then? Let's go have a look at it."

It looked amazing on her. Even I could see it was designed for height, and Bree has that, at five foot ten. Green's her colour, as well. The damned thing looked as though it had been made for her. Hell, it looked as though it had been made *on* her. Perfect.

I pulled out a credit card at random. "Ring it up."

Bree was having a look at the price, though, and the noise she made this time wasn't nearly as happy. She was doing sums in her head, I could see it. *Shit.* Bree and her money issues….

"What's the conversion rate?"

"Doesn't matter," I told her, and lifted an eyebrow at the sales-girl. The girl had recognised me; I could tell. I saw the way her eyes dropped to my name on the card, the way her face changed, the way she opened her mouth as if to say something, remembered she was working, and closed her mouth again. "Call it the groom's gift to the bride, love, all right? You gave me the best guitar in the world for my prezzie, now it's my turn. No, don't argue, Bree, we're having it."

The salesgirl took the card, and went off with it. Bree was quiet, but there was trouble in her face. I tilted her chin down toward me, and kept my voice low.

"Okay. Look. This isn't the time and it really isn't the place. I don't really want to argue about it right now, anyway. But we're going to talk about the money thing, Bree. I know why you're this way about it. I get it, all right? The thing is, the situation that made it this way, that doesn't exist anymore. And the state of California would agree with me, not you. What's mine is yours, I thee endow and all that, and bloody hell, you're going to have to learn to accept presents gracefully."

She opened her mouth, probably to blast me, but I grinned and shook my head at her. "Here comes your coat. You can make me miserable over it later, all right?"

Her face changed. "John, I wasn't trying to—"

"Here you are, Mr. Kinkaid, if you'll sign here, please?" The salesgirl had said something to the rest of the salespeople, back behind the glass counter; there was a little cluster of staff now, all peeping at us and whispering, trying to look casual. I signed the sales slip, hoisted the hanger, and led Bree—who had clamped her teeth on her lower lip, and was being very quiet—out of the building and south toward the river, where our hired digs were.

Something very bizarre was happening in my head, as I gave

Bree the coat to hold onto—it weighed damned near as much as one of my guitars—and fiddled with the keys to the two locks: I was writing a song in my head.

"John—" It was the first thing she'd said since we left Harvey Nichols. Her voice sounded shaky.

"Hold on a minute, love, okay?" The damned locks were fighting back, and my mind was elsewhere, but I got them sorted out and pulled the front door open. "Sorry—there seems to be a song lyric coming together in my head, and I want to get it down before it goes."

"A song lyric?" Her eyes were wide. "But you never write lyrics. What's it about?"

"You. Us." I was feeling around in my pockets. "Shit! Have you got any paper in your bag, and a pen? Here, we'll explore in a few minutes, okay? I need to do this first. Is that a closet? Let's hang this thing up—crikey, how can anything that soft weigh so much?"

She hung the coat up, and got her small spiral notebook out for me. The place was wonderful, but I didn't know that until later; right that moment, I wasn't paying attention to any of it. Hell, I wasn't even seeing it. All I wanted right then was a flat surface and a place to park my bottom before the lyrics faded out....

"Here. Chair." Bree pushed open a swinging half-door, into a good-sized kitchen. "Table, too. Sit."

"Ta." I was writing, nice and fast.

*Baby, I've watched you counting the pennies—your money, my money, separate rooms....*

The kitchen was a good size; it was light, too, painted a soft pale yellow. I wasn't paying attention, though, not right then. Bree was checking out the appliances, being quiet, giving me space.

*Always seemed so worried you'd be left without any, you know I'd give you gold, you know I'd give you silver, babe I'd give you anything: sun, stars or moon.*

I had no clue where the hell it was coming from. I'd written three songs with Mac when he'd been staying with us back in the autumn, but my contribution had been exclusively the music. I've never written lyrics—I end up sweating over them, saying rude things under my breath. I think in terms of chord structure, not word structure. I can't even read poetry; it makes me feel a complete mental defective.

Right now, though, words were pouring out. What's more, I could hear the music I wanted in my head, full rock and roll but not heavy, sort of mid-period Beatles by way of a power ballad. And I was already hearing what Mac would do with the vocal.

*Cool foggy nights, we'd go out strolling, listen to the waves out at Ocean Beach, other nights I was off rockin' and rollin', piling up the gold, piling up the silver, babe I don't have anything that's out of your reach.*

Bree had left me alone in the kitchen, scribbling down words like a speed freak with a Waterman. I felt a breeze on the back of my neck; she'd opened a door or a window somewhere.

*Well there's more to us than money, honey, more to us than paying for the day by day—you can take it to the bank, but it just seems funny, Take what you need, don't ever leave, I know you don't want it but hey—take it anyway.*

I set the pen down, and took a long deep breath. The song wanted a closing verse, but right now, my hands were tingling and needed a rest. MS never lets you forget about it, not entirely.

I raised my voice. "Oi! Bree?"

"Upstairs." She sounded too far away for my liking, and I got up in a hurry. "Come up."

The stairs were steep, but that's standard for a converted mews house in this part of London. Up at the top there was a hallway, a corridor thing with a choice of doors. The first one was a split bath and loo, and those doors were open. The third door was shut.

I opened it, and walked into a bedroom, with a high ceiling and a big canopy bed and some pale springtime London light coming through the windows.

My wife was standing in a patch of sunlight. She was wearing the coat I'd just bullied her into accepting as a present. That was all she was wearing.

"I'm sorry." She leaned forward, eyes the colour of the stone in her ring, and the coat swung open. Bloody hell. She doesn't apologise easily, either, but this was looking to qualify as one of her best apologies ever. "I really am sorry, John. I know I'm a pill about the money. I know things are different now, and I'll try not to be stupid about it. And I love my coat. Thank you for giving it to me."

"Glad you like it." My heart was doing some interesting things, the beat rate going up. So were other bits of me. "Bree, do you know what KORWIGH means? K-O-R-W-I-G-H?"

"No." She was unbuttoning my shirt, and was leaning up close. Her hair brushed my cheek. "I've heard it, but I don't know what it means."

"It's, what do you call those damned things—an acronym." My voice went up and came back down again; she'd got the shirt off, sliding it off me and down on the floor, and now she was working on the belt buckle and the trousers. "Initial letters, yeah? It means 'knickers off, ready when I get home.'"

"I'm not wearing any knickers."

"I noticed," I told her, and I got my hands under the coat, and I turned her around, hearing her make a noise and feeling her knees sag, and we headed off to check out the big canopy bed. Because, yeah, this was what a honeymoon was all about, and maybe afterward, back at our posh digs in Mayfair, I'd put on one of the fancy bathrobes they give you, and pull out one of the guitars, and play my wife a tune.

# Chapter Three

"(beep) JP? Cheers, mate, it's Luke. Look, I'm coming up to town tomorrow—Solange wants some shopping time down the Kings Road, and I'm not mad enough to trust the girl with my credit cards. Do you want to have a meal, or are you and Bree not getting out of bed the entire trip? Ring me back. Oh, and Mac said something about the house in Camden—do you need help with that? Let me know. (beep)"

"Anything interesting?" Bree was at the sink, doing the washing up.

"Luke, ringing up to offer help with the house. He's coming up today with Solange, and wants to hook up. I've got another two messages to check—hang on."

"(beep) Johnny? Mac here. I'm assuming we're still on for meeting up at Howard Crescent at around noon, unless you and Bree want a lift. Ring me and let me know. I had a brainwave about your old flash *stage gear, by the way, assuming it's still there—I'm thinking maybe a charity auction. Oh, and Luke's coming up with Solange today, and wants dinner. (beep)"*

We'd settled into a nice holiday routine in the mews house: not all that different from home, really. It was Tuesday morning, I'd had my interferon shot the night before with no problem at all, I'd read the paper, and I was just having the last of my breakfast and morning coffee. If the rest of the day wasn't going to be spent going to the Camden Town house and showing me and Cilla's old digs to Bree for the first time, it would have been a nice mellow day, you know?

My house—Cilla's house, for the last quarter century—is right at the edge of Camden, in North London. It can't decide whether it wants to be Camden, or Kentish Town, or maybe even not-quite-Highgate on its posh days. The whole area's dotted with nice little crescents, small short curving streets. Most of them have these big Regency or early Vic houses, end to end. Ours was right in the middle: 18, Howard Crescent, London, NW1. Good address.

It's a beautiful house, actually. All the houses in the Crescent are similar, nice clean lines outside and gardens at the back. When we first bought it, after I'd officially joined Blacklight and had the tricky question of income nicely sorted out for the foreseeable future, we'd hired a trendy architect to come and update things. The house has four bedrooms on the first floor, so we'd taken the ground floor and opened it out, leaving a kitchen, a pantry, a loo, and one huge room for just hanging out. There's also a guest room on the ground floor, for those nights when someone would be too stoned to either find their way home or climb the stairs.

When I'd left for San Francisco permanently, I'd basically told Cilla that the house was hers. Thing is, we'd never got properly divorced while she was alive, so I still owned it. The problem was, I didn't want it, and I had no clue what we were going to find when we got there. But I was glad I'd had got my point about accepting presents gracefully across to Bree, because, even though she didn't know it, she was about to be given a much pricier prezzie than the cashmere coat.

"(beep) Hey, JP, it's Ian. We heard from Cedric Parmeley's people— whoops, sorry, make that Sir Cedric Parmeley. 'Playing in the Dark' is a go—Parmeley did some final tweaks and submitted it to the Cannes judges, and it's been accepted. I just got a call from the film's European distribution agent, and they want to know if we'd be up for a one-off gig during the Festival, a big outdoor thing. They're talking about Blacklight headlining, maybe a jam with the guys from Isle of Dogs and Typhoid Harry, assuming any of those people are still around. They want to do it at Frejus. Since everyone's in town today, I was thinking we might go out to dinner, have a band meeting, get a consensus. Ring me back. Cheers. (beep)"

"John?" I must have made a noise, because Bree's head whipped around. "Is something wrong?"

"Nothing at all—just the opposite, actually. Looks like we may be playing at Frejus. Do you know about it? It's this Roman ruin, a huge amphitheatre down in the South of France. Bleedin' gorgeous, music out there in the mountains under the stars. I always wanted a shot at playing there, but the chance never came up until now." I grinned at her. "During the festival, too. You're going to need to buy a smashing new bathing suit for this one, yeah? Not to mention a killer dress for the show and one for the premiere, as well. Look, love, would you mind if we did dinner tonight as a kind of band meeting? Everyone's actually in the city at the same time for once, and Ian wants to talk about it."

"Works for me." I saw her shoulders relax. Bloody hell, I hadn't even noticed she'd tightened up.

Truth is, I was surprised and worried by how fast she'd assumed there was a problem. I mean, we were right in the middle of what was panning out to be a damned near perfect honeymoon—I had no clue why she'd be edgy, or assume that a phone message was going to mean bad news.

But I wasn't dealing with that one, not right now, not today. We had enough on our plate for the day, and I wanted to cope with the house stuff first. Yeah, right, I know, baby steps after twenty five years together sounds insane, but there it was. The actual marriage was only half a year old, and I was still feeling like a newlywed.

We'd been planning on taking a cab up to Camden, but when I rang Mac back, I found he'd got a hired car and Dom had arrived, so we all went up together.

I probably should have expected it, but I got pretty damned tense myself, the closer we got to Howard Crescent. I'd had a few years where that house was home, really home, you know? My bed was there, my guitars were there, my wife was there. But I'd closed down quite a few of those memories when I'd left, just shut them down and walked away. I hadn't given it so much as a backwards glance until now. And I hadn't been inside in twenty years. Cilla'd been going steadily downhill all that time, losing it, deeper into her addictive shit.

Riding up in the hired car, listening to Mac and Bree talk about restaurants and vaguely noticing that the driver kept glancing at us in the driver's mirror, I did a few sums in my head. I'd arranged for five thousand quid every month to be paid straight into Cilla's account, plus the annual taxes on the freehold. I'd paid out well over a million pounds over the time I'd been gone, and never noticed.

And this had been personal, kept away from Bree having to deal. She was in charge of most everything to do with money, whether it was mine, hers, or ours—but not this. This had been handled straight through Blacklight's London office. I may have been too damned self-absorbed for too many of those years, but I wasn't completely dim. There was no way I was rubbing Bree's nose in Cilla's existence every month.

One more thing I needed to deal with, and that was talking to the finance people. I'd had them stop those payments, except for making sure the rates and taxes were kept up, after my mother-in-law reminded me about it, back in September. In American dollars, that was roughly eight thousand a month, for seven months. Hardly worth noticing in terms of what I see after a Blacklight tour, but still a nice chunk of dosh, you know? And it was just sitting there in the London house account, doing fuck-all. There must be something I could use it for....

"Johnny? Wake up, mate. We're here."

While Mac paid the driver, I was going back and forth between sorting out the keys, and keeping one eye on Bree. I'd finally put it together: the best way to tell what's going on with her is to watch her shoulders. She's got very broad shoulders, and a long neck; when she tenses up, everything contracts down. It makes her look like a turtle, as if her entire upper body is some kind of shell, and it's visible for miles, at least for me.

I'd got the keys because the New York City Police Department had sent me Cilla's effects. It was weird, and a bit unsettling— they'd sent me her wedding ring separately, in its own envelope, with a note about when she'd been cremated. Her purse— complete with keys, her cancelled passport and a few other personal items—had arrived separately, about two weeks later.

There were people out on the Crescent, an old bloke walking his pug, a gardener trimming roses down near the end, a nanny pushing a pram with a sleeping baby in it. And out of nowhere, something really bizarre happened: I saw a ghost, and it was me.

There I was, twenty five years old, skin-tight black trousers and boots and a guitar case in my hand, walking out the front door and straight down the path, and it was me coming toward me. And Cilla was up on the first floor, waving to me out the

45

window, and there was a gardener, trimming the roses and a nanny pushing a baby in a pram toward Camden Road, and I was blowing a kiss back over my shoulder, heading off to somewhere to make music.

It was uncanny. It really was like seeing ghosts, one overlaying each other, as if everything was a sort of film and there was no break in time, no break in continuity, it was all some sort of movie and I couldn't tell what was real….

"John?"

I jumped about a mile. I'd stopped in the path, just stopped dead, and I hadn't known it. I focused my eyes and there was Bree, just standing there on the path to the house, her shoulders hunched into bunches of locked muscle, her entire body contracting. Dom was at Mac's back, and there was Mac, just behind Bree. He'd got what had spooked me; I could tell.

I looked up at the house. The windows were shut tight, and there was paint peeling in a few spots. The ghosts backed off, and there we were, present tense, right now, alive and real.

"Right." I got the keys in one hand, and took Bree's hand in the other. "Here we go. Bree, love, I've got no clue what we're going to find in there. It was messy but okay last time I saw it but by now, the place is probably a tip. I sent her enough every month for a dozen housekeepers, but who knows? Here, let me get this unlocked."

The first thing that hit, once I'd got the door open, was the smell. Not too surprising, really; no one had been in there since Cilla'd gone, and that meant the better part of a year. The windows were all shut, and wherever the sunlight came in, you could see dust in the air. It didn't smell nasty—any spoiled food was probably petrified by now. It just smelled stale, dusty, a house where no one lived, that no one loved or cared enough about to come in and air the place out. It smelled abandoned. It smelled empty.

"Bloody *hell.*"

I'd been so busy sorting out the smell that I hadn't looked around. But Mac's voice, tight and strange, got my attention back onto the reality of the big empty room.

When I'd seen it last, twenty years ago, I hadn't been doing much noticing. Cilla had got me over from the States by telling me she was ill, but there was nothing wrong with her. It had all been bullshit, to see if she could manipulate me to hurt Bree, and she'd managed it. I'd told her this was the last time, that I wasn't coming back; I'd send her enough money to live nicely on, more than enough, but from that point on, she was on her own. I'd stuck to it, too.

But there had been someone I cared about, and wanted to see, on that visit in 1985, someone who actually was sick: my old sessions mate Jack Featherstone, dying in his wheelchair from complications of progressive multiple sclerosis. All my attention had been there.

Still, I'd have noticed if the place looked then the way it looked now. I remembered the walls being just as we'd painted them, a sort of cream colour, and a few abstract paintings, by local artists. Cilla'd liked abstract art; I thought it was rubbish, but it made her happy, and I didn't give enough of a damn to argue about it. I'm not an art bloke.

The paintings were gone. Instead, the walls were covered with a collection of stuff that made me go seriously cold.

There were gold records up there, every gold record for anything I'd had anything to do with, right up through about 1986. They were on the usual plaques and behind the usual glassed-in frames, and they were hung all over the place—it looked as if they'd just been flung up there by someone and left where they'd stuck. They were mostly up high, but even from down here on the ground floor, I could see the nails, just pounded into the plaster and wood.

47

There were sheets of newsprint on the walls, as well, not in frames or anything, either—just the paper, glued straight onto the walls. Melody Maker, Rolling Stone, NME, even Guitar Wizard; I recognised the magazine layouts, and the articles. All of the articles were about Blacklight. All of them had at least one photo of me.

The worst of it was the photos. There were photos on the walls, photos I'd either long since forgotten or else hadn't known about at all. There were at least thirty of the damned things, some small and some blown up huge; they were jammed up, jostling for position, some of them lopsided.

Every one of them was a photo of me and Cilla. Me and Cilla holding hands, me and Cilla coming out of a club, me and Cilla at a party….

I stood there like a mannequin, just staring, my mouth half-open. My skin was crawling.

From a few feet behind me, I heard a whimper. I turned around fast.

Bree's eyes were wide, and she didn't seem to be blinking. Mac had already moved up next to her. He wasn't touching her, not at all, but there was something protective about that gesture, and I got there in a hurry.

"Come outside, love. You want some air. Come along."

I led her toward the kitchen, where the doors out into the garden were. I didn't want her out front on the Crescent, with the old man, the gardeners and their roses, the nanny and her pram, all Cilla's neighbours wondering about us.

"*Damn.*" Dom craned her neck, looking up at the glued-on magazine pages, the gold records, the dozens of photos. "This place is like some kind of sick-ass shrine. JP, dude? Your ex? Chick was a total freak. That woman wasn't right in the head. This is some scary shit, man."

Weirdly enough, the back garden was in decent shape. I'd expected a jungle, or maybe the plane trees and the big yew at the back of the garden to have gold records or voodoo dolls dangling off them or something, but everything looked fine. The wrought iron benches and table we'd got when we'd first moved in were still out there. I found out later that Cilla had a gardener, paid automatically out of the house account, and no one had stopped him coming after Cilla'd died. So he'd been coming twice monthly, all this time, letting himself in through the side gate at the end of the path on the north side of the house, clipping the hedges, pruning the roses, whatever needed doing, and then quietly leaving. I didn't know it then; I just knew I was grateful, because Bree was the colour of old cheese, and I was afraid she was going to pass out. I wanted her sitting out in the open air, with trees around her and high walls, and nothing to look at but growing things.

Mac had followed us out, and he and I locked eyes over her head. He mouthed a question at me—*should we check upstairs?*—and I nodded. I had an arm around Bree's shoulders, and if we're talking about tense, this was it. It was like holding on to a curvy boulder, at least for the first minute or two. After that, she started to shudder, just hard sharp shakes, her body jerking as she tried to control herself.

"I'm sorry, love." I kept my voice down; if the neighbours had seen us pull up, we might just be playing for an audience, up there in all those houses, behind all those curtains. "I'm so sorry. What we just saw, that stuff—it wasn't like that, the last time I was here. I'd have warned you. You know that, right? And if you honestly can't cope—"

"No." I'd been expecting some tears, but there weren't any. She just sat there, shaking. No tears, and crikey, I'd have been happy to see a few, something normal. Her voice was very choppy, as if she was having trouble getting enough air to talk. "It's yours. I can cope with your house."

49

"No, it's not, Bree." The words were out before I could stop them. "It's yours."

*Shit.* This wasn't how I'd planned on doing this. Of course, I hadn't planned on walking into some damned perverted shrine, either. I was badly shaken myself, you know? Off balance. Still, I couldn't have said anything stupider, not right then.

"No." She sounded as flat as I've ever heard her. "Yours. Why would you say it was mine? It was Cilla's, and yours. Now it's yours. Don't say it's mine, don't you dare say it's mine. It's not mine."

Her breathing was shortening up. I rubbed her arm. "Bree, breathe. Come on, love, just breathe. You've gone way the hell too pale. Duck your head if you need—"

"I'm fine." She got up, pulling away from me, swaying on her feet. "Let's get this over with. Let's go get it done. Let's figure out what has to happen to clean it out and then we can clean it out and once it's cleaned out you can do whatever you like with it. I'll do the kitchen, and the closets. The walls, all those photos, those gold records—I'm not touching any of that. They're yours. It's all yours. Not mine."

"Bree—"

She turned and walked back into the house. Her shoulders were so far up, her neck had damn near disappeared. My stomach was doing more acrobatics, but I followed her in, and began with the stuff on the walls I could reach. I could hear her, moving about in the other room. All things considered, this probably wasn't a good time for conversation.

The photos turned out to have been stuck up on the walls with dabs of some sort of industrial strength glue. I'd got three of them torn mostly off, and discovered that the magazine stuff was completely glued on, when Mac come back downstairs.

"Johnny, we're going to need a scraper of some sort, if you want this stuff gone. Also a good long ladder, for some of the gold records."

50

"Right." I heard my own voice, grim and tight, and reached for another photo. I pulled it free of the wall; there were little holes all over the place, where she'd had other stuff hung. What in hell had been going on in her mind? "Where's Dom? Still upstairs?"

"Yeah, that's what I came down to tell you. The big bedroom, the one with the antique bed and the walk-in closet? Treasure trove, mate, at least from a charity auction point of view, anyway. It's got all your stage gear from the *Pick Up the Slack* tour in it. Christ, you were a flash boy back in those days, Johnny. Trying to out-peacock me, were you? Or was that Cilla's little notion? Anyway, Dom's doing an inventory. You might want to save one of those embroidered jackets to give the Hall of Fame—they weren't thrilled with the black thing you gave them at the induction, were they? Not too noticeable, basic black."

"Right. Good idea."

He glanced over his shoulder toward the kitchen. "Look, Johnny. I'm not your mum or your marriage counselor, but are you sure you want her dealing with this? I mean, I don't give a fuck about your history with Cilla, and I nearly had a heart attack when I saw those walls. How's Bree coping?"

"Badly." I straightened up, and took a deep breath, and then couldn't let it out again. Everything was suddenly tight, aching, tingling, everything at once, both hands, both feet, back of the neck all of it. "Oh, shit!"

"What?"

The damned MS was flaring, tremors moving up both legs, a nasty twitch on the left side of my face. Things were spasming and I thought back to the morning: sitting at the table, checking my messages, eating breakfast. I put a hand out toward Mac.

"I need water—I forgot to take my damned meds this morning. Bree's in the kitchen. She always carries extra meds for me."

Bree was actually in the pantry, the good-sized room off the kitchen. It's got most of the built-in shelves in the house, and it was where we'd kept everything that needed a shelf to live on, from linens to tins to spare light bulbs. She was doing just what Mac had said Dom was doing upstairs: taking inventory. I noticed she'd got on top of it well enough to take out her little notebook and that Waterman pen she always uses, and I could see there were already two pages covered in lists.

Good. I wasn't going to push anything right now, but if she could just get a handle on this place, it would be a brilliant way to make the past, my past, get a few of its teeth out of her neck, you know? And honestly, that's all I was trying for.

She fussed over me, making sure I got my meds, rinsing out a glass from the cupboard over the sink. There were birds out in the garden, singing in the trees. She rubbed my neck for a few minutes, not smiling, and went back to the pantry.

I gave it a couple of minutes sitting before I felt human enough to start on the walls again. Mac got a brilliant idea and rummaged around in the kitchen drawers; he found a couple of cooking tools, spatulas or something, and they were perfect for scraping, so we got some old dishcloths from Bree's stack in the pantry, soaked them in hot water, and headed back out into the main room to tackle the newsprint.

Out of nowhere, someone in the kitchen screamed.

It was so totally unexpected, so unreal, that when I heard it, I didn't react straight off. Bizarre, yeah? I just stood there for a moment, thinking, *Right, it's that ghost thing again*, remembering the first time I'd come back, Cilla with something nasty on one ovary, something that ruptured, a scream from the other room and I'd gone in and she'd been on the floor, writhing in her own blood. Not real.

I was still thinking that when a door slammed upstairs, and Domitra came past me so fast, I barely saw her. Mac had already moved, the doors swinging wildly behind him.

*Not a memory. This is real, this is right now. Cilla's dead and gone and Bree's in the kitchen. That was Bree who screamed.*

I moved, then. I ran into the kitchen, and that picture of Cilla on the floor was moving across my eyes like some sort of mist. But of course, Cilla was gone, long gone. It was Bree, it was here and now, and she'd screamed.

She wasn't on the floor. She was standing and swaying back and forth, about to topple; her face was a colour I'd never seen it before, old fireplace ash grey, basically. She had her left hand clenched around her right wrist. Her mouth was open. I couldn't see a damned thing wrong.

"Bree! What in hell? What is it? What's happened?"

She opened her mouth, and tried to say something, but nothing came out. Then, slowly, she turned her palm out, and showed me a single drop of blood, welling up from the soft tissue between her thumb and first finger.

I was completely bewildered. Unbelievable, yeah? You'd think I'd have sussed it, but no. I looked at her hand, and mercifully, before I could say anything at all, she said, much louder than she had to, "I want my mother."

"What?" What in hell was I missing, here? Mac was slamming drawers open, saying over and over, "Directory, where in hell's the fucking directory" and Dom was saying "Whittington, that's nearest, the hospital at Swiss Cottage is too small, it has no casualty ward."

I still couldn't see what everyone was making such a fuss about. One tiny drop of blood, it couldn't be serious, but Bree was freaked as hell and that was enough for me. I went over and got my arm around her waist, and looked at her palm.

It was tiny, nothing at all. If it hadn't been for that one drop of blood, I wouldn't have known where to look.

"I want my mother." Same flat loud voice, but something was moving about under it, something completely unlike Bree, and it was enough to stop both Mac and Dom in their tracks. "I want my phone. Where in hell is my phone!"

"Here."

I got it out for her. She got it open, fumbling with it, punching in numbers; her hands were shaking the way mine do, when the MS is at its worst. Mac and Dom, who seemed to be less clueless than I was, exchanged a quick look.

"Mom?" There is was, the thing moving in her voice that I hadn't recognised: pure panic. I'd never heard her panic, not once in all this time together. "Mom, I'm sorry I woke you but I was cleaning out a closet and I reached in and there was a needle—no, a syringe, and it's still got old stuff in it and I'm scared, I'm so scared, what should I do, tell me what to do? Mom? Please, please...."

Past and present. Oh, God.

It was the one thing I hadn't considered: Cilla, keeping her works stashed in the closet. I'd found them there myself, years ago; that was why I'd run to Kent, to stay with Luke and Viv at Draycote. I'd found them there myself once. I hadn't remembered. I'd let Bree tackle the damned cupboards, and I hadn't thought to warn her.

Miranda's voice crackled through the phone, fast and sharp. Bree's knees went, suddenly. And I was there, hanging on for dear life, calling something out to Mac, but he was already on his own cell, talking to the casualty ward at Whittington Hospital, telling them they'd need to get a blood panel set up, we were bringing someone in who'd accidentally punctured herself with a syringe, yes it had belonged to a known drug user, no we didn't know what state of health the user had been in last, no the user had died and been cremated, yes we'd bring the syringe in as well, yes we needed an ambulance and yes, we understood that they'd need to test for Hepatitis B, Hepatitis C, and HIV.

I've been through quite a lot in my life. Illness, addiction, withdrawal, alcoholism, three murders, playing with the best musicians on earth, seeing the world at the top levels of comfort, love, loss, the lot.

The two days that followed that visit to the casualty ward at Whittington Hospital in Highgate were the first time in my life I'd ever experienced terror, the real thing, the sort of thing that jolts you out of any complacency you might be stupid enough to try and hang on to.

And I got one other thing out of the worst two days of my life: I learned how to apologise, just as Bree had learned how to apologise. It's not something that comes naturally to either of us, you know? But we were learning, and about time, too.

They took Bree's blood at Whittington, and explained what they were going to be checking for: two flavours of hepatitis, a couple of other, smaller things, and HIV. That was when the fear began to set in, not the bone-shaking stuff quite yet, just the first sting of it.

I'd got hold of her left hand and I wasn't letting go of it. Her wedding ring and the engagement ring, with its emerald in the centre and the inscription hidden inside—*B from J: the light's always burning*—were warm and sharp against my skin. It made her real, close, someone I could touch, and stay with, and keep.

They looked at her hand, cleaned it, and dressed it. They asked her to describe how she'd sustained the injury—their words, not mine, I don't know why I remember the phrase so clearly—and she told them. Turned out she'd reached into the pile of towels, and the damned thing had gone straight through the soft tissue of her hand, in at the palm side and piercing all the way through to the back of her hand. It had been stashed between the towels. Mac had picked it up, just before I'd reached the kitchen; I hadn't seen it, not until he handed it to them. Not having had the visual cue didn't make me feel less terrified, you know? Or less guilty.

Because it was drugs, they also had someone from the police come in, and ask a few questions. Once he'd got that I hadn't been near the place in twenty years, that Bree had never even been to London before, that this was just bad luck, that we were on honeymoon, that we were who our passports said we were, he suggested that we might want to work with the local drug squad people, to clear the place out.

I agreed to that without any thought at all. I had more sense than to ask Bree what she wanted—really, I was afraid if I did, she'd start screaming and not be able to stop. All I wanted that moment, personally, was to dowse the entire place in petrol, toss a lit book of matches into it, and watch it burn to the fucking ground. If I never saw 18, Howard Crescent again, that was going to be fine with me.

The terror began to set it as they were telling us that the test results would take forty-eight hours to come back. That hit me, woke me up, good and hard. Two days, I thought, two days of not knowing, of wondering, of waiting, not being able to do a damned thing, to be any use at all.

I thought about hepatitis C, what it did to the liver. I know something about it because the literature on my interferon, the kind they use for MS, also had some gen on the interferon they'd specially refined for Hep C patients. It was harsh, ugly stuff, with some brutal side effects. Hepatitis, especially the C version, destroys the liver, and it does it slow and painful.

And then I thought, Christ almighty, what if it's AIDS?

Something went straight through me at that point, a picture of Bree losing weight, becoming skeletal and weak; I saw all the things that go along with AIDS in a worst case scenario. It moved through my head like a horror flick, playing over and over, nailing me to my chair, not letting me leave the theatre.

I'd moved to San Francisco, the centre of the original epidemic, in 1980. I remembered the pictures in the windows of the bars and shops and bath houses in the Castro, bare arms with suppurating sores, warning the locals to look out for something called Kaposi's sarcoma. I thought of Bree fading, weakening, dying over months or years, covered in those sores.

At that point, I basically shut down for forty-eight hours. I had just enough left to decide that I wasn't going to let her see how scared I was.

I'd been shut out of a lot of early grief that had come into her life through me. She'd protected me by just not telling me about it, not when it happened, and not later, either, unless and until I forced the issue. I'd started out resenting that, been given a good hard boot in the arse by circumstance and providence in the form of Domitra, and finished up understanding it. It was just Bree.

I'd been scared half off my nut when she'd had to go in for cancer surgery. But this was different. This was directly my fault. It was my doing. If she got sick, if she died, it was my doing. I was responsible. I'd made her come with me when she clearly hadn't wanted to. I'd let her put her hands in those piles of stuff. My doing.

I hadn't thought about it, and I hadn't warned her. There was a fifty-fifty shot that I was going to lose her.

Of course, we didn't go out to dinner with the band that night. I told Mac I'd go along with whatever they decided about Frejus, just tell me when and I'd be there, but right now, I was taking Bree home to the mews house. They got us a taxi and we left Mac and Dom at Whittington, ringing for a taxi of their own— they'd let the hire car go. Mac had promised he'd let everyone know what had happened, and why I wasn't there. I basically forgot about the band and everything else the minute we'd got into the car.

Two days. It was completely miserable and yeah, I know I sound selfish, but when I say miserable, I'm talking about Bree.

She tried to be normal, tried to be herself. We have these patterns, these things we fall into, and always have done, you know? Of course she sussed that I was blaming myself, and she was worried, what with the MS and the MVP, and she didn't want me worrying myself into a heart attack, or some rubbish. And to Bree, not worrying me came first. It always has.

So she tried the same old pattern, telling me everything was fine and not to worry, but this time, I wasn't having any of that. If putting on the act had made her feel better instead of just me, I'd have gritted my teeth and gone along with it, but it didn't. She was doing it for me, and just then, nothing in the world mattered less than I did.

So she got two days of me fussing over her like a hen. Morning of the third day, right around the point when we started thinking we might hear back from the people at the haematology lab, she dropped a bombshell on me.

We were side by side on the sofa. I remember it was raining, light and soft, spring rain, the kind that comes down easy and smells like the season and washes the oil and muck off the London streets. We'd had breakfast with the windows cracked open, enough to let the springtime in, not enough to let the damp in with it. Her cell phone was on the table, mine right beside it, waiting.

I'd already had the call from Mac, letting me know that the gig at Frejus was on, we'd have ten days to get it set up and rehearse at the amphitheatre, check the acoustics. It was all very rushed, but they wanted the gig for the night before the official opening night at the festival. There was no word on whether the remnants of the other two bands were in, as well, but at that point, I didn't much care. I was ready to be where they wanted me to be, play what they wanted me to play, but I just didn't have the attention to spare for it right then.

So we were sitting there, just hanging out and trying to relax.

And out of nowhere, Bree suddenly looked up at me.

"John—listen. I need to say something—I need to get it out, to ask you, to find out—shit, I don't know. It's going to sound sick. You're going to think I've gone out of my mind, and maybe I have. But I just have to say it. Okay?"

"Right." My heart stuttered, but I ignored it. "I'm right here, love. What's going on, then?"

"Do you think she knew?" Her voice was very quiet, low, as if she thought someone or something might be listening and didn't want her thought to be overheard. "Cilla, I mean. Do you suppose she guessed that she wasn't coming back? That I'd be there? Do you think she did it on purpose? She told me in New York that she wanted to watch me die—she told you that too, on that voicemail she left you. Do you think she's in the house, still, somehow? Watching, maybe laughing?"

All the hair at the back of my neck was prickling. Whatever I'd thought she might be going to say, it wasn't this. I looked at her, trying to sort out if she was seriously asking me if I honestly believed that Cilla'd had some sort of premonition, and had laid a booby trap for the girl she'd hated so long.

And damn it, she was serious. I could see it.

"No." I sounded calm, and very sure of myself. Good. If I wasn't showing the goosebumps, how thoroughly creeped out I was, that was good. "I don't think she had a clue she was never coming home. I don't believe in ghosts, not that kind of ghost, anyway. And by the way, love, I don't think you've got AIDS, either. I know you haven't asked my opinion, but I just thought I'd mention it."

"You don't?" Her mouth twisted suddenly, painfully. "Why not? Because I think maybe I do. I think she wanted me dead and maybe she's going to get her wish. So, why don't you think so?"

She obviously thought I was just being reassuring, and really, I had been, but suddenly there was something right there, something I'd forgotten, and I had an answer for her, after all. I reached out and got hold of the bandaged right palm, and kissed it.

"Back in New York, you told me Cilla had a nosebleed. You said her blood got all over your hands. Do you remember, Bree?"

She was quiet, not saying a word, letting her hand stay where it was, very passive. But her eyes were fixed on me. She didn't seem to get where I was going with it. She nodded, a small nod. She was holding her breath.

"You're a cook," I told her. "I've never known you to not have at least one good scrape or two on your hands. You use yours as much as I use mine, and that's quite a lot of use, yeah? And you said she bled all over you. I remember those nosebleeds, from the coke days—there's a lot of blood. So if she had AIDS, or hepatitis, you'd have got it from her then."

"Maybe I did." Her voice wavered. "Oh God, John, I never even thought about that. Maybe…."

"No." I shook my head at her. I had it clear in my head, now, sorted out. "Because they did a blood panel on you, when you went in for cancer surgery, remember? They might not have checked for AIDS, true, but I'm betting they'd have scanned for hepatitis, both varieties. And actually, thinking about it, HIV as well. Anything where the doctor might be at risk, they'd want to know. You could call your mum, and ask her."

Her lips were quivering. I bent over and kissed her, full on the mouth, tongue tip to tongue tip, the way we both like it best.

"And if you've got AIDS, lady, then I've got it, as well. It's not as if we use condoms, right? If we've both got it, then okay, we can work it out and deal with it together, just like married people. Isn't that what marriage is about? Loyalty to each other, loyalty working both ways? Dealing together?"

There were tears on her cheeks, and I brushed them away.

"I'm sorry, Bree," I told her. It came out, no thought, no planning, the apology I'd wanted to give her since I'd seen her standing there with a bead of blood on her palm, and hadn't seen what the fuss was about, and nearly said so. "I should have thought back to what happened after my own rehab, when I got deported. I should have remembered about her stashing her works between the linens—it's not as if I didn't know. I should have sent you off to Bond Street to try on some Jimmy Choos, and gone off to Howard Crescent by myself first. I fucked up, I just didn't think, and I'm so sorry. This has been two days of hell for both of us, and the truth is, love, only one of us deserved to go through it."

She opened her mouth to say something, and her cell phone rang. She was only on for about twenty seconds, and this time I watched her shoulders the whole time.

So I'd guessed what the news was before she told me. When she'd picked up and flipped the phone open to answer it, her shoulders had been hunched, drawn in for protection, warding off bad news. It took all of twenty seconds for them to relax.

She laid the phone down, and looked at me. I was already smiling.

"Negative." Her lips had curved up in an answering smile. "Negative for all three. Cilla may have been a junkie and a tramp and a dupe and who knows what the hell else, but she didn't give me AIDS or hepatitis. And I am so damned relieved, I could just get up on the table and dance, but I know you don't dance, so why don't you tell me what you'd like to do instead, by way of celebration? Or is that too easy?"

"Pretty easy, yeah." My eyes were stinging, sheer relief. "I say we go out and you indulge me by letting me buy you something pricey and flash, maybe some new shoes, just to prove that you've forgiven me and show me you're still willing to pamper me by letting me blow a lot of dosh on you. Then we eat something, come back here, and I make your eyes roll all the way back a few dozen times. Sound good?"

"Oh, hell yes." Her eyes were shining. "I can hardly wait. Maybe we can switch the order around…?"

"Anything you want, love. But first let's ring a few people and share the good news—it's not fair to keep them dangling, when they've all been so worried. Mac and Dom can tell the rest of our friends, and you can ring your mum, once it's a decent time back in California. Give Tony and Katia a ring, as well, let them know, and check on the cats, while we're at it. Oh, and tomorrow, we can start packing—we're off to Cannes at the weekend."

# Chapter Four

"(beep) JP? Ian. The band needs to meet at the amphitheatre at two this afternoon. I spoke with Benno Marling and Harry Johns, and they'll be along with their lot later on—the plan right now is the two bands combining to cover some of their bigger hits. They haven't got enough personnel left between them for individual sets, so they're opening, an hour maximum. We get first soundcheck—headlining for ninety minutes, an hour fifteen plus encore. Can you be outside at right around one? There's a car coming to get you. (beep)"

"Perfect." I glanced out the window. The weather was gorgeous, the way it always seems to be in the South of France once you get past the Mistral, about March. "Soundcheck at the amphitheatre at two. Did you want to come along?"

"Not unless you want me there." Bree was about as relaxed as I'd ever seen her. "I thought I'd go wander the open-air market in

St. Raphael, maybe get some fish for dinner. It's so damned fresh, it's still squirming. They carry it up from the sea in baskets, just caught. I've been jonesing for some."

"Sounds good, love, but let me see about the rest of my messages first. There may be something on for tonight—I've got the feeling we're supposed to be somewhere, but I'm damned if I can remember where it is."

"*(beep) Yes, good morning JP. This is David Walters from Blacklight London. Just wanted to remind you, tonight is that private dinner for the band and their families with Sir Cedric Parmeley. He's hired the casino at the Hotel d'Ange, in Les Sirènes sur Mer. Everything begins around nine, and will go on as long as anyone wants to use the casino. He's requesting black tie, so it's dress all the way up. Limo will be at your place at eight. RSVP to me, and I'll update my lists. Cheers. (beep)*"

"Ah. Better hold off a day on the fish, love, okay?" I glanced over at Bree, who had a glass of fresh orange juice in one hand and was dreaming out at the Mediterranean in the distance. She'd picked the oranges from the tree outside the front door— the damned things were the size of a baby's head, and were sweeter than the roses in May, thin-skinned and fragrant. There were lemons, as well, and she'd been muttering about making an old-fashioned lemon curd, whatever that was. "I knew I was forgetting something. Turns out we've got a do tonight at a casino, full posh dinner, the lot, band and families, so you get to be my plus-one, lady. I'm betting you've got the perfect dress for it in the closet, somewhere."

She swung around and rested her chin in one hand. "What kind of do? You mean Blacklight's playing?"

"Not playing—eating. And probably gambling, if I happened to enjoy gambling. Good thing I don't, right? It's not as if I haven't indulged in enough addictive behaviour in my time. You can if you want to, though. Hang on a minute, and let me ring David

Walters back to tell them we're coming along."

I made my call, got through with no trouble, and set the phone down. Bree had her legs stretched out, taking in the sun. She has long, long legs, Bree does, and they were tanning up nicely. She does a lot better in the sun than I do.

"Yeah, so, tonight's event is courtesy of our charming host, the barmy director, Sir Cedric himself," I told her. "He's hired a casino and probably a decent chef. This one smells like an excuse to impress the local media, and drool down whatever healthy young cleavage happens to be hanging about the place. Black tie."

"Okay. No problem, John—I can go fancy. Tomorrow, though, I'm cooking for us, damn it." She nodded toward the tall doors that led back into the villa. "What's the point of having a kitchen like that, if we keep eating out all the time? What are you grinning about?"

"Nothing."

I'd wanted Bree to get used to some of the Blacklight side benefits I've always taken for granted. Over the past few days, circumstances had got together, gone into a huddle, and decided to pick my wife up and drop her straight into reality, at least the way a successful touring band defines reality. The short notice of the Frejus gig had meant a major acceleration of Blacklight's resources. After total immersion in the reality of emergency band spending, Bree wasn't even going to remember what that fancy cashmere coat had cost me.

The first reality check had come with the jet. The circs were straightforward enough: we needed to get to the South of France in a hurry, and for that, the logical thing was a private corporate jet. So our management had hired us one, right after the London staff had hired us a bunch of villas. They'd been smart enough to not even bother about looking at hotels. Around festival time at Cannes, there isn't a hotel within three hours any direction that hasn't been booked for a year. Your only hope is private villas, unless you fancy sleeping under a tree on one of the hillsides in the mountains, or in your car. So everyone in the band had got their own villa, because why would you double or triple up if you have enough money not to?

The downside, if there was one, was that we were scattered all over the area. Cal and Barb Wilson were farthest east, overlooking the sea at Villefranche-sur-Mer, on the hill between Nice and Monaco. Luke and Solange were farthest west, at St. Tropez. Stu and Cyn had a nice penthouse in Nice, looking out at the Promenade. Mac and Dom were in Les Sirènes sur Mer, close to Antibes.

Ours was on the hill just above St. Raphael, walkable down into town or up into Frejus, if you happened to be a mountain goat, or maybe in shape for the Tour de France. It had a pool, and antique furniture, and a custom kitchen as good as Bree's back home. There was a fruit orchard, and lavender growing in one corner of the garden, and some purple flowering vine that smelled to high heaven, around the doors and windows. I'd caught Bree out there a few times, just staring at the garlic as big as tangerines, and the wild herbs; I had no idea what any of them were, but I could smell them from ten feet away. The villa had five bedrooms, and it could have easily fit the rest of the band, but we had it to ourselves.

I'd known it was going to ping Bree's socialist working-class-hero sensibilities. It wasn't as bad as I thought it would be, probably because she'd reacted so hard to the jet that there wasn't much outrage left to spare, even for Bree.

The jet—right. When we got into a hire car and headed out to Gatwick Airport, Bree'd thought we were boarding a commercial flight. At least, that's what I found out later; I never thought about it, really. We had to get there fast, there were sixteen of us, we hired a corporate jet. Seems logical enough, really. Blacklight's operations and travel people seem to think so, and that's why we pay them, to handle all that. Besides, we'd been doing it for coming up on thirty years.

From the outside, it was a basic plane, a 737, I think. I don't know a lot about them—as far as I'm concerned, a plane is a plane, a metal tube with wings and engines, designed to get me long distances in a reasonable time. This one was different from the ones Bree'd flown before, though.

She started out edgy, straight off, when she realised that the band personnel were going to have the plane to ourselves. After we boarded, I really thought the top of her head was going to explode.

If you've never flown a private corporate jet before, you might not realise that the interior's usually been tarted up. The one Blacklight Corporate had chartered for us carried eighteen passengers plus crew, had white leather chairs, a couple of bedrooms, satellite telly, and a general vibe of such decadent luxury that I took one look at my old lady's face and found myself hoping she wouldn't start yelling "Up against the wall, motherfucker!" or something.

All her redder hackles were up and humming like piano wires; you couldn't miss it. Any minute, she was going to start singing the bloody *Nationale* and start hunting up comrades so that she could start the revolution. It's hard to explain—she's not even a communist, it's just that she can't deal with ostentatious wealth. Somewhere in her head, she associates it with greed, and greed equals evil, in her book.

She sat there and simmered, all the way to France. We were about twenty minutes from landing at Nice when Ian, bless him, wandered over and parked himself in the chair next to her, and proceeded to clue her in.

"Not bad for an economy flight," he asked her. "Is it?"

He wasn't joking, either, and she could see it. Her eyes went wider than usual.

"*Economy* flight…?"

By the time we taxied up to the gate and were ready to get off our posh ride, Bree'd been given a crash course in the economics of why a corporate charter was the cheap way to go. Basically—I got this from Ian later—London to Nice, entire package, ran about twenty thousand dollars. If we'd put sixteen people on commercial flights at short notice, flying first class, we'd have spent closer to thirty thousand, and possibly even more. But air charters like ours charge by the air hour, not by how many people are flying; it's a flat rate. So the result was nice savings. And luxury, in this instance, actually equaled economy.

It was perfect. The math made so much sense, it took all the socialist wind straight out of Bree's sails. And that was without ever having to remind her that, when I'd been laid up in hospital in Boston after my heart attack, she'd flown the detective who wanted to question her up from New York by chartered helicopter—at a cost of slightly over six thousand dollars—because she'd refused to leave me alone in a hospital bed, to please the police or for any other reason.

What Ian had started, the South of France finished off. Bree liked London, was interested and amused by it, but I got the feeling she could shrug it off if I hadn't been from there, and hadn't loved the place myself. France, though, that was a different story. She and the south fell for each other from the moment she got off the plane and smelled the sea, and lavender growing in the garden.

The place just seduced her. I never heard a word about the extravagance of two people in a villa with five bedrooms; all that happened was some amazing sex, followed by some brilliant meals, and then more sex. Hell, once she realised we weren't overlooked by any neighbouring villas, she started swimming nude and wanting to make love outdoors. I was delighted to oblige, so long as it was late enough in the day to not get a sunburn on my bum; like I said, she does better out in the sun than I do. It was a lot of fun.

She wandered off into town on her own, with a basket over one arm, for a few hours of market browsing, while I headed up the hill to the amphitheatre in a hired car, with Little Queenie and my Les Paul Deluxe. We had two days before the festival started, which meant we had two days to sort out the concert. Actually, we'd already done most of it, deciding on which songs worked for an hour fifteen worth of music plus encore, getting our roadies and instrument techs flown in, making sure the rig was in place.

The last details had been put together the afternoon before, so today was the big run-through and soundcheck. The acoustics in a Roman hillside amphitheatre, originally designed to seat thirteen thousand screaming bloodthirsty spectators on stone benches while they watched gladiators, are different from playing the Meadowlands or Wembley Stadium, you know?

The soundcheck went perfectly. No surprise there—we'd been doing this together nearly thirty years, and Mac and Luke in their old band, Blackpool Southern, had been doing it since I was too young for O levels. We adjusted EQ, went over the set list, checked the echo of drums against the mountain, and let Ronan Greene, our amazing sound designer, tell us what the differences would be with ten thousand people sitting on the benches. I had a nice reunion with my Scots guitar tech, Jas, and introduced him to Little Queenie. Once he got over the shock of seeing me with something that wasn't a Gibson, he got familiar with the new axe, and crooned over her.

We finished up by running through two songs—the set opener and closer—top to bottom. When I looked up, I saw we had company.

It had been a long time since I'd seen Benno Marling, founder of Isle of Dogs, but I recognised him at once. There was no mistaking that eagle beak he used for a nose, and no mistake on the high forehead, either. The nose looked even beakier and the forehead looked even higher, now that he was completely bald. His face was so well-known from the sixties, it took me a moment to remember that I'd never actually met the bloke before.

"Nice." He must be in his mid-sixties by now; Isle of Dogs had topped the charts in 1965 and 1966, sneaking into the cracks on the rare days the Beatles and Stones had been on holiday, or off with the Maharishi, or something. He'd long ago stopped wearing the flash velvet suits and Slim Jim ties. Just as well, because a teddy boy in his sixties, even a retired one, would be a complete menace and a very bad joke. "You lot have your shit all down, don't you? Here's hoping we can give a decent gig ourselves. We'll see when Jimmy and the blokes from Typhoid Harry get here."

His singing voice was just like his speaking voice. I'd listened to him a lot when the band was popular; Isle of Dogs had a superb guitar player, Jimmy Wonderley, a blues fan and a bit of an innovator. Wonderley hadn't been as big an influence on me as someone like Bulldog Moody, but he was up there.

I'd have liked to hang out a few minutes longer, listen to their soundcheck, but Parmeley had cut things close by inviting everyone involved to the casino. I saw Harry Johns and the two remaining members of Typhoid Harry pull up as my driver was closing my door and getting ready to head out. Harry didn't look to have aged nearly as badly as Benno had, but of course, Harry was probably twenty years younger than Benno to start with. Besides, he'd always worn his head shaved, so there was no sudden-bald shock thing going on there.

The bloke with him was their bass player, and one look told me he wasn't going to be up for much; he had that sick look all longtime junkies get. I wondered what they were going to do for a drummer, since theirs had OD'd in a cheap Miami motel room a good long time back, and I couldn't remember if Benno's drummer was here or not. I wasn't even sure they'd played together in twenty years.

Still, there was no point in worrying about what the opening and closing acts in Parmeley's movie were likely to do. Blacklight had its act together, and that was all I really had the mental room to worry about right now. In two days, the band that was supposed to be long gone by now was going to take the stage in front of a packed house at an amphitheatre built just around the time they'd been perforating Julius Caesar on the Ides of March.

And no matter what our predecessors did, or the band who was supposed to take over for us did? We were going to kick ass, just the way we always had done and hopefully always would.

I actually got home in time for some kip, which was a damned good thing; my feet were doing their wretched little tingle thing, and my face felt tender. That's never a good sign, not where my MS is concerned.

Bree was already back, and had got her clothes for the party ready. She was feeling energised and chatty, but she took one look at me, and that was over fast. She always knows when the MS is acting up, no matter what I do to downplay it and not worry her.

"Bed." She was already pouring me out a glass of spring water. "Here, take your meds. You don't need to even think about getting a shower and getting dressed for another hour or so. Did you eat anything? Damn. Okay, no problem, I'll get some soup together for when you wake up. Come on, John, you need a nap."

She turned down the covers and watched me curl up. There was a nice light easy breeze coming through the window, and I could smell the sea, and Bree was right there in the next room if I needed her….

When I woke up, nearly ninety minutes later, the meds had

had time to do their thing, and I was feeling much less shaky. She'd laid my tux out, and was getting dressed in her own posh bathroom, so I let her know I was up, and doing better, and headed in for a shower.

I was just adjusting my tie, trying to get it to sit flat, when Bree came out. I looked up and saw her in the mirror, and right there, I nearly decided to ditch the casino and the dinner in favour of staying home and pinning her to the bed, or the pool, or anything or anywhere else I could pin her. Looking back, I wish to hell I had done.

She looked smashing. Her dress was this coppery brown velvet thing, with a sort of green shine to it. It hugged her everywhere it could possibly hug, sleeves and hips and thigh, and then did this sort of fishtail thing at the bottom back. It had a high neck and long sleeves. She'd put her hair up, and her mouth was juicy with deep red lipstick. She'd put on very high dinner sandals, bronze snakeskin stilettos. The heels were so skinny, I don't know how they didn't snap when she walked. She looked like a movie star from the thirties or forties.

"Wow." Everything below the waist was making itself heard. "Bree, baby, if you're trying to convince me to stay here and not let you up for a couple of hours, you're doing a brilliant job. The lipstick's a nice touch—you ought to wear it more often. Here, turn around, let me see the whole look. New gear?"

"Yep, bought the dress yesterday. And if you wanted to nail me, you left it too late." She puckered her lips and twirled once, and I felt the rest of my blood supply deserting the north end of me in favour of the south. The dress was backless, and there's just something about Bree's back, especially when there are also buttons under it or around it, that has that immediate effect on me. "You like the lipstick? Good to know. I figured I had to do something to compete with all these French babes. I thought I needed more ammo than just the Jimmy Choos. The women here all seem to have perfect asses and adorable pouts."

"They do?" The bottom back of the dress was as huggy as the rest of it, what I'd once heard Mac refer to as an arse-loving skirt. It was also cut down to the crack in her ass. I thought for a moment that, for once, she'd done without buttons, but they were there: tiny tortoise-shell things under her spine, and more running up each tight sleeve. "Are you sure we haven't got time? I could just lift the skirt up over your head. Are you even wearing knickers under that thing…?"

"Dream on, honey." She was grinning. "I spent the better part of half an hour getting my hair to cooperate, and if you think I'm going to let you—what are you—John, stop, don't—oh, *man*, you don't play fair, ohgodohgod…."

She managed to redo her makeup before the limo showed up, and really, I'd been careful not to mess her hair. So we were both hungry and sleek and in really good moods. Bree was actually looking smug.

The drive down was beautiful, the sea off to the south and the sky full of stars. It was weird; I'd gone half a century, more than that really, without noticing much, but this trip, I was noticing and it was having a very unexpected result: I kept writing song lyrics. I'd gone half a century without doing that, either, but, well, there you go. Fragments, snippets that became verses, kept popping into my head and I kept scribbling them down, and turning them into complete songs. Maybe that's what happens to ageing musicians who go on honeymoon.

The driver pulled up outside the casino, and opened the door for me first. I thought that was peculiar, because isn't the lady supposed to get first attention from the help? But then I got that I was supposed to offer Bree my arm, because there was a red carpet, and lights, and people with cameras.

"Whoa." Bree had her hand on my arm. She sounded stunned, and she was talking out the side of her mouth, keeping it low.

"What the fuck? Did we just warp into the Academy Awards, or something? Is some snotty talking head with breast enhancements going to come over and diss my dress for a cable TV network? Because if this is just a private party, no big deal, why are those photographers taking pictures of us?"

"It's better than the Academy Awards, love. This is the Cannes festival. And over here, we call them paparazzi."

"Smartass."

"Damned right I am."

I slid my hand down her arm, got hold of her waist, and jerked her lightly around, and down for a kiss. Flashbulbs popped all over the place. I was grinning like an idiot. Bree probably didn't realise it, but I'd just signed the death warrant for whatever was left of her invisibility in my world.

"There you go. It's official—we're married. The morning newspapers will all say 'JP Kinkaid, guitarist for legendary rock band Blacklight, in a tuxedo by Armani, and his lovely wife Bree'. Having fun? Because if you are, you might as well play to the cameras."

"You're shitting me, right?"

"Not at all. The morning papers, I swear." We'd passed under a canopy, up red-carpeted steps, into the Hotel d'Ange. "Right, here we go—showtime. Luke! Oi, mate, over here. Solange, you look gorgeous."

She did, too. She raised a little ache in my heart, especially in the gear she had on. Solange had opted for retro glam, a seventies thing with a poufy short skirt, embroidered in gold thread, and a metallic gathered strapless top. She'd have been right at home out on the dance floor at Studio 54, back in the day. Turned out the dress was vintage designer. It looked familiar, for some reason.

"Ta, Uncle John. This was my mum's dress—Daddy said I could bring it along if it fit, and it does, so I did. Isn't it amazing?

The label says Zandra Rhodes—she was a trendy designer back then, right? My mum had three dresses by her." She caught sight of Bree and her own dark blue eyes went very wide. "Oh, wow! Aunt Bree, that dress is hot!"

"If we're talking about hot, infant, it's pot meet kettle." Mac had come up behind me, sleek and formal. "You look scorching. I love the upswept hair—you've gone all golden and sophisticated."

It was ridiculous, how easily he could switch from his usual flash to dead elegant. The room was crowded with people, but I could see all sorts of female faces turning his way. "Dom, you'd best keep an eye on my goddaughter, here. Bloody hell, this place is absolutely swarming with beautiful women. What is it about France, anyway? Do they put something in the prenatal vitamins?"

"It's because we're all tourists, that's what. French men, they take these chicks for granted. They're the norm, the women are. You know?"

Dom was dressed so unusually for her that it took me a moment or two to actually suss out what was different: she had on billowy silky trouser things that reminded me vaguely of the Arabian Nights, and a short loose jacket I might have worn myself, back during my flash rocker days in the seventies, if it hadn't been a sort of cantaloupe colour. She had low shoes on with it, and I suddenly got it: the girl was dressed for work, insofar as black tie allowed. She might have been Mac's plus-one, but she was also his muscle, and it showed.

The place was filling up in a hurry. We tracked down dinner in a private room off the main floor of the casino, a long buffet with food good enough to earn a thumbs-up from Bree. The crowd—there must have been over two hundred people—ate, and talked, and drank. I looked around and spotted Benno Marling in all black, talking with Jimmy Wonderley, his guitar player; I made a mental note to go find someone to introduce me.

There was also a lot of gambling going on. I saw Solange settling down at a roulette table, next to a geezer with two scary-looking bald blokes guarding his back. The geezer put some money on a slot, and Solange watched him. He reached out and patted her hand, and for some reason, maybe because he held her hand too long, I wanted to bash him. The entire thing felt like a bad remake of *Casino Royale,* or something….

"Isn't that Cedric Parmeley, teaching Solange how to play roulette?" Stu Corrigan and his wife Cyn had come up next to us. Cyn, one of those Nordic-looking blondes, was in something beaded. She was frowning across the room. "And if it is, why are his two watchdogs staring at Mac as if he was dinner?"

Cyn was right. The geezer was Cedric Parmeley, reminding me of the difference between sixty and eighty-five, and the two black-suited heavies with him weren't watching their boss, they were watching Mac. Mac, completely oblivious, was having a lively conversation in rapid-fire French with someone I'd never seen before, female of course.

I turned my attention back to the two suits. They both had seriously unpleasant expressions on their faces; as I watched, one of them leaned over to the other one, and whispered something, and jerked his head toward Mac. The other one smiled, about as nasty a look as I'd ever seen on a human face.

"They're not looking at Mac." There was something in Bree's voice, a kind of trouble, or maybe just recognition of trouble to come. "They're looking at Dom."

Right that moment, Solange Hedley got up, and said something to Cedric Parmeley. It looked like a nice basic thank-you and farewell moment, perfectly casual, and she started off into the crowd.

Cedric Parmeley got to his feet and started after her, the two heavies no more than a hand's reach behind. The look on Parmeley's face was ugly, a kind of smoothed-out thing. He looked as if he might go off drooling any moment.

"Shit!" I don't know why, but every nerve ending I had, with or without MS-depleted myelin, was yelling. Something was off; something was wrong. I could feel it. "Where's Luke?"

Bree'd caught it, as well. She waved a hand wildly, and got Dom's eye. Bree tried to semaphore, said something profane under her breath, and started after Solange, who seemed to be heading off in search of a loo.

"Bree, wait—"

It was no good. Even in four-inch stilettos, she was too fast for me. But Dom was with her now, catching up and taking the lead, the pair of them slicing a way through the crush of tuxedos and pricey evening dresses. I looked around, trying to find Luke. I couldn't see Solange, or Parmeley, or his muscle.

The whole thing happened very fast. There was a yell, a crash, and then a scream of pain, all coming from the other side of a pair of roped-off velvet curtains.

For a few seconds, everyone and everything seemed to get caught in place. That scream hadn't been a girl's sort of noise. The pitch belonged to a full-grown man, in serious discomfort.

And then Luke was there at the curtains, saying something, but he was separated from me by a good thirty feet and a good fifty people. A split second later, Solange erupted through the curtains and into her father's arms. He had her protectively circled in one arm, and she was in tears, the front of her mother's Zandra Rhodes vintage dress torn where someone had tried to separate it from its wearer, the edge of a lacy strapless bra showing.

There was a moment of silence, total and absolute. Solange broke it. She was nearly hysterical, completely freaked out; dark blonde strands of hair had come loose, as if someone had got a hand into the do and held, hard. Fragments and snippets of her voice slammed across the room at me, at Cyn and Stu Corrigan, at the crowd around us.

"...he grabbed my dress...he tried to pull me into the loo...those bald men wouldn't let me out...Daddy...?"

I sucked my breath in and got my wits back. Luke, his face murderous, took a step toward the doorway. I'd never seen him looking like that; both hands were balled up into fists, including the one at the end of the arm he had round his daughter. I had a sudden flash of him breaking a few knuckles across Parmeley's jaw, and being unable to play the show. Of course, if he did that and the two watchdogs did what they were obviously paid to do, he'd need backup, or maybe a wheelchair.

I think it was right about then that all hell broke loose.

If you want to know what came first, I can't tell you. The local gendarmes asked me the same thing later, much later, but I have no idea what the sequence was. The first thing I really remember seeing was Cedric Parmeley, his right wrist twisted up at a very odd angle, staggering out from between the curtains, mouthing something and blubbering like a baby. After that, it all sort of went bad action movie on me and ran together, you know? Sergio Leone on acid.

I remember a sort of small whirlwind, a melee of movement: it was the two bald blokes, and Dom. Dom backed out of the curtained alcove fast, and she was in full fight mode, first time I'd ever seen it. I spared one tiny corner of my brain to be thankful it wasn't me she was preparing to take down, but I was damned if I could summon up any sympathy at all for the two goons who were trying to surround her. Because it was obvious, even to me, that they wanted her in the middle, and she wasn't having any.

"Come to poppa, bitch," one of them told her, and added a racial epithet I hadn't heard used in years, and could have done quite nicely never hearing again. He had a thick cockney accent, pure East London, and a bumpy nose. "We're going to add a bit of blue to all that black."

She ignored both the invitation and the insult. Too busy keeping both of them within the range of her vision, I'd say.

The second goon didn't bother with language. He just slashed out suddenly, very fast, a smooth professional move that scared the shit out of me, and I saw something glint in his left hand, and my heart stuttered hard.

The fucker had a knife.

What I didn't see was Dom's kick, because honestly, it was too fast. Her face was stone, pure concentration, and one second there was a knife in the suit's hand and the next, he was empty-handed, or at least, no knife, because both hands were spasming as he tried to cover his demolished groin. I felt my own nuts tighten up in a moment of sympathy, but that didn't last long; the bastard had it coming. The knife hit the floor, and Dom kicked it away, into the crowd, well beyond his sight or his reach, assuming he'd been in any shape to deal with it.

People were yelling, the room emptying out as people backed away toward the exits, and Mac was heading for his bodyguard at full speed, cutting through the crush of people. I thought I saw Jimmy Wonderley in the crowd near the door, but I couldn't be sure. It was total chaos.

Mac yelled something at Luke—*get her out of here*—and I saw Luke nod. I thought, for a mad moment, that Mac was talking about Dom, but then I saw Luke lead his daughter toward the main doors, without so much as a look behind him. He stopped to take off his tux jacket and drape it over her torn dress on the way out. He's a very good dad, Luke is.

Right around then, I realised I was moving myself, not away from the fight, but towards it. There was a voice in my head, asking me what the fuck I thought I was doing, it's not as if I could do anything but get in Dom's way. And if course, my brain provided the immediate answer: *where the hell is my wife?* There was no sign of Bree, and now I was beginning to lose it.

I looked up just in time to see Bumpy Nose—he really looked

as if he'd been on the wrong end of too many schoolyard punch-ups—launch a kick at Dom, but she was a lot faster than he was, and the kick met air. Before he could get his leg back on the ground, she'd got hold of his foot and given it a hard twist and jerk. Bumpy Nose screamed, and went down hard.

His mate seemed to have good recuperative powers, because he was up on his feet and reasonably steady again, even after that slam to the groin. Bumpy Nose hitting the ground seemed to be a signal to his mate to lose what was left of his tiny little excuse for a mind, because he went for Dom.

I can't imagine, now, what he thought he was on about. He just went full throttle, pure hate. Maybe he didn't respect her fighting skills because she was black, or maybe it was because she was female. Either way, the bloke was a fucking moron, a lovely demonstration of Darwinism at its finest, doing its whole survival of the fittest thing.

She actually let him get almost within grabbing distance before she moved her right leg up and out, and did whatever it was she did to his left eye. I know there was blood and I know my stomach tried to do a tango with itself, and I know the bloke gave a screech that was too high to be coming out of that big a body. He hit the floor and, as it turned out, hit it hard enough to dislocate his shoulder. We found out later she'd nailed him high on the cheekbone, cracking the lower part of the eye socket, whatever that bone is called. Couldn't have happened to a nicer bloke, except maybe his partner.

As much as I'd love to be able to say Dom hadn't even broken a sweat, I'd be lying. She was panting and heaving for breath, seeing Mac out of the corner of her vision, waving at him to get the hell back and out of her way. She was so damned busy that I couldn't be sure whether she'd spotted Bumpy Nose, down on the floor behind her. He seemed to have decided to ignore his twisted ankle, and he'd managed to get back to his feet. He didn't stay there very long, though, just long enough to reach into his pocket and pull out something small, and dark, and metallic.

You don't need to be standing on a sore ankle to use what he had in his hand. At that range, he couldn't miss. I opened my mouth to yell something, I'm damned if I know what, but I never got it out.

The goon's eyes suddenly went very wide. He was still three feet out of Dom's range, but he stopped where he was. There was a look of surprise on his face. Something seemed to have gone wrong with his right arm, because he dropped the gun.

And then he went down to his knees, and then flat out on his face. He was writhing and whimpering and moaning, trying to get words out and not getting it done, just twisting like an eel. There was a dark sticky patch high up on the back of his suit jacket, right where his back met his right shoulder, just outside the armpit. The dark sticky stuff was blood, and it was oozing out of a small round hole.

I just stood there, totally disoriented. It looked like a bullet hole, a perfect little circle. But the only one with a gun that I knew of was the bloke who'd just hit the deck. I looked at that hole, at the sticky dark blood around it, and out of nowhere, I remembered Bree, standing in the kitchen of Howard Crescent with the tiny hole in her hand, the hole from Cilla's leftover works, swaying on her feet.

And there *was* Bree, right behind where the first goon had gone down. She really was swaying on her feet, but this time it was because she was lopsided, one shoe off and one shoe on. That was a four-inch difference—quite a lot to balance, you know? She was holding a bronze Jimmy Choo dinner sandal in her right hand. The sandal seemed to be missing quite a lot of its wooden stiletto heel; there was a long steel shaft still attached, but the wood that had covered that reinforcing metal spike had broken off at an angle, leaving nothing but the shaft. She looked down at the writhing bloke at her feet.

"You fucking racist piece of shit." Her voice was absolutely furious. "You and your asshole horndog boss owe me a new pair of shoes."

# Chapter Five

It took us hours at the Les Sirènes lockup before we were able to get Dom and Bree out of jail. The entire thing was a cluster-fuck of bloody epic proportions.

Part of the problem was that Parmeley was local. He'd lived there for thirty years or more. He bought his wine and cheese and pâté from some bloke down the road who probably called him Ceddie. They knew him; he was *Monsieur Le Directeur.* And they didn't know us.

There was also the fact that, while the French are generally willing to cut a pretty woman a good deal of slack, it helps if the pretty woman isn't snarling at them and calling them rude names. Bree was uncooperative, to say the least. Turned out she'd seen the gun in the second bloke's hand, seen him turn it toward Dom, and buried the heel of her shoe in the bloke's back.

She'd only meant to sting him, to make him drop the gun, or at least that's what she told me later. Thing is, there's a lot of Bree, and she's quite strong; hell, she's had years of helping me carry Marshall amplifiers, and she tosses her stainless steel cookware about with no effort at all.

So she'd stung the bastard, all right. She'd hit so hard, she'd broken off nearly two inches of wooden stiletto heel covering on impact, and buried the uncovered steel shaft in his muscle, or the soft tissue at the back of his shoulder. He'd been taken off to hospital and was undergoing surgery, and the gendarmes were discussing whether or not to charge her with assault, because it was pretty clear that she'd done enough damage to keep him from playing bodyguard again for a good long while.

And while it was true that Parmeley had tried to rape Solange, with a little help from his scumbag bodyguards, Luke couldn't enter an attempted rape charge against Parmeley without shoving Solange into the limelight, and putting her through hell. He didn't want to do that, and honestly, neither did the rest of us. We all remembered those flashbulbs, out there on the red carpet.

Where it suddenly got tricky, and what it turned out was triggering Bree, was how they were dealing with Dom. Because she was in an entirely different situation—she was a professional, you know? She was there doing the job she was paid to do, which was to protect her employer. Her employer had asked her to keep an eye on his goddaughter, and when the subject of that request had been molested in an alcove, she'd reacted and done her job. It doesn't get much more straightforward than that. When you add to it that the French have a high respect for propriety, for people doing what they're supposed to be doing, I think we were all expecting that they weren't even going to bother with Dom.

We were wrong. They were bothering, all right. It was right about then that I began to get a nasty taste at the back of my mouth, and the nastiness came from my suspicion that there was a racist streak at the bottom of all this. They were leaning on Dom because she was black.

And Bree—who, unlike me, has at least some rudimentary school French—had sussed it out, and was chaining herself to the ramparts. All that lovely outrage she'd been made to discard over the luxury chartered plane and the fancy villa had just come roaring back, and this time there was a legitimate reason for it. She had a major "*à la lanterne!*" vibe going; any minute, she was going to start talking about the *sans culottes*. My wife was spitting piss and vinegar in two different languages. She had some serious blood in her eye.

It was ridiculous. It was simple enough: Parmeley had grabbed Solange against her will, Dom had intervened, and Parmeley had a fractured wrist and maybe a lesson learned. Personally, I'd say the bugger had got off light, all things considered. She could easily have broken his neck.

I don't know whether Parmeley was completely nuts, drooling and good for nothing except dicking around with his precious films, or whether it was because the girl who'd broken his wrist wasn't white. But whatever was going on in his head, he was pressing charges against Dom for assault. And Luke would have to file a counter-charge against Parmeley to get him to back off, but he couldn't do that without shoving his daughter into a publicity pillory. We were stuck.

So we were there, at the local lock-up, until nearly three in the damned morning. They'd actually taken Dom and Bree off into a different room. Normally, that would have twigged me a lot sooner, but there was so much noise, and so much going on, and people snarling at each other in French and so much damned hand-waving, that I got distracted. And at first, I thought it was just to get their statements, anyway.

I finally caught on what was happening at about one in the morning, when my legs started tingling and shaking, and I realised I needed my meds. They were with Bree—she'd actually brought them along in her fancy little purse—and I got someone to translate. When they refused to let me see her, and sent a copper off to fetch the meds, it suddenly sank in that they'd put Dom and Bree in custody, in a fucking cell.

Of course, I completely flipped my shit. I got my cell out and rang Ian. If I hadn't been so flipped out, I would have been surprised that he wasn't here already, but I was half off my nut. Turned out he was at the local casualty ward, making damned sure there was a statement ready for the local media who'd followed the action out that way.

He sounded nice and frazzled. I let him know, at the top of my lungs, that these fucking wanking sons of bitches had locked up Bree and Dom, that Parmeley was a rapist, that if they didn't let both Mac's bodyguard and my wife out within thirty minutes I wanted every lawyer Blacklight Corporate could get their hands on down here, that the bloke Bree had taken down had a gun and had been about to use it, that had to be illegal and they ought to be giving her a fucking medal and instead they were locking her up, and I wasn't going to stand for it, and on and on. I was shouting, good and loud, but right about then, Mac showed up.

"Johnny, take a breath. It's taken care of." He looked at the copper behind the desk. Even as furious as I was, that look surprised me—it was like a laser, full of contempt. I'd never seen that from Mac before. "Sir Cedric is on his way over from hospital. He's dropping all charges against Dom."

Next to me, I heard Luke give a sigh of relief. He'd taken Solange back to their villa, got her tucked up and sleeping, and come back again. I wasn't quite ready or willing to calm down just yet, and anyway, Ian was yapping at me through the phone.

"Ian, Mac's here—I'll ring you back—okay, you'll send a car? Brilliant." I stared at Mac. "Right. How'd you get the little weasel to see sense?"

Mac grinned suddenly, not his usual grin. This one was tight, a bit sardonic, and I suddenly got how angry he was.

"Easy. Pure cheek, really, and I was very high-handed, but I meant it. I told him if he didn't drop all charges, Blacklight wouldn't play Frejus tomorrow night. He's not happy about it, but he's doing it."

"High-handed?" Luke met Mac's eye. "Is that some new way of saying common sense? Nothing high-handed about it. Right now, I'm not inclined to play the gig anyway, Mac, and I'm going to need convincing to do it at all. Why the fuck should we go out there and do a publicity gig to benefit Cedric Parmeley? He tried to rape my daughter, and his hired goon tried to kill Dom. The bastard had a gun. Why should we play?"

I opened my mouth, and closed it again. Stu and Cal had taken their wives home, after making us promise that we'd ring them up if they were needed. I wondered what they'd say about walking out of a show, but that was stupid, really, because I knew damned well they'd do it in a heartbeat, after what had happened tonight. And in case you're wondering about it, so would I have, without a blink. The bastard could sue if he wanted to. Blacklight owed him absolutely nothing, not after the shite he'd pulled.

Right now, though, there was a piece of vital information Mac didn't have, and I shared it with him.

"I'm with you and Luke. I don't give a toss for his bloody movie. The only question I'd want answered before we backed out entirely is how much we'd be letting the fans down. But in the meantime, Mac, we've got something else to deal with. Your bodyguard—not to mention my wife—are both in jail cells, behind bars. They won't let me see Bree. They've locked them both up."

Mac went very still. That doesn't happen often—he's one of the most mobile human beings on the planet: kinetic, constantly moving about. So, when it does happen, it's impressive.

When he finally did move, he turned to the copper in charge, and, as far as I could tell, ripped the bloke a new arsehole. I haven't got a clue what he was saying, because, unlike me, Mac went to university and he does speak French. Right then, he was speaking so fast, I doubt I'd have been able to follow it anyway.

So I just watched the cop's reactions, and after a minute or two I stopped worrying and had to smother a grin, because the cop was visibly wilting. He tried to interrupt once or twice, but Mac went straight over him, and the cop's hands stopped waving about, and went limp and quiet. The French talk with their hands, so that said it all, really.

Parmeley showed up just as Mac was finishing his demolition of the cop. He trotted in, his hand in a cast and resting in the bottom half of a shoulder sling, and headed straight for Luke. And I suddenly realised, all those things I'd been thinking about him being basically incompetent and drooly had been right. I don't know whether he was completely disconnected from reality or what, but whatever the cause, Sir Cedric Parmeley was officially bonkers.

"Good morning, Luke, how are you?" He beamed up into Luke's face. I remembered the voice from long ago—high, chirpy, with some odd inflections. It was more tremulous than it used to be, but that was the only change. "I haven't seen you in forever, have I? How's the luscious Vivian? Not here with you?"

Luke just stood and blinked at him. So did the rest of us.

It was completely surreal. I couldn't imagine what had been going on in Parmeley's head. He'd spent the earlier part of the evening trying to assault Luke's daughter. He'd got his wrist snapped like a twig for his pains. His hired macho racist muscle had got their arses publicly kicked by a pair of women, one of them black.

And now? This. His brain had apparently booked a package tour to another planet. None of us had anything to say, because what was there, really?

Mac got his voice back first. "Cedric. Tell these nice police officers that you aren't filing assault charges against my bodyguard, or against my guitarist's wife. Tell them that now. Because if you don't, Blacklight won't be playing your gig at Frejus tomorrow night. And us not playing, that'll mean very bad publicity for *Playing in the Dark*."

Parmeley pouted. It was a real pout, not the sexy thing French women practice from birth on up; he pushed his lips out like a podgy baby about to cry, and stamped his foot. My skin was moving on my bones.

"Come along, Cedric." Mac sounded as if he was talking to someone's stroppy toddler. "Tell them, or we won't play. Get on with it. I want my bodyguard out of jail, and I want her out now."

Of course Parmeley did it, just turned to the bloke in charge and rattled off a string of French, and that was that. But I noticed that the coppers didn't seem too happy about it, and when they brought Bree and Dom out, the staff spoke fairly politely to Bree, but were terse with Dom, to the point of rudeness. I also noticed that Parmeley didn't so much as glance Dom's way.

I'd been right. There was some serious racist bullshit going on here.

It was nearly four in the morning, and all I wanted, at that point, was to find a car and a driver and get the hell back to our villa for some kip. Mac was head to head with Dom, the two of them whispering back and forth, both of them nodding. I turned my own attention to my wife.

"Are you all right, love? Did they hurt you?"

She didn't answer. She was glaring at Parmeley, her lips compressed down into a thin line. She looked about to commit a felony of some sort, and I couldn't help thinking that the middle of the Les Sirènes police station was a bad place for it.

I got her around the waist, and realised she was back down to a mere two inches taller than me; she was barefoot. I found out later, the coppers had taken her shoes, as evidence or something. "Bree? Talk to me, love, please."

She didn't get a chance to answer me. Cedric Parmeley had plumped his way over to us, and stood there, looking up at Bree, peering, squinting.

"Good heavens, JP." His voice was much too loud, squeaky, insinuating. "Aren't you naughty! I'd never have thought it of you—road nookie, I mean. Isn't that pretty little blonde wife of yours going to be cross if she finds out? What's her name again? Priscilla? I thought you two were joined at the hip."

I know I'm not the world's most socially adept bloke. But right that moment, not even Mac knew what to say—we just stood there, gawking like stuffed trout. Bree was breathing entirely through her nostrils; her shoulders had hunched up so hard and tight, I was afraid she was going to explode. If she'd had her other shoe in her hand, she might have planted the heel right between Parmeley's eyes. And Parmeley himself just stood there, leering up at us.

We were saved by the bell. Yeah, I know, total cliché, but that's what happened. The front door to the station had a little bell over it, and it tinkled, and we all jumped. A bloke in chauffeur's livery stuck his head in, and looked around at the lot of us.

"*Bon soir.*" He cleared his throat, and, thank God, switched to English. "I am here from the limousine service. I am to ask for a Mister Sharpe and a Mister Kinkaid. Mister Ian Hendry called to ask that I come and drive you all home."

"(beep) JP? This is Ian. Listen, I've got some news for you—a situation, really. There's going to be a private screening of 'Playing in the Dark,' tonight at seven, the final cut that's going to the jury. It's at the Theatre deVille, down in Cannes. This is courtesy of the French Riviera Convention Bureau—they've got their knickers in a twist over

*what happened last night, and this is their idea of damage control. I
wouldn't even be suggesting any member of Blacklight go near this, but
there's been a lot of rumours flying around about what happened last
night—there were paparazzi for miles at the hospital. I issued a statement, but there's a problem: I've already heard Solange's name being
whispered among the local media. This would be a good way to bury
the gossip before it really starts—we don't want her on the front page.
Let me know if you're willing to go, and we'll arrange a car. (beep)"*

"Shit!" This was just about the last thing anyone needed right
now. "Bree, love, do me a favour and talk me out of throwing this
damned phone into the pool, okay?"

"Not until I know why." She looked tired, and drained, and
dispirited, somehow. It wasn't the late night; she'd done enough
rock and roll shows to have stayed up until dawn many times in
the past. I hoped she wasn't feeling guilty about having sent
Bumpy Nose off to emergency surgery by way of her high heels.
"What's going on?"

"A last pre-festival showing of Parmeley's flick, in Cannes tonight." I saw her mouth drop open, and held up a hand. "Hang
on a minute, love, okay? My reaction's the same as yours, believe
me, but here's the thing—Ian wants us to go, as a show of solidarity. He says the place is buzzing about what happened, and
he's heard Solange's name. He thinks this ought to quiet things
down. And honestly, Bree, if we dislike all this, can you imagine
how Luke feels? He gets to worry about headlines starring his
only child, and she hasn't done a damned thing to deserve it. So
anything I can do to make his life easier, I'm up for doing, you
know? He's my mate—he'd do it for me. But you don't have to
come along, if you don't want to."

"Fuck. You're right, of course."

She looked disgusted. It was emotional blackmail, we both
knew it, but really, I'd meant what I'd said. Luke's gone out of his
way over the years to kick the log jams out of my path, and I owe

91

him. And Bree knows that. Besides, he's my mate. "So, we go, I guess." She sounded resigned. "If you're going, I'm going."

I'm glad, now, that we had a very good day, glad that we spent it entirely alone together. We went into St. Raphael, walking down from the villa, me stopping to rest at sensible points, not overdoing it. We bought fresh fish and fresh veggies, and stopped at the local *patisserie* for a sweet. Walking back up to the villa, we sat down side by side on an ancient stone wall along the road, just looking out toward the sea, letting the day move on as we sat still, the occasional car or cyclist passing us.

I had my arm around Bree's waist, and she sighed, a small tired contented noise, and leaned up against me. We didn't talk; we didn't have to. It was one of those moments, the ones that make me wonder about blokes like Mac, who don't do the whole being connected thing. Being connected, it's what keeps me alive, and sane, and even happy, sometimes.

An early dinner, a nice snog, a quick nap. We got dressed, not as fancy as we'd gone for the casino do the night before, but still on the formal side. At least, Bree did; there's not much differ-ence between the levels of my usual clothes, since they're mostly different levels of black, grey, white and whatnot, anyway. Bree says I'm the world's most monochromatic dresser, which is fine, since it sets off her love of rich colours.

We saw the paparazzi outside the Theatre deVille before we saw the theatre itself. The vultures were smelling blood, smelling a story, and if Ian was right, it had Solange Hedley's name all over it.

"Assholes. Miserable worthless assholes. God, I hate them."

Bree was looking out the window, and there was something in her voice that might have been genuine hate. She doesn't hate easily, it's not her natural state, but when she does, it's scary, you know? I saw the driver's head jerk up, as he checked her out in his mirror. "Leeches. Would you look at them? Every last one of those scavengers is out there hoping for something bad to happen. Why can't they go be hired mercenaries, or hitmen? It would be cleaner."

I didn't answer that, because there was nothing to say. She was right: Rumour, trouble, that was their meat, someone or something falling, hitting the ground, coming to earth, something they could take pictures of and write captions for and share with a world hungry for that sort of rubbish. And I was glad we'd agreed to come along for this, agreed to put up a show of solidarity, take the fangs out of what these people wanted to do to Solange Hedley, to all of us.

This may seem naive, but the last thing I was expecting was to see Cedric Parmeley there. Right, I know—where the hell else would he be? It was still his flick, and even though this do was just the local Convention Bureau, their idea of wing and prayer, trying to smooth out a situation that might have damaged the entire Festival, I honestly hadn't thought for one second that Parmeley would be there.

But of course, he was. I just hadn't thought far enough about it. If the idea was to shut the local rumour mill down cold, throwing a screener and not inviting the director would have been a piss-poor way of going about it.

I spotted him straight off when we hit the theatre's lobby. I'd barely had time to say something rude and profane and probably actionable in the presence of minors, when I saw something a lot more worrying than Parmeley.

He wasn't alone. Both his bodyguards were with him, flanking him, right there at his back.

It was unbelievable. Bumpy Nose had a bruise on his cheek and his right arm completely immobilised. The other one was wrapped up in a complicated bandage that covered half his head and one eye. The word in the local gossip columns was that the eye itself was mostly undamaged, but the surgeons had worried about stray bone chips. So he was swathed in a mass of bandages that made him look like an extra from "The Mummy", or something. That had been one hell of a kick Dom had nailed him with.

Bree had stopped in her tracks. I glanced at her, and felt my stomach wanting to move. She and Bumpy Nose had locked eyes over Parmeley's shoulder.

There was nothing in that look, the one he was giving her, nothing I could read. He was a professional, someone who knew how to size people up, knew how to stonewall it. But Bree—she had hate in her face, and a challenge, as well: *fuck with me or mine and I'll plant the other heel in your back, asshole.*

They just stood there, not more than a dozen feet apart, stares locked up like a couple of lions facing off over a dead antelope. Any minute, someone was going to start passing the hat and offering odds. Personally, my money would have been on my old lady, but the truth is, I didn't want to have to place that particular bet.

"Oh, bloody hell! Are you fucking joking!"

I jumped half a mile. Mac had come up next to me, Domitra at his shoulder, and now the whole eye locking thing was going on in stereo, because Dom had seen the other bloke, the Mummy one, and he'd seen her, as well. If I'd thought Bree and Bumpy Nose were looking unloving, it was nothing compared to what was happening with Dom. And people were staring at the staring.

I got one hand under Bree's elbow, and put my lips up against her ear. She'd jerked her eyes around to the Mummy bloke, caught his eye, and now they were measuring each other.

"Look, love, we're supposed to be watching a flick, and keeping Solange off the gossip sheets. And you're standing like Evander Holyfield before a title fight. Ease up, would you? Look, Dom's moving along."

"Dom's moving along because Mac is. She's doing her job. But, okay." I saw her shoulders relax, and I let my own breath out. "What I want to know is, what are those two pigs doing here? And don't say their jobs."

"Not a clue, and honestly, Bree, I don't give a damn, you know?" We'd passed them, gone through the lobby doors and into the theatre itself. "They can fuck off and die, for all of me. Oh, look, there's the Isle of Dogs lot. I keep meaning to get someone to introduce me to Jimmy Wonderley. Remind me about it after the showing, will you?"

The place was filling up, but there were two rows roped off as reserved; I saw Ian, a few members of the Blacklight crew and staff, Cal and Barb Wilson. Mac took a seat one off the aisle, with Dom in the seat behind him, and crew members surrounding him. I had a moment, wondering where Parmeley's pair of yobbos were planning on parking their bums, and then saw Parmeley trot down the far aisle, other side of the house. Good. A nice distance between us and them ought to cut back on the drama.

There was no sign of Stu and Cyn Corrigan, and of course, Luke and Solange had stayed away. I hadn't expected them to show up. I mean, there are limits, yeah? The festival wonks could spin like a toy top, but that didn't mean Luke had to play along. It had taken some work on Mac's part to get Luke to agree to show up at Frejus; parading Solange out in front of Parmeley and the media, that just wasn't going to fly.

There was no announcement, nothing. The house lights dimmed and went dark, the screen flickered to life, and the opening sequences for *Playing in the Dark* rolled up on the oversized screen.

Ten minutes in, I knew we were in trouble.

I saw it in Mac's slackened jaw line, heard it in the muttering from around the place. This wasn't the cut Mac had shown me, back in London. This one had been tinkered with. Parmeley had told our management that he was going to tweak it, but this hadn't been tweaked, it had been manhandled.

For one thing, there were sudden jump-cuts, badly done and amateurish, the sort of thing you might expect from some pompous film school student, arsing about with pricey gear in the school's film lab. That was the first clue. But it was obvious, very quickly indeed, that Parmeley had been screwing with the film in some very nasty ways.

The Isle of Dogs manager, back when the thing had been filmed, had been a bloke called Steve. I'd never known his last name, never thought about it, was only vaguely aware that he existed. He'd died of AIDS in the mid-eighties, which wasn't all that surprising, since he'd apparently had a thing for mainlining cocaine with shared works, as well as a taste for pretty young boys. I hadn't known about either vice at the time, and hadn't cared. Blacklight and Isle of Dogs, we didn't have anything to do with each other. We never played together, and we certainly didn't hang out with each other.

So there really was no reason for my stomach to tighten up when Parmeley's cameras found Steve Whatever his last name was dry-humping a blonde teenager with curls and a bulge in his leather jeans, backstage at a club in Manchester, while Benno Marling watched, snickering, unless it was that the teenager was blank-faced and stoned. And really, my dodgy tum should have saved its outrage, because things got much worse.

Where it began to get really ugly was the incident of the Dogs' roadies beating up a kid in the alley outside their gig. From what Mac had told me, in the cut our management had okayed, that scene had been taken out entirely. Now it was back in, and it had been expanded. And, right, it may have been good cinema, or whatever, but there are people out there who think snuff porn is good cinema, as well.

This was ugly on a level I could barely wrap my head around. It was Jimmy Wonderley who set the two roadies on the bloke out in the alley.

I've got no idea what triggered it, unless it was because the kid—he couldn't have been more than twenty—wasn't white; Pakistani, or maybe Indian. For whatever reason, there was Wonderley, with his hair cut close to his head and a peculiar black tattoo at the back of his neck, nodding and pointing toward the bloke; they'd all come out of the club for a smoke, it looked like, and this kid just happened to be there, and he happened not to be white.

They went for the kid, fists, boots and all. I heard Bree catch her breath, and a moment later, she had her face buried in my shoulder. I nearly vomited up dinner, myself. They were putting on a show, you know? Beating this boy halfway into a fucking coma, doing it with this kind of darkness and glee, and what they were really doing was, they were making sure the camera caught every blow, every kick, every taunt, every name they were calling the kid. They weren't just committing a hate crime—they were performing it.

The kid gave up yelling after a few minutes, and spent the last part of it just trying to protect his head and his face from the flying boots. It worked; they went for his belly and groin, instead.

There was noise from all over the theatre at that point, and none of it was friendly. The place probably had about a hundred people in it right then, and damned near all of them—all of *us*— were shocked. And it's damned hard to shock a crowd of rockers, when all's said and done.

They left the kid bleeding in the alley, just left him there. One of the thugs put the boot in one last time, and flicked his cigarette away. It skimmed off the kid's hand. They headed back indoors to where Jimmy Wonderley was standing, grinning, giving them the thumbs-up.

The bloke was a musician, and a damned innovative one, a blues player. He played Delta blues, the music of southern blacks in America, and there he was, acting like an organiser for the fucking National Front.

The first of the two roadies, the one who'd aimed that last kick and tossed his smoke, reached out a hand, and he and Wonderley did a sort of high-five thing, very complex, all thumbs moving around each other in some sort of macho bullshit pattern. They bent elbows and banged them together. Then the cameraman moved to one side, getting some of the reflections, all very shadowy and atmospheric, and I saw the roadie's face, and I said something out loud, God knows what.

The bloke with the handshake, who'd given the kid that last kick? It was Bumpy Nose.

Yeah, he was a lot younger, but there was no way I was wrong about it. Parmeley's bodyguard, the yob my wife had nailed with a high heel, had been a roadie for the Isle of Dogs, back in the late seventies. He'd also apparently amused himself and his boss by beating up minorities in alleys, and it looked he'd done it with the band's guitarist egging him on.

I turned sideways, keeping a hand on Bree's hair to keep her from looking up, and craned my neck. Jimmy Wonderley had been sitting just across, next to Benno Marling. Now he wasn't.

"John?" Bree's voice was muffled, and very shaken. "Is it over? I thought you said this movie—"

"Yeah, that bit's over, and yeah, I know what I said." I kept my own voice low. A lot of people weren't bothering; there was some serious outrage going on. I had a bad feeling, really bad, that as nasty as what we'd just seen had been, things were going to get a whole lot worse. "This isn't the movie I saw, Bree. Not even close. It's been messed with."

Mac was leaning over, talking urgently to Ian; he caught my eye in the dark theatre, and we nodded at each other. This was total rubbish, absolute bullshit. This wasn't the flick we'd given permission for, and it wasn't anything, so far, that I'd personally be willing to play a gig to endorse. What the hell had been going on in Parmeley's mind? Had he been this deranged when he re-did the film, and sent it to us, or had he lost it within the past month or so?

Isle of Dogs, another twenty minutes of them, most of it concert footage. I hadn't seen anything in the version we'd been sent except our segment, but the editing was a complete mess. The jump-cuts were back, along with weirdly interspersed slices of disoriented editing. There was about five solid minutes of spell-binding music—Benno Marling's always been amazing onstage—was followed by the song being cut off in mid-lyric, cutting to backstage conversation.

And then they were done, and here we were, and after a few minutes, I had one hand on Bree's arm, because I honestly thought she was going to lose it, flip her shit, run screaming into the night.

In the studio, casual jamming, conversation. The studio segment I'd seen at Mac's had run about eight minutes, and had followed a logical pattern. It had made some sense, you know? Not this. We got maybe three minutes of straight rehearsal and then it cut off in mid-flow and we cut to a hotel, Dallas I think, for the tour that hadn't happened for months after that rehearsal. One look at that footage, and I knew that every warning bell in my head had been right.

The camera cut to me, with Cilla, the two of us, sitting on our hotel room bed, with a mirror between us. There were lines of coke from edge to edge. My wife, in her black lace gloves, had the silver straw she'd always used. She lifted the mirror, snorted a line, leaned forward, giggled. Her hand slipped down between my thighs, and the camera followed that, a nice juicy close-up. I set the mirror aside, laughing, pushing her down on her back, laying a line of coke across the base of her throat, snorting it, saying something, getting hold of her….

It was obscene, a nightmare. I haven't got a clue what I'd been thinking, allowing a camera in our room for that; I'd probably been so fucking stoned, I'd have sold tickets. But whatever, there we were, me and Cilla, twenty feet tall and right on the edge of shagging, right there on the screen, for everyone—including Bree—to watch. And there was fuck-all I could do about it.

I turned my head. All I got was Bree's profile. She was staring up at the screen like someone looking at a hypnotist, or maybe a vision of Hell. She wasn't touching me, not anywhere, not hand or elbow or anything at all. She was just staring. I wasn't sure she was even aware I was there. I could have waved a hand in front of her, and she probably wouldn't have noticed.

I swallowed, hard, and managed to get some words out; I had to say something, anything, try to do something, to get her eyes off what was happening onscreen. Problem was, I was staring up at it myself, just not believing what I was seeing up there.

Cilla'd got one hand inside my trousers. I'd got a leg over her, pinning her down to the bed and I had one hand up her skirt, pulling it up around her waist, we were both laughing, the laughter breaking, the camera handler aiming the thing to get us in profile, the two of us kissing….

"Bree." I heard my own voice, too loud, not loud enough. "Close your eyes. You don't need to look at this. It wasn't in the cut I saw. Come *on*, Bree, don't watch this…."

It was no good. I might as well have been talking to an empty chair. She wasn't hearing me, or seeing me; she wasn't moving and she didn't seem to be blinking. She looked like a rabbit facing a cobra.

The only small blessing was that Cilla and I didn't actually get naked, at least not completely. We did get a lovely shot of Cilla taking her top off, slow and deliberate, taunting the camera, and me disappearing between her breasts, nibbling as I went, laughing, the two of us breathing hard, low voices.

I heard myself laugh, my cheek up against Cilla's. It was a sound Bree knew very well. I thought I heard her say something, and I jerked my head around. I wasn't the only one; damned near everyone in the theatre who wasn't a mate of mine had turned to stare at Bree. The people we were close to were carefully not looking at us. Looking back at it, I don't know now which was worse. At the time, all I thought was that we were in hell, we were fucked, hosed, in major shit.

I took a moment, and turned to my wife. I didn't know what I'd see—I didn't dare not look.

She'd closed her eyes, finally. I was about to be really happy about that, but then I realised that she was shaking, just shuddering, long tremors from head to foot. There were no tears on her face, but her lips were moving, as if she was saying something to herself, under her breath, maybe a prayer for strength, maybe something else.

Two hundred people were staring in the dark at the woman who'd been a part of my life from, basically, right after this abomination had been filmed, the woman who'd opted for invisibility all this time. Right now, she'd been completely exposed. I'd left her no place to hide.

I remembered how I'd kissed her for the cameras last night, remembered how pleased with myself I'd felt, because that had blown any hope she still might have of staying invisible all to hell. Feeling those eyes on us, all I wanted was to turn back the clock a day, and let her be whatever she needed to be.

Then, mercifully, the camera moved off and there was another of those jump-cuts, and we were back in the studio. More jumps, more moments that hadn't been there in the cut I'd watched in London. There was Mac with a pair of girls, obviously gearing up for a threesome. I doubted he minded that being shown.

Concert footage. Cilla, again; the camera bloke had liked her, probably because she wanted nothing better than to be on display, Mrs. JP Kinkaid, the rocker's wife, in her short skirt and her spiky hair, cocaine on her upper lip, always dangling off my arm. There was a shot of Viv Hedley, dancing in the wings, laughing, leaving me dizzy and grateful that Luke, and Solange, had stayed away. Then more concert footage, including Hurricane Felina, and after that, at bloody last, we were done with Blacklight's footage and on to Typhoid Harry's stuff.

I don't remember anything about Typhoid Harry's segment. All my attention was on getting through the film, getting my wife the hell out of there, and then letting Ian and the rest of the band know that there was no way in hell I was having anything to do with *Playing in the Dark*, not the way it looked here. The festival organisers could sod off—I was going to fight it with everything I had.

The lights came up. There was a smattering of confused applause, as if people had no idea how to react. Mostly, they looked staggered.

"I want to get out of here. I have to get out." She wasn't meeting my eyes; her voice was tiny, just a thread. "Take me home. Please, John? I want to go home, get me out of here, just get me out...."

"Damned right I will. Hang on."

I jerked my head, and Ian was right there; I must have looked pretty demented myself. Next to me, Bree had ducked her face—she couldn't even bring herself to meet Ian's eye. "We need a car. And by the way, Ian, that's not the film I saw, not the film I agreed to, and there's no way I'm going out and play a show to endorse that. I hope we're clear?"

"Absolutely." He looked pretty shaken. "Cars are out front—already waiting for you. I'll ring you in the morning."

Bree and I didn't say a word to each other the entire ride back to St. Raphael. I got hold of her hand, and she let me, but there was no return pressure, none at all. She wouldn't meet my eyes, either; it was as if, after all those years of trying to perfect the ability to step back and become part of the woodwork, she'd lost it right at the moment she needed it most.

We got home and she headed indoors, too fast for me to catch. The hired car hadn't even finished the three-point turn to get it pointed back down the hill before she'd vanished upstairs. I got to the bedroom in time to hear her bathroom door slam shut, and the lock turn, and then the shower running.

I didn't know whether to hope she was in there crying, or not. All I particularly remember wanting, just then, was to find everyone concerned with the entire mess, and throttle them.

When she finally came out, I took one look at her face, and my heart went straight down to my shoes. She was calm, remote. It was just like old times, old patterns; we'd been trying so damned hard to break out of that rubbish, the old hide and protect thing she did, me just letting her do it even though I knew it was costing her. Forty minutes of film seemed to have undone everything we'd managed since Cilla's suicide.

"I've got a major headache." Her voice might as well have been coming from the other side of the moon. "I'm going to take one of your pain pills, and go to bed. Don't forget to take your meds."

"Bree—"

It was no good. She turned and was gone up the stairs, before I could get another word out. At the top, she turned left instead of right, and I suddenly got it: she was sleeping in one of the other bedrooms. She wasn't doing it as punishment—Bree doesn't use sex as a weapon, not ever. But I don't think she'd done this twice in twenty-five years, and it scared the hell out of me.

I stayed up awhile after she'd gone, thinking, remembering, wondering if other men who'd been married more than once had the past constantly getting straight up in their faces this way, arsing about with the present, messing up everyone's lives. The best I could come up with was that this was on me, payback for all those years of just going along and being passive, not divorcing Cilla, letting myself believe it wasn't hurting Bree. Not very comforting.

I got a guitar out, and played for awhile, but things were aching, and my chest felt tight. After awhile, I gave up and gave in. I took my meds, and headed upstairs.

I stood outside her door for a few minutes. There was no sound at all; either she'd doped herself out of it and was fathoms deep, or she was simply so far away from me that I couldn't hear her.

I laid a hand on the knob—after all, she was my wife. But Cilla had been my wife, as well, and tonight, one of those damned landmines I'd always known was lying about had blown up in both our faces.

I wasn't blaming myself, you know? Not for what had happened at the theatre, because I'd been blindsided by it, as well. But if Bree wanted a night away from me, the least I could do was give her that.

I went to bed myself, alone, in our room. I didn't sleep all that well; after a while, I found myself dreaming about storms, stormy weather, the sky getting dark and colourful, clouds off toward Africa banging against each other, lightning, a big banging roll of thunder....

I opened my eyes, wincing against movement outside the tall windows. The sky outside the window was dancing with light. And the entire villa was shaking.

I pulled on trousers and headed outdoors. I don't know why I was expecting Bree to be outside before me, but she wasn't; no sign of her. I looked off the hillside, toward Les Sirènes sur Mer. The sky was on fire, but it wasn't lightning.

104

Something in the distance was burning. And I didn't think that huge clap of thunder I'd heard was entirely in my dreams, either. Something had blown up, something was burning. You could nearly taste the ashes on the breeze.

I watched it for awhile. There was still no sign that it had woken Bree, even though there were sirens in the distance, a lot of them. Probably a gas main had gone, or something; I just hoped it wasn't some sort of terrorist thing. That was the last thing the festival organisers needed....

When I went back indoors, finally, something caught the corner of my eye: the green light on my cell phone was blinking. Someone had rung me up, at four in the morning.

"(beep) Johnny? Bloody hell, are you sleeping through this? It's Mac—there's a light show going on just down the road, and it's Cedric Parmeley's villa. The damned thing's gone sky high."

# Chapter Six

The police, two coppers from Les Sirènes sur Mer, showed up not long after noon.

We'd had a busy morning, burning up the phone lines, or at least I had. I'd let Bree sleep in; she'd said she was taking one of my muscle relaxants or pain pills, and since she wasn't used to meds of any sort, she'd easily sleep twelve hours. Besides, she'd been emotionally drained to begin with.

By the time she finally came down and made herself coffee, it was nearly eleven. I'd been on the phone with everyone and anyone since I'd got Mac's voicemail, seven hours earlier, and my own voice was beginning to go, from all the talking.

"John? Have you had breakfast?" She sounded dragged down, and lethargic. Not surprising, really. If you aren't used to drugs, they can kick you hard. Really, she sounded more as if she hadn't slept than if she'd overslept. She looked absolutely exhausted, as well; there were dark blue shadows under her eyes. Last time I'd seen her look this wasted and weary had been after spending a long few days dealing with Cilla's heroin withdrawal, nearly a year ago now. "Oh—sorry. I didn't realise you were on the phone."

"Carla, hang on a minute, will you?" I looked up at Bree. She had her back to me, measuring out coffee. "Morning, love. You slept through the explosion, did you?"

That turned her head around. She didn't seem to want to meet my eyes. I'd been so up to my eyebrows in the aftermath of what had happened to Cedric Parmeley and his villa, I'd nearly forgotten about his dirty movie.

"What explosion?"

"Cedric Parmeley," I told her. "He seems to be dead. Carla, look, I'll ring you back later, or if there's anything I need to do, anything to sign to get this fucking thing taken out of competition, ring me back. Right. Cheers."

I clicked the phone off, and plugged it into my charger. I'd given it quite a workout this morning.

Bree was staring at me, not moving at all. Behind her, the coffee was dripping; it smelled wonderful. "What? What do you mean, he's dead? What explosion? What are you talking about?"

"His villa blew up. It woke me up, right round half past three—the entire coastline lit up. Really amazing—the house was shaking. I thought it was terrorists or something at first. I'm glad you slept through it." I jerked my head at her; there was no way I was sharing more bad news until she'd woken. "That coffee smells brilliant. Enough for two cups?"

That got her moving, of course. She poured me a cup first, got herself one, and sat down. She seemed awfully fragile this morning, and I didn't like it. She was sipping coffee, but it didn't seem to be reviving her. I took a mouthful of my own, and tried to remember if I'd taken my meds yet. My right leg was trembling and a bit twitchy. Damn. But it was going to have to wait—there was something that needed saying, first.

"Bree. I've got something to say to you, and I want you to just listen, all right?"

I saw her swallow hard, but there was no coffee involved; I'd scared her. I hate doing that, it's never intentional, but I had to say it.

"Okay. I'm listening, John. And I have something I want to say to you, when you're done."

"Right. I'm not going to talk about that damned film, not now. Nothing I can say, really, is there? That was then, this is now, and I would never have let you walk through the theatre doors if I'd known that was up there. You ought to know that. For whatever it's worth, Bree, I'm just as sick over it as you are. I've already told everyone out there—including the festival organisers—that I've withdrawn my consent. If that damned thing gets shown on a single screen from this point on, the lawsuit will hit them so hard, they'll have whiplash. The whole band's behind me on this one. So is Ian, so is Carla, so is the entire organisation and you know, I'm not surprised."

She watched me. I reached out for her hand.

"They're my mates, Bree." I looked at her; her face was stony, but she had had her teeth set into her lower lip. I kept my voice quiet. "They're your mates, as well. More than that—they're family. Mine, and yours. We've been there for each other whenever possible since I first met them, and we aren't likely to stop now, you know?"

"I know." She did, too. I could see it. "I'm sorry, John. Since we're being honest, I'll just say that I don't want to talk about that damned movie right now, either. I know we have to deal with it at some point, I'm not ducking it forever, but last night was—" She stopped.

"I know, Bree."

"No, you don't know."

She lifted her face, and I nearly lost it. I remembered that look of desolation, but it hadn't been there in so damned long, not since the day I'd left her behind in San Francisco, not nineteen yet, and gone back to London, to take care of Cilla. Her voice was quiet, as low as it ever gets.

"Watching that thing last night, I wanted to die. It felt like being stripped naked in public. It felt like a gang-rape. My soul hurts. Right now, I can't make up my mind what I want to do more, find a hole to crawl into and hide in, or find a good shrink and spill it out to them, or maybe just curl up somewhere and cry until I die of exhaustion. I can't deal with it yet and I'm not going to try. I'd just screw it up. It's too fresh in my head right now—if I close my eyes, I'm back in that theatre and you're up there on screen, kissing her, whispering, laughing, and there are all those *eyes* on me. And I can't. I just can't."

She stopped. The desolation was still there, in her face. "I need time and space, John. And that's all I wanted to say, really."

I reached out and got hold of her left hand. Her rings were right there, where they belonged. She may have locked herself away from me for the night, but my ring was right where I'd put it. And for the first time since the movie, she squeezed my hand back. "You've got both," I told her. "As much as you need. I'm sorry, love. Not for the film, really—that was in another place and time and reality, yeah? As much as I hated seeing that, it's got sod-all to do with us, with today. But you've had a haunted sort of honeymoon, and I hate that. I wanted this all perfect for you."

"Nothing's perfect." She lifted her hand, with mine still wrapped around it, and suddenly kissed my fingers, letting her lips rest against my own ring for a moment. "Or maybe—I don't know. I just need time to process stuff. Anyway, tell me about Cedric Parmeley. I took two of your pain pills last night; you

109

could have had Blacklight set up next to my pillow, full PA with Mac standing on my night table, and I would have snored through it. What the hell happened? You talk and I'll make breakfast—have you eaten? Taken your meds?"

I filled her in, with as much as I knew. Cedric Parmeley's villa, along with a couple of smaller buildings close to the main house, had gone up in a massive explosion at about half past three that morning. There'd been fire brigades from every neighbouring town, and it had burned so hot and so fast that by the time the fire brigade from Marseilles had been able to get there, there was nothing left but a few piles of smoking ash. The two outbuildings had burned just as hot, and both had been totally destroyed; one of them was actually Parmeley's film vault, where he'd kept all his film masters. It looked as if his entire library, the archives of all his films, had been wiped out.

"Wow." She was juicing oranges, and letting eggs warm up to room temperature for omelettes. "Do they know what caused it?"

"They're being cagey, but it had to have been deliberate, you know? I was talking to Ian, and he said the word was that the villa had to have been wired, or something. Same stuff terrorists and commando types use. C4? Something like that. Anyway, a bomb of some kind." I took a deep breath and a mouthful of orange juice; this was going to upset her. "They found two bodies inside the villa."

She'd been whisking cheese and heavy cream into the eggs, melting butter in the omelette pan, but that stopped her in mid-stroke. She'd gone very pale.

"Oh, God, John. You said one of them was Parmeley? Do they know for sure?"

"Haven't heard yet, but it seems likely, doesn't it?" I'd had the full description of what they found from Ian, and I was damned if I was going to pass it on to Bree. She was pale enough as it was. "Middle of the night, he lived alone, except for his nasty little skinhead protection. Word is, it was Parmeley and one of his bodyguards. That's all I know about that right now."

She went back to whisking eggs, and pouring them into the heated pan. "God, that's horrible."

"One more thing I want you to know." I finished my juice, and set the glass down. "We're not doing the Frejus gig. Ian and the PR staff have been down arguing with the Convention Bureau and organisers all morning, and I don't give a rat's arse what they say or do, we're not doing it. Blacklight put an official statement out this morning, and ads in all the papers. We're not endorsing the film. Until they take it completely off the table and get rid of any connection between the gig and the movie, we won't play."

"I'm sorry, baby. That sucks. I know you wanted to play there, and really, it looks like a perfect venue."

She meant it. Everything that had happened, the film, what had to have been a taste of hell, and what was she regretting? That I was going to be disappointed, that I might not get to play Frejus. There are times she just floors me.

"Nothing's perfect, remember?" I reached for a napkin and a fork; she slid a plate in front of me, and I took a mouthful of omelette, moist and beautifully fluffy. She'd stuffed the thing full of cheese, fresh herbs, cream, the local garlic. "Right, okay, so I'm wrong. This omelette is perfect—damn it, is that my cell, or yours?"

"Yours. Keep eating—I'll get it. Hello? Oh, hi—Mac, what's wrong? Mac, calm down, what…." I saw her face change, fast and drastic, and put my fork down in a hurry. "But—that's nuts! That's completely insane! Why—"

Mac's voice rattled. I held my hand out for the phone.

"Johnny?" His voice was almost unrecognisable. "I'm down at the lock-up in Les Sirènes sur Mer. A couple of local coppers came up to our villa about half an hour ago, and arrested Dom."

"What the *fuck?*" I inhaled wrong and nearly choked on a

sliver of garlic I'd missed swallowing. "Arrested her for what?"

"Collusion, or conspiracy, or something. They found another body at Parmeley's villa—it's that bloke Bree parked her high heel in. This one was behind some bushes, and he wasn't burned. Someone knocked him out—they're claiming it was a blow to the chin, that there's a bruise on his chin. They think he was kicked unconscious."

He stopped suddenly. This was insane, ridiculous, completely fucked up. All my nerves were prickling.

"Mac. What the hell do they mean, collusion? Collusion in what? How did the bloke die?"

Mac was trying to control his voice, and he wasn't having much luck. "Someone slashed his throat, from behind. Knocked out, throat cut—I don't know what the hell they mean by collusion, or why they think Dom has anything to do with it. The copper in charge, Inspector something or other, Italian I think, had this smug little grin on his face—it was as if he knew the charge was bullshit, knew I knew it, and didn't give a damn. He was enjoying himself. I've got Blacklight Corporate on it, getting lawyers in. I'm demanding they set bail. I've got a meeting with our embassy rep as soon as I've done here. Domitra is not spending a single night in their bloody jail, not if I have anything to say about it. Something's going down here, Johnny—they want to know about my political associations."

I opened my mouth, and closed it again. I could hear something from outside, the hum of a car, climbing the hill to our villa. Bree stared at me a moment, and went outside, still holding her orange juice.

"Johnny?"

"Yeah, I'm here." I heard myself, sounding about as grim as I'd ever been. "Someone's just driven up to our front door. Small black car, two blokes. I think your coppers have arrived."

The man in charge of finding out who'd blown Cedric Parmeley halfway back to England and who'd killed Bumpy Nose was a skinny little bloke called Lucien Santini, and I honestly don't remember disliking anyone at first sight quite as much as I disliked him. I'm generally quite easy with most people, but it's never a good sign when you shake hands with someone first time out, and have to force yourself not to wipe your hand on your trousers, you know?

It probably didn't help things that I recognised him from Mac's description, straight off. Santini introduced himself, told me his sidekick's name, something French rather than Italian, but that's all I remember about the other copper, except that he seemed uneasy, on edge—not at all comfortable.

One thing I did notice was that Santini took himself really seriously. It was damned near eighty degrees already and he was sweating in long sleeves and an oversized jacket, big patch pockets, and white cotton gloves. Bloody copper was straight out of Central Casting.

"Monsieur Kinkaid?"

"Yeah, I'm John Kinkaid." He was straight off an Inspector Clouseau film, little moustache, oversized coat, twitchiness and all, except that he didn't look harmless, or comical. "What can I do for you?"

What it turned out I could do for him was introduce him to Bree. He made the request—I *would like to speak with Mrs. Kinkaid*—in English, but I noticed his accent was getting stronger by the word, and I started to wonder, right around then, whether the red flags he'd set flying in my head might not be more than just nerves. His eyes were on Bree the whole time. She'd sat down with her orange juice in one of the outdoor chairs on the garden terrace, and was watching us.

And then, out of nowhere, there were ghosts in the garden. I looked at Santini and suddenly, I was back in New York not quite a year ago, facing off against Lieutenant Patrick Ormand, NYPD Homicide, seeing the same look in Ormand's eye when he'd looked at Bree that I was seeing on Santini's face as he looked at her now. Too many teeth, the smell of fresh blood, wounded prey for him to play with. What the hell was all this…?

"Right. This is my wife, Bree Godwin Kinkaid." I must have sounded the wrong side of peculiar, but I couldn't shake that picture, same thing I'd felt about Ormand when he'd decided Bree would look good in an orange prison overall, or maybe strapped to a table for lethal injection. The little shit was damned near licking his lips. The alarms bells in my head were clanging away even louder than the fire brigade sirens this morning.

Bree got up and nodded at him. I noticed she didn't offer a hand, and right then, the alarm bells got even louder. She's got no taste for touching strangers, but she'll usually do a quick handshake, just as part of the social niceties. And when she's the hostess, it's automatic; she'd shake hands with Attila the Hun, if he was a guest in her house. The fact that she hadn't offered a hand to Santini said a lot about her reaction to him.

"Hello." I barely recognised her voice; she'd gone totally parky on the bloke, chilly as winter. Distant, remote; she hadn't even got this *grande dame* with Vinny Fabiano, when I'd asked her to accept his apology for groping her, and hell, she'd kneed Vinny in the nuts. "How can I help you?"

He wanted to see her passport. Right, okay, standard stuff— this was France, and the French are all ID-happy and always have been. It's one of the first things you get told when you're visiting, even if it's just a day trip from Dover to buy wine at Le Havre or Calais, is to keep your identity papers with you at all times, because they can nick you if you don't.

She set her glass of juice down, headed inside, and came back about twenty seconds later with her passport. Santini took it from her, looked at it, and closed it.

"Mrs. Kinkaid." His accent was suddenly thicker. "I must ask you to accompany us, to our office in Les Sirènes sur Mer."

"What!"

I was gobsmacked. Bree'd gone very still. She'd locked eyes with the bloke, and there were those ghosts again, Bree in a pricey green dress covered in vomit, locking stares with Patrick Ormand a few hours after she'd pushed open the door of my dressing room at Madison Square Garden, and found a dead bloke.

"Like hell she has to accompany you." *Right. Calm, Johnny my lad. Stay calm. You lose it and you'll make this worse.* It was no good—I couldn't do it. "She's not going anywhere."

"John—"

"There are questions that must be answered. We have a man who was killed, a man with a cut throat."

"So?" She had all the calm I seemed to have lost. "What does that have to do with me?"

He said something in French, or it might have been Italian—I'm no good with languages. He wasn't smiling, but he wanted to; the corner of his mouth was twitching. The little shit was enjoying this. I'd been right. He was a sadist. "This man, this Leonard Cullum, was an Englishman, a bodyguard in the employ of Sir Cedric Parmeley. He has a deep wound in his back, and witnesses have told us—"

"He pulled a gun on someone we know." Bree'd gone very pale. "He was about to shoot an unarmed woman in the back. I stopped him. Is this supposed to be a civilised country? Because I wasn't aware that shooting someone in the back was legal in France, Detective—I'm sorry, I've forgotten your name."

"My name is Lucien Santini." He jerked his head at his mate, who was standing there, just standing, looking miserable. He hadn't said a damned word. "And you must come with us, to answer questions. You will be permitted a phone call."

"She's not—"

"You seem to have difficulty understanding me." He turned away from Bree, finally, and there we were, faces superimposed, me and Patrick Ormand, me winning the first round, but this was right now, I wasn't going to win this one, and they were going to take Bree. "We are considering the probability that Mrs. Kinkaid was involved in this man's death."

*Knocked out, throat cut.* Mac's voice rang in my head. *I don't know what the hell they mean by collusion.*

"John. It's okay." She was chalky, but her voice was steady. She must have seen blue murder looking out of my eyes. "I'll go down. Don't—"

"Are you seriously going to stand there and say you think my wife had something to do with this?" Right, John. Unclench the fists. Don't take a swing at him. Oh, God.

"Ah, you finally understand. *Oui.* Yes. That is what we think." The smile was there, under the moustache. He wasn't biting it back, not now, and there was Mac's voice in my head again: *The copper in charge, Inspector something or other, Italian I think, had this smug little grin on his face—it was as if he knew the charge was bull-shit, knew I knew it, and didn't give a damn. He was enjoying himself.*

Bree leaned out suddenly, and kissed me. She'd seen it in his face, seen that I got it. "Call someone. Get someone in who can handle it, John, okay? Please? I had nothing to do with it, and neither did Dom."

She turned her head, and looked steadily at Santini. "And you know it, don't you? You're up to something. It's going to be interesting to find out just what."

He grinned at her, and I took a step forward. I think I was going to deck him, just bloody bash him. Bree had a hand out, an arm in front of me, keeping me back.

"Call someone." She was perfectly calm, but she shot a glance at Santini, and the contempt in her face was like nothing I'd ever

116

seen there. "Get us some help. And then, for heaven's sake, come down to Les Sirènes sur Mer and get me—and Dom—the hell out of their disgusting little jail."

She climbed into the back of the car, ducking her head. As they pulled off down the drive, she turned her head toward me, and I thought I saw her lift a hand, waving goodbye.

I gave myself two minutes, just two minutes, to make certain I wasn't going to have a heart attack, because it felt that way. And then I picked up my cell phone, dialed the country code for the US and the city code for San Francisco, and rang Patrick Ormand.

# Chapter Seven

I didn't know, when I rang up Patrick Ormand and asked him to come help, that the French police aren't authorised to hold anyone for more than four hours, unless they've officially charged them with a crime. No reason for me to know that—it's not as if I'd ever got popped for anything in France.

Truth is, even if I'd known, it wouldn't have helped. I was half out of my mind and anyway, I didn't know whether they'd charged Bree with something or not. That slimy little shit Santini had said he had questions because he thought she might be involved, but he hadn't said anything else. Mac had made it sound as if they'd actually slapped some sort of murder charge on Dom, and he'd said conspiracy, collusion. Both of those words involve more than one person, and Santini had come up there knowing damned well he wasn't leaving without my wife.

So, yeah, I was flipping out and panicking, but panic wasn't going to do anyone a damned bit of good, and it wouldn't help Bree. So I pushed it away and concentrated on getting my shit together.

I got off the phone with Patrick, and rang Carla, and yeah, it was half past four in the morning in Los Angeles, but I wasn't about to wait. Of course Carla was right on it, as soon as I'd given her the details—it didn't take her ten minutes to get back to me. Patrick Ormand would be flying San Francisco to Paris, with a connector to Marseilles, first class all the way. He wasn't going to have much chance to breathe between now and whenever he got here, but I couldn't summon up a lot of sympathy for the rush. I was just sorry they'd got rid of the Concorde. The bugger couldn't get to France fast enough for me.

I gave her Ormand's number, asked her to grease as many wheels as she could, and was told that not only would she be ringing him and a few other people up momentarily, she'd be getting a flight out of Los Angeles herself, just as soon as she let the London staff know what was going on. That took some serious weight off my mind. There was going to be a shitload of coping with the press necessary on this one, and no one does that better than Carla.

After I'd rung off, I sat for a few minutes, breathing deep and trying to get my brain working properly. Things had begun to hurt—there was an ominous little jerk going on in my right leg, a sort of electric twitch that reminded me of the myokymia that hadn't hit me for nearly a year, now. There were tingles where there weren't supposed to be any, and my heart rate didn't seem to want to slow down. It was really bizarre; I was having this sort of running conversation with myself, telling myself to go Zen, talking to myself: *come on, John, do what you always do when the MS sinks its teeth in your arse.* It's the way I handle the annual MRI, the way I cope with nights when the disease is being noisy

119

and I'm trying not to disturb Bree. Right now, it wasn't working, and right now, I couldn't give the MS any room at all.

"Okay." I heard myself talking out loud. The sun was good, warm but not hot, and there were oranges on the trees, and I was damned well going to get Bree out of that miserable jail, bring her home, get her to take a long swim in the pool, and maybe make love to her under the stars. "Showtime. Ian, Mac, the rest of the band. Lawyers. Right."

I rang Ian first. That turned out to be a good idea, because he'd just got off the phone with Carla. Apparently, she was handling it, but she was being mysterious about it, and Ian seemed to think she had something up her sleeve. It wouldn't have surprised me—you could have asked for a space shuttle and she'd have had one parked out front of the hotel twenty minutes later—but there were practical things that needed doing, the first being that I needed a lawyer to see about bail for Bree, and a car to take me to Les Sirènes sur Mer.

Ian told me the lawyers were on their way and probably already there, for Bree and Dom both, and the car would be arranged as soon as I rang off and let him get on with it. It was probably all in my head, imagination, but even just that much dealing with the situation seemed to have taken some of the edge off the shakes in my legs.

I got on to Mac next. He was back at his own villa; he'd also rung up Carla, and she'd told him about me wanting Patrick Ormand out here, someone who knew the score, knew how things worked, someone with muscle and cred to cover our backs and find out what in hell was going on. Mac thought it was a brilliant idea, and didn't give a fuck what it cost Blacklight as a corporate entity or us personally, either. Just as I was feeling smug over having done something smart, he dropped a small tactical nuke of a question on me.

"Johnny, I don't know if Carla's had time to think about this.

But here's the deal—the damned film festival kicked off today. Where's the bloke going to stay? Have we got a place to put him while he's waving his hands about and performing legal abracadabra, or whatever?"

"Gordon *Bennett!*" Mac was right. It hadn't even occurred to me; this was the reason we were scattered across the Cote d'Azur in the first place, because it didn't matter who you were, or even who you knew, you simply didn't come swanning into Cannes during the festival, and expect to find a hotel.

"Johnny?"

"Yeah. Right. Fuck." I sounded good and bitter. There was an obvious answer, probably the only answer, really, and of course I knew it, but truth to tell, the idea made me want to smash things. "You just had to bring that up, did you? For Christ's sake, Mac, don't suggest what I think you're about to suggest, all right? Please? Because I've had enough bullshit today and I honestly can't cope with any more, you know?"

"Sorry, Johnny." He probably was, too. Not sorry enough to offer to host Patrick Ormand, mind you. "But really, you and Bree know him a lot better than I do. What?"

"Nothing." I suddenly had the picture of Patrick Ormand, lounging about the place, sipping fresh orange juice Bree'd squeezed for him, getting up before I did, hanging out with my old lady, lounging around the pool, probably in a fucking Speedo, showing off his abs, while I was still upstairs sucking down meds for the damned disease, and trying to get my middle-aged arse in gear…. "Mac, the truth is, there's nothing in the world I won't do for Bree, but the thought of having Patrick Ormand gazing at my wife over the breakfast table makes me want to kill something."

"Oh, I doubt he would, really. He's got very nice manners, for a copper." There was something in Mac's voice that might have been amusement. "Come on, Johnny, you're taking the piss, right? You don't seriously think he wants to get into Bree's knickers, do you? And you aren't really thinking Bree even realises he's got a willy, are you? Because I don't think she's ever noticed there's any man alive that isn't you."

"Yes. No. Oh, fuck all, Mac, I don't know. And right now, it doesn't matter. I'll ring Carla back and make sure he knows he can stay with us." A wasp went past me, hovered around the top of the glass of juice Bree'd abandoned when Santini had taken her off in his car, and settled there. I swallowed, hard. "I'll do that now, while I'm waiting for the car Ian's sending. Look, where are you? What are you doing about getting Dom the hell out of there?"

Turned out he was also waiting for a car and word from Ian about bail, and the arrival of some suits from our band's pricey law firm. I thought that, come the end of the festival, the local hire-car drivers were going to love us, we were throwing them so much business. We agreed to meet up at the police station—it was in Les Sirènes sur Mer proper, and of course the drivers would know just where to find it. I'd just rung off when the phone buzzed in my hand.

"JP? It's Luke." There was an odd crackling on the line. "Look, I wanted to let you know—I'm not in France right now. We've cleared out."

"What?" I was feeling around in my pockets: money, right, credit cards, yeah, no problem, keys to the villa, the car was supposed to be here shortly…it suddenly hit me, what he'd said. "Wait a minute—where in hell are you, then?"

He took a deep breath. "Italy. Look, JP, it's this way—I talked to Ian, and also to some of the people in our London office, and since we aren't playing the Frejus gig tonight, we all felt the best thing was to get Solange out of here. Because I don't know what's going on up where you are, but our digs, where we'd been staying, has got paparazzi swarming all over the place. Ian let us know about Parmeley's villa before the sun was even up this morning, and suggested I get my daughter out before the vultures set up shop. Best idea I've heard in days, so we grabbed some gear and rented a car, and headed for the border. We're in Florence, en route to Venice. I'm not having Solange harassed, and that's that."

"Bloody hell, Luke, don't sound so damned defensive! What, you honestly think I'd be narked? I'm with everyone else, it's a good idea, and yeah, keep the bastards away from Solange. Me, I need to stay where I am, since they've got Dom and Bree in jail on murder charges—and look, I've got to go. My car just arrived. Keep your cell phone with you, mate, and shout if you need backup."

I probably shouldn't have been surprised to find the rest of the band gathered in the main room at the station. After all, I'd given Bree that lecture, about how they were our family, just before Santini and his lapdog showed up. But it raised a warm hard lump at the back of my throat, seeing Cal and Stu, shoulder to shoulder with Mac and Ian.

There were also a couple of blokes in button-downs. That was a dead giveaway: either they were suits from a film distribution consortium, which was always a possibility this time of year, or they were lawyers. No one else wears that kind of gear in the South of France in this weather.

We'd walked into a zoo, a wall of sound, and it turned out we were in for a wait. The lawyers were French, the coppers were French—there was no sign of Santini, which was interesting, even though his unhappy-looking sidekick was there—and the media trying to cram inside was French. So of course there was a lot of hand-waving and high shrill voices and *oui* and *non* and all the rest of the usual stuff that goes on whenever more than one Frenchman gets together in one place. They never seem to stop moving, you know? It makes me tired, just watching them.

123

It didn't help that I didn't understand more than about ten words of the language. I was relying on Mac, and so were Stu and Cal. He didn't let us down; he had about three minutes of rapid-fire rattling on in French, first with the lawyers, then with the stone-faced woman behind the desk. He didn't seem to me to be bothering with charm at all, but after about two minutes, the stone in the lady's face had softened up, and damned if she wasn't showing a flash of dimple and pout. I suspected she was out of luck, though. He was distracted, and really cross, and not noticing. Just goes to show how worried he was about Domitra—it takes a lot to get his mind completely off sex.

"Okay." He turned his back to the desk, making sure we were all paying attention. "Here's what's going on. They aren't charging them, at least not yet. Short version, Bree and Dom are both still sussy, but that little shit Santini hasn't got anything like evidence to hold them. They're asking us not to leave the jurisdiction. It's going to take them about an hour to process the release papers, and I don't know about you lot, but I want something cold and smooth and comforting, and maybe even a sweet to go along with it. There's a *brasserie* right across the road. Anyone else? Because I'm off. They'll send someone over when they're ready."

Of course, we all went. We pushed a couple of tables together, just outside the main doors. There were paparazzi all over the place, and I thought at first we hadn't got a hope in hell of being left alone, but Ian got up, and said something short and sharp to the first of the blokes who headed in our direction. To this day, I haven't got a clue what Ian said, but whatever it was, it did the trick: the bloke backed off to a reasonable distance, and so did his mates. The waiter came out, took our order, and left us alone.

"Okay," Stu said. He looked as if he hadn't slept enough, and Cal looked knackered as well. We were all pretty well in an advanced state of wilt. "First off, did Luke ring everyone else? He said he'd let everyone know—he got Solange off to Italy this morning, and he's staying away until this mess is sorted out. He did? Good."

"Ian, where do we stand, in terms of the Frejus gig?" Cal was keeping one eye on the doors to the cop shop across the road. "I know it's not our responsibility, but we've got fans who wanted to see us, who paid to see us. We were supposed to be headlining, and personally, I'd like to see some sort of statement put out in the press, something about us not wanting to disappoint our fans, maybe a make-up date down the road, something that's not associated with all this bullshit."

"Already done." The waiter came back, and Ian drained half his glass. "Half-page ads in all the local rags tomorrow morning, with notices sent to the local media as well. It won't be out before the show, but it's the best we could do. Nice simple release. It just says that due to the unfortunate events, gig postponed indefinitely, full refund on tickets, and so on. Radio and TV have the same statement on today. And it's up at our website, as well."

"So basically, what you're saying is, we're in limbo?" I had a glass of juice, nice and cold. When Bree was out of there, I was taking her up the hill to St. Raphael, and we could eat leftovers, and I'd juice some of our own oranges, and spend the evening wrapped round her. It was likely to be the last evening we had alone together, since Patrick Ormand would probably get here in the morning. "Gig postponed, possibly forever but not actually cancelled, makeup gig possible, we—that would be Mac and me—don't get to get the hell out of here, Dom and Bree still prime suspects? That the meat of it?"

He nodded. "Don't look so glum," I told him. "What about the film, Ian? I already had my lawyers slap a cease and desist on it, so it isn't getting shown, not without a lawsuit, not that nightmare we saw last night. Have we got an official statement about that? Something from Blacklight Corporate? And by the way, has anyone got any idea what happened? Because the film I saw at Mac's, the day of Chris Fallow's funeral, that wasn't what we saw last night. That wasn't what Bree got blindsided with last night."

My voice must have gone dodgy, because Mac lifted a hand. "Calm down, Johnny. I don't think Bree believes you're capable of that sort of cruelty. The girl's not stupid. But it's a good question, the official band stance, and we really ought—oh, bloody hell! Heads up, people, we're about to have company."

He was staring over my shoulder. I twisted round in my chair, and saw Benno Marling and Harry Johns heading our way.

My first thought was that Benno had aged since last night. I know, not possible, but it looked that way; he'd been smooth, and now he wasn't. I'd thought my own mates looked wasted, but Benno had them all beat. He was sagging: shoulders, jaw, face. Everything looked loose, and tired, and old.

And then it hit me: he *was* old. Isle of Dogs had been big in the mid-sixties; he had to be five years older than Mac at least, and probably more.

"Christ." It was the first word out of Benno's mouth. He stood there, a foot away, with Harry at his heels like a junked-out junkyard dog. "This is a bit of something special, innit? This cockup?"

"Pretty spectacular, yeah." Mac nodded. "There's a couple of empty chairs behind you. Care to sit?"

"Ta." Benno must have felt my eyes on him, because he turned around and stared at me. He had really pale eyes, that sort of washed-out blue you see in old flicks about the Nazis. They gave me the creeps; they were as flat as his voice. "You're JP Kinkaid. Always wanted to meet you."

I didn't know what I was going to say, but the words were there, and they were out. "Well, now we've met. And that's a coincidence, really, because I always wanted to meet Jimmy Wonderley, at least until last night. Not anymore. Got his rocks off setting his pet roadies at beating up Pakistani teenagers be-tween sets, did he?"

Everyone was quiet, staring at me. Cal and Stu edged their chairs closer to mine; it was a nice show of solidarity, my mates at my shoulder. Harry Johns was watching us, not saying anything, looking uneasy and puzzled. And I suddenly got it, that he wasn't just cooked on smack; he was dim. There simply wasn't anything in there, no mind, no thought, nothing. Whatever it was he had, it was simple instinct.

He had a talent for stamping round onstage, shouting pissy song lyrics that boiled down to stroppy slogans. He'd been the right age at the right moment in time to make that work for him. But times were different, all that was gone, and he was useless, as useless as Santini's silent little tagalong, good for nothing but sitting and following and looking uneasy. He was like a walking ghost.

"Jimmy, yeah, that's right. He always had it in for the darks—really didn't like the bloody Pakis." If the grit in what I'd said had got through Benno's skin, it didn't show. "Jimmy was always a yob, that way, always looking for his bit of fun. On the bash. You know what I mean?"

Behind him, Harry suddenly giggled. I thought about last night, Bree with her face in my shoulder, with Bumpy Nose—what was the bloke's name? Len something or other? putting in the boot, doing his macho little handshake deal with Wonderley. I felt my hands ball up into fists, and saw Ian, across the table, tense up. I don't know what I would have said, or done, but Mac cut in.

"Look, don't know if you'd heard, but we're not playing Frejus. The flick we saw last night wasn't the one we agreed to, so the Frejus gig is off for now. Sorry, but that's the way it has to be. And our other guitar player's left, anyway."

"So's mine." Benno snaked a hand out, and poured himself

some water. He looked at me. "Good thing you don't still want to meet Jimmy. The fucker's gone, scarpered. Haven't seen him since that film rolled, last night. So we can't play. The Typhoid boys don't know our stuff, and they're crap musicians anyway."

Mac opened his mouth, but I cut him off. I'd been watching the police station doors and I was on my feet, shoving past Benno, brushing through the mass of paparazzi as if they were paper cut-outs. Across the road, the doors to the police station had swung open, and there were people coming out, heading away from the jail and right at us: the lawyers we'd sent, and Dom, and Bree.

Patrick Ormand, along with a bloke from Interpol's offices in Marseilles, rolled up the gravel drive to our villa the next afternoon, and I made a mental note to have a word with Carla. He was behind the wheel of a brand new Ferrari, bright red.

"Damn." Bree's eyes were wide. She was in the pool, not nude for a change, so I suppose that was something. Problem was, the swimsuit was actually more suggestive than nothing at all would have been; it was a sleek grey thing that made her legs look about ten feet longer than they are. It was also cut low enough at the back to nark the censors. I thought for a moment about asking her to please pop back indoors and for fuck's sake put on some clothes, but I swallowed that, hard and fast. *Right, Johnny. Don't be a berk. You asked him to help and you told him to come and you let Carla know to do it up as luxe as possible. Just belt up, Johnny. Grit your teeth. Smile.*

I took some deep air in, and tried for zen. I must have made some noise, though, because she glanced at me. "What?"

"Nothing. Just wondering how much that rental is costing us. Looks as though Carla splurged with the chequebook."

I got up and headed over as Patrick killed the motor, but not before he gunned it once, letting the entire universe know he was driving a bloodbeast of a car. I could have throttled him, the macho berk.

I gritted my teeth, and got my face in shape to smile at him. It took some doing. I had a sort of running mental mantra looping in my head: *he's here to help, mustn't kill him, not until he does his job, he's here to help, what in hell was Carla thinking, a bloody Ferrari, what's wrong with a damned Citroen or something, mustn't kill him, he's here to help.*

I was just getting a handle on it when I heard a splash from behind me. So much for staying calm about it.

I was aiming brainwaves behind me, hoping she'd pick up on them—*stay in the pool just stay in the pool no, right, of COURSE you won't you're the hostess, at least go inside and put some fucking CLOTHES on, oh bloody hell, right, shut up, Johnny, don't say a word, he's here to HELP....*

No joy, of course. She wasn't doing any mind-reading today. She'd climbed out and was rubbing her hair dry with a towel, and her legs were shining with pool water. Patrick did a small double-take and I reminded myself that I couldn't hold his head down in the pool until he drowned, nice as the idea was.

"Hey." He was all the way out of the Ferrari now, and his friend was unfolding himself from the passenger seat. "JP, thanks for having me. I've got some luggage crammed into the trunk of this thing—oh, sorry, let me introduce Pirmin Bochsler. Pirmin's an old friend of mine from Interpol, and he's going to be handling their part in this mess. I thought the first thing we ought to do is sit down, just the bunch of us, and pool whatever knowledge we have. Pirmin, this is JP Kinkaid. And this is his wife, Bree Godwin—Bree, how are you? Not in jail too long? You look a lot better than most parolees."

"That's Bree Godwin *Kinkaid*, ta."

They all turned to stare at me for a moment, including Bree, and I felt myself go red. That had come out sharper than I'd meant. I held out a hand.

"Right. Nice to meet you. Interpol's really getting involved? I knew Patrick was planning on getting a foot in the door through you blokes, but this sounds as if there really is something in it, that your lot ought to be handling."

"It seems that is so, yes." Swiss Germans have the strangest accents—thick and soupy, with the emphasis in slightly different places from actual Germans. His eyes kept flickering over my shoulder to Bree, and then back to me again. I glanced back myself, and saw the she had one leg up on the low stone wall that separated the flagstone terrace from the flower beds. She was rubbing down with a towel, showing off miles of skin, all of her back, and altogether too much cleavage. I felt my own body temperature go up, but whether it was reacting to how hot she looked or because both men weren't even trying to hide the stares, I honestly couldn't tell you.

She looked up just then, as if she'd finally caught the thoughts I'd been aiming straight, and gave me the kind of smile I love best. It's intimate, warm, as if we were talking without a word anyone else could hear, as if the moment was a joke we both know the punch line to, but which never gets stale or old. She doesn't give me that look very often, and I wasn't sure why I was getting it now, because if she could overhear my thoughts, she probably wouldn't be smiling.

And then, out of nowhere, I heard Mac's voice in my head. What was it he'd said, when I'd copped to not wanting Patrick Ormand sharing the breakfast table with my wife? Something about Bree not even being aware that there were other blokes in the world....

"Hi there." She was done rubbing herself down, and wrapped the towel around her waist and hips. About bloody time, too. Of course, that didn't do anything about the cleavage. "Patrick, thanks for coming. John told me he'd called you for help, after they let me out of the Les Sirènes sur Mer jail, and I'm surprised you didn't hear my sigh of relief on whatever plane you were on. And hi—it's Pirmin, isn't it? Like the Olympic skier from Switzerland?"

"Pirmin Zurbriggen, yes." It was amazing. He was shaking her hand and she'd made a simple little remark and all of a sudden, he'd stopped looking as if she was a tasty munch and was looking at ease, like he'd kicked away playing copper, just part of the family. "He comes from near to my own village, in fact."

"Does he really? That's very cool. You know, you both look hot and thirsty, and I'm not surprised. Pirmin, here, have a seat. Patrick, why don't you get your stuff and bring it inside? John can show you your room, and I'll get some cold drinks together—juice or lemonade all right?"

"Right." I couldn't help it. "Good idea. And maybe put some clothes on, love, yeah?"

She looked at me over her shoulder, that smile again, and out of nowhere, it hit me right between the eyes: she knew exactly how jealous I was, knew what I was on about, and she thought it was funny, because she knew it was pointless, and stupid. Mac had been dead right, spot on. He'd nailed it: I'd met Bree when she was sixteen years old and I'd been with her damned near ever since. She really didn't see other men as anything to want, to desire; she didn't see Patrick Ormand, or Pirmin Bochsler, or Mac himself, as men at all.

It was nuts, but it was true—in her eyes, in her head, in her world, there was just me. And I'd been assuming that forever, not even thinking about it because, bone-deep, I'd always known that was the way it was. So why was it suddenly getting to me? Why worry about it now? What was I missing?

I needed time to process that, sort it out, but I wasn't getting time, not just then. Patrick had wrestled two small pieces of luggage out of the Ferrari's boot, and followed me inside, and up the

131

stairs. He stopped in the main room, and looked around, and gave a long, low whistle.

"Damn." He looked around at the antique furniture, the parquet floors, the paintings, the floor to ceiling windows, the grand piano in its own bay. "This is—wow. Makes me wish I was a rock and roll star. I'm in the wrong business. Must be nice, to have this kind of money."

"Well, you drove up here in a bleedin' Ferrari." I didn't sound particularly sympathetic. "And I'm paying for it. So sit back and enjoy the perks, yeah? By the way, how were the flights? Carla do you up first class? No worries?"

"Worries? You mean, problems? Are you kidding me?" He followed me upstairs, and down the hall to the guest room that was farthest from our bedroom. "She pulled off a miracle. After dealing with your LA public relations point person, I'm not sure why you guys aren't bankrolling a campaign for her to run for president. She'd do it better than most."

That got a laugh out of me. "That's why we pay her as much as your average small company CEO makes every year, and that doesn't include tour bonuses. She bought her bungalow with her bonus from the tour we did before this last one—nice big place in the Hollywood hills. Here we go, mate—this is your room, for as long as you're here."

I opened the door, and he followed me in to a nice big bedroom, with its own terrace and bathroom. "Bree got it ready," I told him. "Hope this'll do you. What miracle did Carla pull off this time?"

What Carla had done was to call in a favour I hadn't known we were owed. Mac had done some famine relief promo spots a few years back, and the chairman of that particular relief fund had been the ambassador from Norway. Carla had got it into her head that Patrick would be able to get the job done a lot faster, and with fewer bumps in his path, if he had embassy credentials

132

to fall back on, especially from a member nation of the EU. So she'd got hold of the Norwegian embassy in France.

The result was that, when Patrick had stepped off his posh flight at Charles DeGaulle Airport, he'd been whisked through customs with diplomatic credentials, and put on a small chartered jet to Marseilles. And since he'd told Carla who to contact before he ever left San Francisco, she'd got that done, as well. She'd even had the sense to ask Pirmin and his mates to ring up SFPD and request Patrick specifically. There wasn't a single thing she'd missed.

So here was Patrick, on a one-week paid leave from SFPD Homicide, with Diplomatic Corps credentials in one hand and Interpol credentials in the other. Basically, she'd got him hooked up with as close to an all-access backstage pass as exists in international criminal investigation. Juggling all that official paperwork, it was surprising he could find room in either hand to hold the keys to the damned Ferrari.

We ended up with Bree cooking us a scratch meal for dinner. At least, that's what she called it. What it actually was, was some mixed seafood thing with rice in a sauce: a kind of *paella*, she said, served with bread alongside. I had a moment of feeling my molars grinding at the back, when she told us we needed bread and Patrick got very gallant and offered to run her down the hill in the Ferrari. If she'd said yes, I'd have had to stay home, since the car only seats two people, but she said no, not a problem, she wanted me to call Mac and Dom to come over and discuss what was going on, she was sure they wanted to hear about it as much as we did and anyway, they were concerned even more. They could bring bread with them.

Mac was enthusiastic about the entire thing. He was also surprised we weren't hip-deep in reporters. Apparently, he and Dom hadn't had a moment's peace since the news broke. Honestly, I couldn't imagine why we weren't being bothered. I was just damned glad about it.

"You're coming? Brilliant," I told him. "Bree wants you to bring along a couple of—what was that again, Bree? Oh, right, baguettes—hang on. What? Ah. She says, if you've got cheese, as well, that would work. See you shortly."

We found out why we weren't being bothered by the media when Mac and Dom's driver dropped them off. Apparently, the elderly woman who owned the villa at the foot of our hill had a pair of Rottweilers, and also—having lived in close proximity to the Festival all her life—a deep loathing of the press. So, this time of year, she made a habit of letting the dogs run loose; Mac had seen her as they'd turned onto the road, and stopped for a word. Since we were up in a cul-de-sac, the only other way in would have something really insane, a helicopter or something. They probably thought we weren't worth it.

Truth is, I hadn't even noticed there was a villa down there, much less a pair of enormous fierce guard dogs, but then, I really hadn't had a reason to notice. Right now, though, I was damned glad about it, and I don't even like dogs very much. But this pair was earning their keep.

"Now that's what I call proper dogs. Bree, love, remind me to bring them down some raw meat, or dead reporters, or whatever it is Rottweilers eat." I was setting cutlery out on the dining room table; Bree had plates and little bowls of olive oil out already, and our guests were drinking fresh juice and mineral water. Mac had handed over an armful of baguettes, still warm from the ovens at the local *boulangerie*; the driver had gone in to get it, while Mac and Dom stayed in the car. The entire house smelled brilliant.

Considering the circs—Bree and Dom sussy for murder, Patrick showing his muscle in the best spare bedroom, a bloke from Interpol sorting through the mess, and all the rest of it—dinner was nice and peaceful. There were undercurrents, yeah, but that was mostly me, I think.

Bree'd brought the big pan of fish and rice out to the table, everyone helped themselves, and after one mouthful, Pirmin started eyeing my wife again, and I had to bite back a grin. Patrick was eyeing her as well, but since he'd already had Bree's cooking back in San Francisco, a grin wasn't what I was biting back. And of course Mac was watching the whole thing. I couldn't shake the feeling I'd been seriously underestimating our lead singer for a good long time. He saw quite a lot.

We'd nearly done with the meal when, out of the blue, Bree asked a question. It seemed to have nothing to do with anything, but maybe the Rottweilers had made her think of it.

"Mac," she asked, "how did Dom hook up as your bodyguard? I mean, how does a person go about finding a bodyguard? What made you think you needed a bodyguard in the first place? And why a girl? Because I think that just rocks, a guy having a woman as his hired muscle, but, well—how? Why?"

Dom was grinning. She doesn't do that very much, you know? Laugh, yeah, she'll do that. But I'm used to seeing her game face, so just a big grin, that made me blink. She looked really relaxed, and beautiful with it. "Ha! It's a good story. Mac, you tell it, man."

Everyone had leaned back in their chairs. I saw Pirmin focusing on Dom, measuring her, taking what looked to be some sharp mental notes.

"It was in Paris, about, what, ten years ago now? No, nine, I think." Mac lifted an eyebrow at Dom, who nodded. "Nine. It was my birthday, middle of November, pissing down cold rain, and I'd gone off to have a quiet little night on the tiles, just me. Listen to some music, maybe dance, have a few drinks."

"Oh, that's such bullshit. You were trying to find a chewtoy for the night." Dom shook her head at him. "If you're going to tell it, tell it true all the way, man. You were looking for nookie. You know you were."

135

"Well, of course I was, angel. I'm *always* keeping an eye out for nookie." He lifted his glass toward her. "Besides, special occasion, wasn't it? Just a little birthday prezzie, from me to me, something to unwrap. Anyway, I wandered round for a bit in the rain, and fetched up in this trendy nightclub off Montparnasse. All blue lights and the DJ spinning things backward and strobes and overpriced drinks, you know? The main thing was, though, that it was nice and dark, and no one knew who I was. Just what I was looking for, right then."

"Trying for invisibility? You?" There was an odd note in Bree's voice, and my head jerked sideways. "I know the feeling."

"Yes, Bree. Me. Sometimes, invisibility is as good as it gets." He'd stopped smiling for just a moment, and I saw their eyes meet, and something, I don't know what it was, moved in my heart—he'd seen something, got to something, that I was still sorting through. "Anyway, I got a table near the door, and right at the next table, there was this absolutely mouth-watering woman, fantastic bones, legs up to her neck, sort of light cocoa, and, it turned out, the most amazing bum. She was wearing a tube top, in November. Totally smashing. She was gorgeous."

"Not was," Dom told him. "Is."

"So, you hit on her?" Patrick sounded casual, no sign of the cop in his voice, but that was bullshit. He was watching them, his eyes going back and forth between Mac and Dom, analysing, calculating, seeing what was real and what might be show. It was pure copper, pure predator, pure Patrick.

Maybe it was part of whatever was cycling round the table at that point, awareness, just getting stuff, understanding stuff. I don't know. But I suddenly got something myself, a clear little jolt to the brain, insight: The warm moments Patrick Ormand had, the moments when I could relax enough to like him, were too few and far between to compensate for this side of him. And that was always going to be the way it was.

"Of course I hit on her." Mac was grinning at his bodyguard. "I slid over to her table, and we got to talking—she had brains to go with the bum and the tube top and everything else. So I bought the lady a drink, and asked her name, and she said, Savannah. Oh, and by the way, whether my arse-saving friend over here wants to admit it or not, the lady was flirting back, and flirting hard. We had a drink, and got out on the dance floor—they had some industrial tech stuff playing, all about the hips and not much else, perfect for what I wanted. Anyway, we got back to the table and I asked her if she'd like to come out on a crawl with me, what with it being my birthday and all. And all of a sudden, there were two of her."

Pirmin tilted his head. "Two, you said?"

Dom was watching Mac. But I realised, out of nowhere, that she'd been doing as much of a watch on the two officials as they'd been doing on her. It was a very strange moment, realising that the only relaxed people at that table were Mac, Bree and me. And I wasn't all that sure about me.

"That's what I said. Two of them, *café au lait* lovelies in matching tube tops." Mac took a hit of his mineral water. "It was dark, and they looked like twins for a moment. Actually, there are some definite structural differences, once you see them together in decent light—Savannah's taller, and her hair was different, even then. Of course, I was lightly sozzled, which didn't really help. Anyway, the second one just sort of materialised next to Savannah, leaned over the table, stared into my face, and said, *No. I don't think so. You should step away from my baby sister. In fact, go away. Go away NOW.*"

Bree, who'd been sipping juice, sputtered and choked. Mac had done a spot-on imitation of Domitra's voice, pitch, tone, inflexion, the lot.

"Did you go?" I thumped Bree on the back, to clear the airways. I was pretty sure I knew the answer.

137

"I'm alive to tell the tale, aren't I?" Mac pointed out. "Really, Johnny, don't be dim. You know the tone of voice and the death glare—of course I did. I nodded at Savannah—she was turning an entirely different colour and I could see there was a huge noisy row about to blow—and headed out into the rain. *C'est la vie*, right?"

He stopped, one eyebrow up, waiting for someone to cue him. I obliged. "And?"

"And I stepped out of the club, and promptly got mugged."

Patrick was gaping. "Holy crap! You mean—"

"I mean mugged, maybe two steps outside the front door. Cheeky bastards, those two would-be robbers were. The club had an alley, running alongside, and they seemed to think they could hustle me in there. Poor dim bastards."

"And?" Bree was watching Dom, not Mac. "What happened next?"

"Well, I was sozzled, as I say. That might be why I got shirty about the idea of being mugged—whatever the reason, I decided I wasn't having any of it. We were halfway down the alley and I yelled at them in French, and one of them pulled a knife, and I thought, fuck, not good, I'm in deep shit. And all of a sudden there was a typhoon in the alley and I jumped back because I thought they'd been joined by reinforcements, and the next thing I saw were two muggers face down in the puddles. One of them was clutching his groin and crying, the other one had what looked like a compound fracture of the arm. It was absolutely pissing down rain. And there was Domitra, tube top and attitude and everything else. She hadn't even broken a sweat."

"Damn!" Bree had a huge grin on her face. "Okay, that's about the coolest story I've heard in a good long time."

"Not to mention the coolest bodyguard, as well. I hired her on the spot, of course." Mac raised his glass in a toast, and blew Dom a kiss. "Here's to you, you arse-kicking brat, you. May your brass knuckles never rust."

"Yeah, flattery, who needs it. That shit don't pay the rent. Just keep writing the cheques, man, and I'll keep your ass out of a sling." Domitra found a whole prawn half-buried in the rice on her plate, and munched it. "Savannah's still pissed off at me. She was planning to take you home and ride you like a rodeo bull. My sister thought you were a hottie, the dope."

I heard a small choking sound from Patrick. He managed to get control of his voice.

"Well," he said, "That's one hell of a story. Is that the way it went down the other night, at the casino? Pirmin had everyone's statements ready for me when I got here, and I've read a few of them, but I was wiped from the long flight and I'd like to get it clear. One of the eyewitness accounts said something about Bree stabbing Len Cullum in the back, and that can't be right."

"Oh, it's right." Suddenly, no one was relaxed; it was New York during the Perry Dillon investigation all over again, Patrick and Bree in eyelock mode. This time, though, she wasn't hiding a damned thing. "It was two to one, Patrick. The bastards had stood guard for Cedric Parmeley while he tried to rape Luke's daughter Solange. Dom got Solange clear, broke Parmeley's wrist in the process, and then all hell broke loose."

"How is that, Mrs. Kinkaid?" Pirmin's eyes were about as chilly as Patrick's, but somehow, that didn't worry me as much.

"One of them pulled a gun—it was in his hand, a small flat thing. I don't know anything about guns, except that I hate them. But he was going to shoot Dom in the back, in the middle of a crowded casino." She turned to me. "You saw it, John. He had a gun."

I was remembering the fight. "Yeah, he did. I saw the damned thing in his hand, saw him lift it—he was pointing it straight at the base of Domitra's skull, Patrick, and he was grinning. Fuck, they'd been grinning the entire time—couple of proper little

Aryans, those two wankers were. I was a few steps away, not close enough to do anything except yell a warning. Damned good thing Bree had those shoes on. Reminds me, love, we'll need to buy you a replacement pair."

"Shoes?" Pirmin was blinking, looking back and forth between us. I suppose the story did sound weird. "What is this, about Mrs. Kinkaid's shoes?"

"Jimmy Choo stilettos," she told him. "Seven hundred dollar bronze snakeskin dinner sandals with four-inch wooden spike heels, and the damned things are ruined. Brand new, too—I bought them to match the dress. They were the only weapon I had, so I got one shoe off and smacked him right behind the shoulder. I was just hoping to startle him into dropping the gun, but I guess I hit harder than I thought, and the little rubber thing on the heel tip must have been loose, because it fell off on contact and flew across the room, and took a couple of inches of the wood wrap on the heel with it. The heel itself—the steel shank, I mean—went all the way in. I suppose that counts as stabbing."

"You stabbed him with your shoe." Patrick was looking at her as if she was a goddess, or something. Pure admiration, the fucking wanking miserable.... "He was about to shoot Ms. Calley, here, so you stabbed him with your shoe. Your *shoe?*"

Bree wasn't noticing. "I told you, it was only weapon I had. And I wasn't trying to stab him, just surprise him. But what I want to know is, why was that little sleaze Santini in such a hurry to arrest me, and Dom? Because he was, Patrick. He was licking his chops."

"We don't know that, not yet." Pirmin was suddenly austere, a bit chilly. He'd gone professional. "But there is one thing I learned, that I think you will all find interesting."

We waited. He'd got our attention, all of it.

"You know, I believe the information is now public, that one of the things destroyed at the villa was Sir Cedric Parmeley's film vault. Well. From the first look the people from forensics took, it would seem that the vault was blown with a blast of C4, from the inside out. There is nothing left of it—even the foundations are mostly gone."

"You're saying it was a prime target." The film, I thought, *Playing in the Dark.* He'd shown it, mangled and full of stuff none of us wanted to the world to see, just a few hours earlier. "I keep thinking the movie he'd submitted has got to be right in the middle of this. Because of the timing, you know? He changed it, put in stuff he'd taken out, the stuff with Len Cullum beating up that kid in the alley—"

"Hang on, JP." Patrick's voice was sharp. "What's this about Len Cullum?"

"He was a roadie for Isle of Dogs, back when Parmeley was shooting the film. Late seventies." I explained about sequence, how it had been taken out, put back in without anyone being told, expanded. "...and I recognised him. The camera cut back to Jimmy Wonderley and his black neck tattoo, doing this fancy handshake thing with Cullum. What? Did I say something?"

Pirmin had made a noise. He and Patrick were staring at each other.

"This tattoo." Pirmin had pulled a notebook out of his shirt pocket, and a small pen. There was something urgent in his voice, and the tension around the table seemed to have suddenly ratcheted all the way up. Patrick's hands had balled up into fists. "Could you draw it, please?"

"If Johnny can't, I can." Mac held a hand out for the pen. "I was right up front, and I got a good look. Anyway, Johnny had his hands full keeping Bree from watching it—it was pretty nasty. Here, pass that over here."

He bent over for a moment, concentrating. "Right. It was something like this."

He drew, a nice clear sketch. Two double circles, thicker out-

141

side, thinner inside, linked in the middle by an upside down thing that looked like a horseshoe.

"Johnny? This was it, right?"

"Right. Two circles, hooked up with—what do they call that, an omega?"

Silence. No response, not a sound, nothing. I glanced up and got a shock; both the coppers were in full stone-faced mode. Two predators, and this time, I had the feeling I ought to be cheering them on.

Pirmin's lips had thinned out. "An omega. And you say this musician had this tattooed on his neck?"

I nodded. Patrick spoke up, nice and soft.

"Well, now." He was smiling, the same kind of smile I'd once faced down on Bree's behalf, the smile of a man who caught a whiff of blood in the air, and got stoned off the smell. "White Omega. When was the last trace of them anyone had over here, Pirmin? Early eighties, wasn't it?"

"I believe so, yes."

"Look, if you don't mind, would you share, please?" Bree looked bewildered. "Who or what is a white omega?"

Patrick lifted his eyes from the drawing, and I got another shock. There was something going on in his face, in his eyes, and his hands, which were usually relaxed, were clenching and un-clenching. There was something in his voice, too. I couldn't fig-ure it out, but whatever it was, it made him seem human, for a change.

"A race hate group. One of the nastiest ones I ever came across. They were mostly here, in Europe, and that was Europe's bad luck. They started out in London, in the summer of 1978, and made the National Front look like social workers. Suspected connection with a series of IRA bombings, and a lot more. Also connections with over thirty hate crimes, most of them mur-ders—there was a day school bombing, mostly Indian kids. If

142

they existed today, they'd be so high up Interpol's list, they'd be sharing a hillside cave with Al-Qaeda. They went underground, disappeared, in the early eighties. We lost sight of them entirely, except for…."

He stopped. I caught Bree's eye, and saw she was reacting the same way I was. This was new, for how we'd ever seen Patrick Ormand. This was personal. And Pirmin was just looking at him, not saying a damned word. Whatever the deal was, the bloke from Interpol already knew all about it.

"Sorry." Patrick wasn't meeting anyone's eye. "Anyway, except for an incident back in Miami, in the mid-nineties. We never knew where the head honcho went—the contact person I knew in Miami wasn't saying, and she didn't live long enough for us to question her seriously. Looks like that might get answered, now."

He turned to Pirmin. "Who has the festival's copy of *Playing in the Dark*? The Cannes police impound it yet?"

"I don't know. They were instructed to do so. Let me find out." Pirmin took his cell phone and his juice, and headed out by the pool. We could see him, pacing and talking, talking and pacing. None of us said anything.

He was back inside less than five minutes later, and he looked absolutely furious. Amazing, since he was Swiss, and the Swiss don't do obvious very well. They're usually pretty stoic and hard to read. But Pirmin was in a flat-out rage, and he wasn't even bothering to try to hide it.

"I have just spoken with the Cannes police, and with this Santini, at Les Sirènes sur Mer." He was breathing through his nose. "Santini asked that the judge's copy of the film be impounded, and sent to him."

"And…?" Patrick already knew what was coming. I could tell. He was as narked as his mate was.

"And it has apparently gone missing. The Cannes police sent it over by messenger; it was logged into the Les Sirènes sur Mer

143

evidence room. And now? No one can find it."

"But—" Mac shook his head. "But if Parmeley's film vault is gone, and the official copy's disappeared, then there's no visual evidence to verify that tattoo."

"That is correct." Pirmin's voice was very quiet. "And that means that, as a starting point, I think it is safe to say that something in that version meant trouble for someone who wouldn't stop at murder."

# Chapter Eight

I wasn't sure, at the time, what got into me that night.

Looking back, I'm pretty sure I know. It would be nice to be wrong about it—it's not something I feel good about. But right or wrong, whatever it was had the sort of effect on the old sex drive that probably put me in Mac's class for a couple of hours, and it would be a stone drag to have that happen as a result of straight-up barnyard jealousy.

Truth is, either way, I'll take it. It left me feeling like I was twenty again, and it left Bree going back and forth between begging me to stop and begging me for more. That doesn't happen as often as it used to, not these days.

Everyone had gone. We'd said goodnight to Pirmin, and Patrick had taken him down the hill and back to his office in Marseilles. Once the Ferrari's engine had finally faded in the distance—the acoustics in those hills are amazing, and anyway, it was a very loud engine—we headed back indoors and started clearing up.

"I wonder what happened to that film." Bree was washing plates, and handing them over to me; I was giving them a rub with the cloth, and putting them away in the cupboard. "The whole thing seems so weird."

"The film that's gone missing, you mean?" I took a wineglass from her; they were crystal things, heavy as hell. "Or why Parmeley messed with it in the first place?"

"I meant the missing version, but they're both good questions." Forks, knives, under the water and over to me. She looked at me over her shoulder. "John, what's going on down here? This place, it feels—I don't know. It's so beautiful, so calm, so casual, but it's like great food with one ingredient that's gone bad. You know what I mean? It tastes fine on the first bite, but then you realise there's something bitter and it leaves something in your throat that you can't wash away. And the next morning, you're sick."

"Right." There was something spot on about how she'd put it. "You talking about the race politics, Bree?"

She turned the water off, and turned all the way round. I could see trouble in her face. "Of course I am. Those cops—they were really nasty to Dom. Santini was almost polite to me, but not to her, and that's not all, John. He had a kid in there when they were booking me, a North African kid. It was for something small, shoplifting or whatever, but Santini acted as if the kid were sub-human. What in hell is going on down here? It is really that racist, and was it always?"

"Well, yes—and no." I thought about telling her she was asking the wrong person, but I did have an answer of sorts. "Always been a bit that way, but it's a lot worse since the last time I had a look-in."

She was quiet. I put the last pieces of cutlery away, and took her hand. "Let's go sit outside, yeah? Gorgeous night, and since we're stuck with a houseguest until this is sorted out, we might as well take advantage of having the place to ourselves. Don't know about you, love, but for me, there's something about having a copper in the room that plays hell with conversation. Have we got any tea in the house? I could fancy a cup."

We settled out in the garden. While she made a pot of tea, I sorted out what I remembered about how things were done down here. She pulled a chaise right up next to me. There were tiny insects buzzing around, and things wheeling about overhead—might have been bats, or owls, or just really huge moths.

We drank our tea, and I filled her in with as much as I knew. The truth is, that wasn't much. I know it's important, that's why I write cheques to Amnesty International and Greenpeace and whatnot, but I haven't lived in Europe for a long time and local politics aren't high up on my list of interests, anyway. Mostly, with politics, I leave it to Mac to suss out what needs supporting or protesting, and then we look at it. We generally do whatever he suggests is needed, because he's usually right when he says something's important enough to get the band's resources and voice behind it.

But France had been in the news about just this sort of thing not two months after we'd got married, so I'd had it in front of me recently. There'd been some ugly race riots, two Muslim boys accidentally getting electrocuted when they hid from cops in a Paris power station. The incident had acted like someone touching a match to a cannon—the riots spread all over France, cars set on fire, police busting heads, the lot. It had got completely out of control.

Reading about that, I'd remembered a mate of Mac's, at a show we'd done not long before my MS was diagnosed, 1997 I think. He'd been active in the French Green party, and I remembered him sitting in the dressing room at a gig we played in Rouen, going on about something called the Front National. I'd never heard of them before, not the French flavour, but Mac had. No surprise there—he'd been rude about the skinheads in the UK music scene since "Anarchy in the UK" first hit the BBC charts, back in the seventies. He'd been so noisy about it, and so prominent in the Rock Against Racism stuff, he'd actually had a couple of death threats.

So Mac checked out the new French flavour, and it was basically the same shit we'd had in the UK, but with different accents. Of course Mac was narked, so we got to hear about it during the next recording sessions. Turned out they were a collection of rightwing nutters headed up by a bloke called Jean-Marie Le Pen, who was the biggest nutter of the lot. They had quite a big foot in the door, down here in the south: mayors in a couple of towns, major support, the lot.

Bree reached out for my hand suddenly. It was full dark now, and I got hold of her hand, pulling it up for a kiss and lacing her fingers with my own. "So there's a long history of it? Has it always been this bad, John?"

"No clue." Her hands were warm. Good. We'd had a long spell where every time I touched her hands, I'd got a chilly little shock, as if the blood in her veins was saying, *right, sod that, I'm not going all the way down there.* "I'm betting not, though. There's been a lot of immigration from North Africa, post-colonial stuff. That kind of thing usually adds to it. Patrick's scary Swiss mate would know—you could ask him."

"Maybe I will, if I see him again. But I don't want to think about it any more tonight."

She'd twisted over on one side. I thought she was just setting her cup down, but she got her other hand over the chaise arm, and on to me, and what she was doing got all my attention. Not sure what it was about the conversation that had got her into that mood, but I wasn't about to push her away and tell her to knock it off, you know? If Bree was in the mood, so was I.

I reached over and wrapped her up, and the next thing I knew, we'd somehow both got onto her chaise, her at the bottom. We were snogging away like a couple of teenagers—or maybe a couple of newlyweds. She'd got both legs wrapped round me, and I was nibbling her neck, her ears, that hollow where her shoulders meet her collarbones. I had just enough blood still flowing north to think about pointing out that we were both still wearing clothes, and that the whole leg-wrapping thing worked a lot better once we'd got annoying things like skirts and knickers out of the way, when I heard a car engine, coming up the hill. I'm not a car bloke, but I knew just which car it was. No way to miss that engine.

Bree stiffened up and made a move in my arms, wanting to straighten up, pull her skirt back down. She hasn't got an exhibitionist bone in her body, and honestly, I haven't got much of that myself. I'm a sideman, not a frontman.

But for some reason, something just sort of kicked. I wasn't thinking about it right then—already said it, not much blood flowing north at that point—but whatever it was, there we were. I had her wrapped up under me and I wasn't letting her off that easy. She'd got me right at the edge....

"John, what—" The Ferrari was nearly at the top of the hill. She pushed at me. "Let me up!"

"Like hell I will." I nuzzled her neck, and nibbled the lobe of her ear. That's a sweet spot for her, and she made a noise, and wriggled, and the wriggling was right up against a few sweet spots of my own. If her bright idea was to get me to stop, she hadn't made a very good job of it.

"I am not necking in front of Patrick Ormand!" It was too dark to tell, but that might have been panic in her eyes. Of course, it could just as easily have been pleasure. Only one way to find out.

"Oh *God* stop please John please-"

"You started it, lady." I was grinning, and I knew it. I had both her wrists caught hard in one hand, but I kept the other hand free and did something with it that I knew would make her eyes roll straight back in her skull. Of course, it worked—I've had her entire adult life to get that particular trick down. She rippled under me, completely silent; I knew that ripple and I was in just the mood to keep it going, as long as I could. This was going to be one hell of a night.

It was full dark now, and the Ferrari was pulling up. I rolled off her, sitting up, taking my time, and got to my feet. I spared a moment to be thankful for loose trousers. It wasn't because I gave a damn what Patrick Ormand thought about it—I cared fuck-all for what he thought. But I was as turned on as Bree was, probably a lot more, actually. I just had better control of it.

Patrick killed the engine, and climbed out. The night air smelled really good, herbs and flowers that bloom at night, with a touch of salt in the air from the Mediterranean, off to the south. It generally does smell good, this part of the world.

I heard Bree pull herself up behind me. From the sound of it, she was trying a yoga technique, to cover up how iffy her breathing really was.

"Oi, Patrick. You get your mate home in one piece?"

I had one arm round Bree's waist and draped on her hip, holding hard. It was nuts. If I don't usually get demonstrative in public, I don't get possessive, either. Tonight, though, something had got into me, and being honest, I needed to let Patrick know whose woman she was. Her hair was a mess, and her skirt was rucked up at one side. She looked like she'd been doing just what she'd been doing, and what she was going to be doing the rest of the night, if I had any say in the matter. All she needed was a few strands of hay in her hair.

I'll admit it, I was digging it. Possessive, yeah; maybe even a touch of the old rooster in there, showing off, the old "Look what I've just had behind the barn". I don't think I'd ever done that before—it's not my thing. But she was responding in a big way, still rippling. I could feel it. She was dodgy on her feet, as well.

"Yes, thanks." He'd noticed—I could see it. "If you two don't mind, I'm going to say goodnight. I want to get a jump on my jetlag. It's going to be a long day tomorrow."

"Sounds like a good idea to me. We're heading off to bed ourselves." I felt myself wanting to grin. "Ready, Bree?"

She said something, a murmur, completely incoherent, God knows what. It sounded like a good-night, but who knows?

I patted her lightly on the bottom, a quick push. Her breath shortened up again and she shot me a look. Both of Patrick's eyebrows were all the way up. I lifted one of mine—it's a handy trick sometimes, that is.

"We're off," I told him. "You've got towels in the bath; we'll see you in the morning."

So yeah, it probably was knowing that Patrick Ormand was under my roof, alone in a guest bed at the other end of the hall, that kicked me into overdrive that night. It wasn't a conscious thing; I wasn't thinking about anything at that point. But it was probably knowing that if either Bree or I had been the noisy type, he would have heard and had to acknowledge it, that got me pissy and perverse and determined to make Bree yelp, whether she wanted to or not.

What I didn't expect was the effect on my own performance, of just knowing who our houseguest was. If you want it in stage terms, I went nuts. I played one of the best gigs of my life, and I never played a guitar that sounded as good to me as Bree did that night.

It was a good hour after I'd kicked the bedroom door shut behind us and pulled her into my arms before either of us came up for air. She was hanging on to me for dear life, and I had a couple of tooth marks on one shoulder. We had this unspoken war going on, a war we hadn't engaged in for a long time and one we were both digging: she was damned if she was going to make any noise, and I was damned if I was letting up until she did.

So there'd been a couple of whimpers, and a couple of times, she had to choke back a scream, something she never does—the girl's not a screamer, never has been, but she'd got close to it tonight. And the simplest way for her to muffle herself was to sink her teeth into something, and my shoulder was right there. One of those bites, she drew blood. It was brilliant. Turned me on even more.

I'd left the bedroom lamp on, wanting to see her, watch her, every damned inch of her. She'd reached out herself, more than once, to darken the room, and every time, I'd pulled her hand away. I wasn't letting her hide from me tonight—I wanted full visibility. I could see a drop of blood on her lower lip; my shoulder wasn't the only thing she'd bit down on, during that amazing hour.

"Son of a *bitch.* John, I don't know what's got into you, but I don't think I can take much more of this. I thought I was going to black out a few times. Have we got a safe word I can say? Please?"

I looked down into her face. I could feel myself grinning like an idiot; that plea of hers, she'd meant it, you know? "Right. Anything for you. You've got about five minutes. Fair warning, Bree, right up front—I'm only just getting started."

She gave a convulsive little heave, trying to knock me off her. I was expecting it, though, and I was ready for it. "None of that," I told her. "Take advantage of it, love. It's one of those nights, yeah? They don't come round all that often, especially me being the wrong side of fifty."

"Just as well. I'd be in a wheelchair if they did." She was staring up at me. Her eyes looked huge. "John, not to kill the mood or anything, but you wouldn't be trying to make me forget all about that damned film, would you?"

"What, you mean by doing you one better than I ever did Cilla?"

I could have thumped myself, soon as the words were out. It was a surprise, that Bree didn't seem to mind.

"One better, or three, or nine." She wasn't smiling, but she'd relaxed; I could feel all of her under me, and the only tension was just where I wanted it, and just where I'd left it. "Because you know, you really don't need to do that. What are you grinning about?"

"Nothing. What a weird idea, though—completely wrong, as a matter of fact. The film never even crossed my mind."

"Then what—oh God John don't do that, you know I—oh God stop don't stop...."

"Sorry, lady. Your five minutes are up."

She actually did lose the battle that night. It had been a while, years, since we'd been that edgy about sex, and I'd nearly forgot what the feeling of a battle going on under all the fun could do to both of us. So there was some noise, and, well, there you go. Petty, right, but I figured it out later: a trophy's a trophy, especially when the bloke you think wants to roger your old lady is down the hall all by himself, hearing it, listening to you get her to that point.

She got me back later, though, and she probably never knew how hard or deep. She was pressed up against me, her face buried up under my chin. Her skin had a nice glaze of sweat to it, and there was moonlight coming through the window, making her shine. I'd got what I wanted, and she'd broken, finally, and begged me to stop. In my head, this was post-encore, house lights up and into the marital green room, you know? Show's over, thanks for coming, everyone get home safely.

And then she muttered something, but I couldn't quite catch the words.

"Come again? No, right, bad choice of words. What did—"

"Curious." She lifted her cheek, and I heard her nice and clear, her voice gone all drowsy. "Just wondering if other men are as good as you are."

It hit me then, right between the eyes, the thing that Mac had said, that I'd been trying to parse out. There it was, not just what he'd said, but what he'd meant: *I don't think she's ever noticed there's any man alive that isn't you.*

Gordon *Bennett.* That's what he'd been getting at: She'd never gone to bed with anyone else. I was it.

I've never been into Mac's style of thing, needing or wanting nonstop sex to get by with. And I was never into the more traditional rocker thing that a lot of blokes who'd got famous were into, pulling women just because they could, because there were always groupies, always someone wanting you as their own trophy shag. I like connection, loyalty, monogamy, all that. Once I met Cilla, I'd stopped messing about, until Bree leaned toward me in the wings at the Hurricane Felina benefit, and after that, there'd been no one but Bree.

But I'd done my share of screwing around before Cilla. Christ, in the sixties and seventies, most of the women I'd met who associated with rock and rollers actively slept around. The more famous blokes they could brag about doing, the more desirable they felt.

"Bree?" There was a voice in my head, one of those little *shut up, mate, just zip it, don't ask, you don't want to know if the answer's not the one you think it is* choruses, running in a loop like a rap dj spinning a disc. There was no way I was paying any attention to it. I wanted to know, to hear it from her, whatever the answer was. "I need to ask you something, all right? And I want a true answer—don't be afraid to tell me, okay?"

"Okay." She'd been half asleep, relaxed and limp up against me. Now, all of a sudden, she wasn't.

"That question you asked me, just now, about other blokes." I

154

stopped, because suddenly, out of nowhere, I felt myself turning warm. I knew just what I wanted to ask her, and I couldn't bring myself to do it. Bloody ridiculous. We'd been together going on twenty-seven years and I couldn't sort out how to ask her a simple question: *am I the only man you've ever slept with?*

So I held on to her, let the words die off, and there I was, mentally urging her on: *come on, baby, you always know what I'm going to say, this would be a bad moment to stop, come on, Bree, help me out here.*

"Are you trying to ask whether I've ever slept with another man?" Her voice was very quiet. "When? While you were off on the road, maybe? Or do you mean when you were back in England, with your wife?"

"Neither. Both." *Relax, Johnny. Just shut up and stay loose. You asked her, and now you can deal with it. You don't get to be narked or freaked or even cross if you don't like the answer.* "Ever, I meant."

She sat up, and looked down into my face. And it came to me, good and hard, that the reason I'd never thought about it was because I'd always taken the answer to the unasked question for granted, taken that absolute loyalty, that fidelity, on faith. If it turned out I'd been wrong all these years, I was probably going to break into a thousand small rough shards and it wouldn't be any consolation at all to know I'd only have myself to blame....

"Idiot."

She didn't sound narked, or scared, or regretful. She sounded amused, and affectionate, and maybe even exasperated. My eyes popped open.

"Oh, for God's sake, John. You look like someone at the dentist's office. You look like you're waiting for a root canal, or maybe word from the governor. Just knock it off, will you please?"

I blinked up at her. She was sitting up, naked and cross-legged, looking down at me and shaking her head.

"You know, you ask some of the stupidest questions, sometimes, it just boggles my mind. What *is* it with you, about me and other men? Because for the record, there aren't any. Okay? Got it? There haven't ever been any, there aren't any, and there aren't likely to ever be any. Make a note, or something. Write it down. Tattoo it on something if you have to. Hell, where would I find the time? You're a fulltime job, and you always have been, even when you'd left me in San Francisco, to take care of Cilla. So just chill out, for fuck's sake."

I pulled her down next to me. Mac had been right, and so had I, taking all that for granted. I thought back to Cilla, to what she'd let slip about herself, about how she'd fucked Blacklight's road manager, when she was selling us all out to a sleazy tabloid biographer for some attention and a few lines of blow. I tightened my hold on Bree.

Luck's a funny old thing, sometimes. Another rocker, a very iconic bloke by the name of Mick Jagger, once sang about not always being able to get what you want, but getting what you need instead. He's got a point, but I tell you what, it's even better when you get both.

"John?" Her voice was drowsy again. Not surprising, really— I'd given her one hell of a workout. My shoulder was pulsing away where she'd bit me.

"What, love?"

"Today, when Patrick and the Interpol guy were talking about that hate group. Did you get the feeling there was something personal about it? Personal for Patrick, I mean."

"I did, yeah. Our pet detective looked almost human there, for a second." I stroked her hair, and reached my free hand out to turn out the light. "Made me wonder if there might not have been a woman in it, once upon a time."

Of course next morning, the universe being what it is, I got handed the cosmic payback for being a petty git about Patrick

Ormand: a hellacious multiple sclerosis relapse, one of the worst I'd had in about a year.

Since I hadn't realised at the time that I was being a petty git, I was really narked about the whole Sod's Law-karma coming home aspect of it. I mean, I'd left Bree happy, as sleek as a seal when she'd fallen asleep. So I hadn't been thinking about having done anything emotionally or ethically dodgy.

I probably should have been expecting the relapse. The disease had been laying way back in the weeds. I'd had some extra tingles, and an episode or two of myokymia and ataxia, but mostly, it was business as usual and my body had let me get on with enjoying my own honeymoon.

So I got a shock when I opened my eyes the next morning, and did my morning ritual. At least, it's my ritual when no one's ringing me up to tell me someone's house has blown up, or letting me know that someone's been bashed with a guitar: I keep my eyes closed for a few minutes, relaxing different body parts, trying to see what's likely to be a drag when I finally do sit up and put my feet to the floor.

Usually, there's a few trouble spots. But when the first thing that happens when I open my eyes is realising that the reason I'm awake is because every inch of me is in pain or spasming, it means a damned long day ahead.

"Bree?"

Her name came out blurry. I remembered her crack about me looking like someone at the dentist last night, and it was too appropriate; I sounded like someone with a head full of novocaine. Right then, I'd have paid anything for a good shot of novocaine. It hurt to talk, the entire jaw was dead on one side and apparently being stabbed with red-hot needles on the other.

I tried again. "Bree?"

"John? Oh, shit!" Of course, she knew straight off what was wrong. "Hold on, I'm getting you some meds."

She was out of bed and back with a glass of water and double my usual morning dose of anti-spasmodic before I'd finished trying to tell her what I needed. Good job, too, because things were bad enough just then to make talking about the last thing I wanted to do.

"Here. Five of these, and I brought you a TyCo too. Sit up—can you swallow? Good, let's get these down. Start with three, and give them a few minutes to kick in. If you need more, they're here. If you take all five and they knock you out, that's good too."

"Ta." It came out as a raspy whisper. I tried to flex one foot, and my whole body winced. I saw a flutter of pain, might have been sympathy pangs, move across Bree's face.

"Oh, man. Oh, baby." She got an arm under my shoulders, and helped me get my head off the pillow. We went nice and slow; I was shaking, up against her. She sounded miserable, and furious with herself. "I wasn't paying attention last night—you never took your bedtime dose. I'm sorry, John, I'm so sorry. I forgot to remind you."

What was she on about, blaming herself? I'd damned near raped the girl, and here she was saying it was on her? I swallowed a couple of pills, and rubbed my jaw. "My fault. Not yours. Distracted you; felt great. Wasn't thinking about meds. Besides—wouldn't let you up."

"I should have remembered."

"Saint Bree." She had one arm round my shoulders, lightly stroking my upper arm. It was very odd; for a very vivid moment, there, it brought back last night, the chaise as Patrick Ormand was pulling up in the Ferrari, me with one hand hard on her hip, possessive, letting Patrick see her in that state, not letting her hide, showing off what I had.

Now we were reversed, or something, and here she was, supporting me, holding me up, nothing but love in that touch. Her motives were a lot purer than mine had been. The guilt mo-

ment—*what the hell were you thinking last night, Johnny my lad?*—
was a kick in the emotional bollocks that almost took my mind
off the physical meltdown I was slap in the middle of.

Not completely, though. This was a bitch of a relapse. In fact,
it was so bad that I had some hopes it was going to pass quickly.
That's the only thing I can say in favour of the corkers—they
hurt more, but for less time.

She'd got the water back on the table, and I realised both my
hands were shaking. Good job there was nothing needed doing
with Blacklight today, because I couldn't have held a guitar,
much less played one. "Are you okay for a few minutes? I should
let Patrick know what's going on, and find out if there's anything
we ought to know about. And you should see if you can get some
food down—a soft egg or something. Give me ten minutes, okay?
I'll get you some breakfast. Here, lay back down, just rest. Egg,
cheese, juice. Maybe a fresh fruit smoothie? We have bananas,
and all the oranges in the world. No, settle back, John! You rest."

I opened my mouth, and she shook her head at me. She was
pulling on the same clothes I'd peeled off her last night, and left
in a heap on the bedroom floor. "Don't argue with me. Just try to
relax. I'll be right back. Ten minutes. I promise."

There was no point in arguing with her. Besides, I wouldn't
have let her see how much I minded the idea of her going tête-à-
tête with Patrick Ormand while I was helpless upstairs, even if I
could have got my jaw to cooperate, not after realising just what
I'd been on about last night. I managed a smile—it felt like a
death mask or something, total rictus—and closed my eyes and
let myself settle back. There was nothing I could do, except ride
it out and wait for the meds to kick in. I heard the bedroom door
shut quietly behind her.

I think I must have dozed, and anyway, I wasn't watching the
clock. So I don't know how long she was gone, but when she
came back, she had a tray with a poached egg and some soft

159

cheese, a smoothie made with milk and fresh fruit, plus a cup of coffee that was clearly for her and not me.

I managed to sit up on my own, and get a mouthful of egg down. The jaw was still numb, but my hands were beginning to work again. The meds were kicking in, finally, and thank God for it. The egg was perfect. "Good. News?"

"You mean, from Patrick? Not really. I pointed him at the fridge, told him to help himself, explained that you were relapsing, said I was sorry for not being able to hang out, and did your breakfast. He knows you're not feeling well." She swallowed some coffee. "Oh, man, I needed that. My whole body is talking to me this morning."

"Not surprised about that. Just—surprised you can walk."

She reached across me, setting her cup down on the tray, and something caught my eye: bruises on her wrists, clusters of dark spots on both of them, where I'd got hold of her last night. I suddenly saw it in my head, that moment on the chaise out near the pool, pinning her down, getting both her wrists held hard, not letting her up....

Christ. Sitting there in bed, her next to me and not even mentioning it, I couldn't sort it out in my head. I felt like a rapist, but the thing is, she hadn't put up much of a struggle. She's nearly as strong as I am—if she'd really wanted me to knock it off, I'd have a few bruises myself. Bree's not quite a valkyrie, but she's not a weak little thing, either.

I got a hand out, and caught hold of hers, no pressure. She saw where I was looking, and went pale—that's Bree's way of blushing. I was still weak as a kitten, but I managed to plant a light kiss on the cluster of bruises.

"Sorry." The tingles in the jaw were still there, still making it tricky to talk, but the stabbing pains had let up, finally. "Hurt you. Didn't mean to. Last night—playing rooster. Cock of the walk. Only just sussed it. Petty."

"What? Are you kidding me?" She blinked at me. "Oh, good grief—is *that* what that was all about? Trying to impress Patrick Ormand with your middle-aged harem of one?"

I nodded. "Yeah. Didn't realise then—sorted it out just now. Hope you at least had fun. I did."

"Wow. That was one hell of a genie I seem to have let out of the bottle last night. And yes, of course I had fun, and you know it." She leaned her cheek up against mine. She sounded honestly puzzled. "Someday, you're going to have to explain to me just what I've ever said or done to make you worry that I'm interested in someone else. Because I just don't get it, John."

"Same question, back at you." The pain meds were working; talking seemed easier. "Why worry about me and Cilla? Ancient history, Bree."

She turned her face away. "That's different. You know it is. You were married, and you were gone, and you were with her, all those months, and you went back, and then you went back again, just because she asked you to. She had the right, she had all the rights, and I had no right at all to—hello?"

There'd been a light knock at the bedroom door. Patrick poked his head in.

"Good morning. Okay for me to come in?"

My first thought was that the bloke was dressed for action; lightweight suit, attaché case, cell phone in its own holder. All he needed was a pair of designer sunglasses and he'd have "international man of mystery" screaming off every move.

I waved him toward the foot of the bed, and Bree moved the bed tray off in a hurry. "Have a seat. Breakfast yet?"

"Just one of the oranges off that big tree outside. I'm meeting up with Pirmin for lunch in a couple of hours. We need to go over some things, agency files on a lot of the people involved in this. I was hoping for a quick word with you two first." He glanced at me, then away, fast. "Sorry to see you aren't feeling well. Is this the MS? Is talking a problem?"

"Yeah. Easing up, though. Took a lot of meds this morning—forgot to take them last night. Why? You want to talk to me? Hang on a minute."

I pulled myself all the way upright, and closed my eyes, feeling out what was still messed up, what still hurt, what was better, flinching away from the pain that was still there, swearing under my breath. Bree'd put an arm round me, nice and light, just supporting me, letting me know she was there. I wasn't happy about going through that drill in front of Patrick Ormand, but no choice, not just then.

The legs were still painful, and they'd probably be shaky until this little episode moved along. The jaw was much better, well enough to talk with, anyway. My left shoulder hurt, just a sort of dull throb, like a drum beat. I realised my bladder was tingling, and I was about to swing my legs out of bed, when I remembered something else: I was stark under the covers. And there was no way I was getting out of bed naked with Patrick Ormand in the room. For some reason—maybe it was that whole man of mystery vibe—I couldn't bring myself to just say, *look, mate, I need a piss, can you get out of here for a minute so I can get some clothes on...?*

I opened my eyes, and focused on Patrick. He was just sitting there, patient, courteous, waiting for me. And here I was, stuck, totally at a disadvantage. Major difference from last night, you know?

"Right. So, what did you want to talk about? Sorry I'm staying in bed, but my legs are dodgy." *Yeah, and if I don't go for a piss soon, they'll get even dodgier.* I aimed a silent thought Bree's way, hoping she'd pick up on it the way she usually does, read the cues, read my mind.

"I wanted to ask you about *Playing in the Dark.*" Patrick kept glancing up, at me, and then his head would jerk, as if he was telling himself to not look. I couldn't imagine what he was on

162

about. I mean, okay, I wasn't wearing pyjamas, but there's nothing weird or off about my torso. It's just a torso. "When I spoke to Pirmin this morning, he told me the festival judges have their original submission copy. But I gather that version was radically different from the one they showed the other night, when the villa went up. So I wanted to ask if you'd seen both versions."

"Yeah, I have." The pressure on my bladder was getting unbearable. *Come on, Bree, help me get him out of here....* "I've seen all three versions, actually."

"Three?" He'd stiffened up, enough so that he was looking at my face now, making eye contact. "There's a third version? No one mentioned that."

"Three." I crossed my legs under the duvet, and Bree stirred suddenly. Good. She was picking up on it, finally. About bloody time. "The original cut, from 1980, the one management for all three bands refused permission for. God knows where that one got to. Then there's the redone cut, the one I saw parts of at Mac's in London—I think that's the one the judges have. That horror show they played the other night makes three. The bloke must have been completely off his nut, messing with—what, Bree?"

"I need more coffee, if you're going to talk about version three. And you're tipping the tray—no, here, let me get it. You need to get up anyway." Bless the girl. "Patrick, why don't we go downstairs? Give John a couple of minutes to do his morning thing, and we can sit outdoors."

"Right. Five minutes." I rubbed my jaw. "Okay, yeah, maybe ten minutes. I need a shave, as well."

"And a Band-Aid." Patrick held the door open for Bree. "Don't know if you realised it, but your shoulder's bleeding."

I made it to the loo just in time, and then took a look at myself in the mirror, and yeah, there was quite a bruise there, dark and scary, with some blood. So that was what had been aching all

163

morning, and that was what he'd been trying not to look at, sitting there asking questions: the spot where Bree'd bitten me last night, trying to muffle her own noise.

I grinned at myself in the mirror. I couldn't help it. It was worth it. That had been some rough sex, rougher than we usually get, and the bite was a fair trade. Seemed the old cock was still crowing, conscience or not.

I had a hot fast shower, put some antibiotic salve and a plaster on the bite, got dressed, and made it downstairs in just under fifteen minutes. Patrick and Bree were sitting outdoors, Patrick drinking juice, just waiting for me to come down, nice tranquil scene. Weird, remembering how pissy that particular mental image had made me just one day ago. Patrick waited for me to get settled, but he was obviously watching the clock.

"About the movie—we've got our hands on the so-called official version of *Playing in the Dark*, number two—I think that's the one your management approved. You said you'd seen all three, JP. What were the substantive differences? Can you remember?"

I filled him in, taking my time, being careful, thinking about it as I went along. It seemed pretty obvious to me that, whatever had happened to Cedric Parmeley and his villa, it had to have something to do with that damned flick of his.

"So you didn't watch some of the official version, and you didn't actually watch the end of the third version the other night. Is that right?" He'd been paying attention, but not writing anything down. It was unnerving, really, the idea that he might have a memory that good. My own's always been iffy, and it gets less reliable the older I get. "The third segment of the film, the one that deals with the late seventies band, Typhoid Harry?"

"Yeah, that's right." I put an arm round Bree. "I was too busy trying not to lose it over what he'd put back in during Blacklight's segment, and trying to get Bree not to watch. It was really

164

ugly—Bree, love, relax, it's okay. Honestly, it's old news and it's long ago and far away."

"I know." She was rigid in her chair, and I saw Patrick glance at her. "It's okay. I'm fine."

"Okay." I turned back to Patrick. "Besides, we were already gobsmacked by the way he'd cut that bit back in on Isle of Dogs, Jimmy Wonderley sending Len Cullum out to beat that Pakistani kid. Mac might have watched it, though."

"Good. I'll call him later today." He emptied his juice. "I need to get going. Pirmin's expecting a call from the pathology people any minute, with positive ID on both the bombing victims. And we're hoping to find some way of identifying Parmeley's other bodyguard. When Ms. Calley injured him, he was taken to the local hospital, so they'll have looked at his papers. France is big on having people carry papers. The trouble is, if he was known to Interpol, his papers are bound to be faked. And we need to find out more about both of these guys. Because if there's a connection between them besides the Parmeley connection, and it's White Omega...."

He stopped. There it was again, that note in his voice, that look, that tensing up and closing off. Something about that organisation had been heavy for him, heavy enough to leave what looked to be the only hole in that damned armour plating of his.

"John?" Bree'd turned toward the villa. "Is that your phone? No, I'll get it, you stay there."

She came back a minute later, and handed it to me. "Sorry. It clicked into voicemail before I got to it."

"Ta." I clicked it to the play function. "Hang on a minute, Patrick, will you? Let me just get this—it's from Ian."

"*(beep) JP? It's Ian. Look, if you've got Patrick Ormand with you, can you give him a message? I'll leave a message on his voicemail, and I have a feeling it's important. I just heard from our London office. They got a package yesterday, from Cedric Parmeley. Not his distribu-*"

tion office—it's straight from him. It's a DVD of 'Playing in the Dark,' and it says, 'final cut.' I told them to send someone down here with it on the next flight out of London. Trisha Ablondi—you met her, she's one of the management team here—should be at your place late this afternoon. (beep)"

# Chapter Nine

"(beep) Oi! This JP Kinkaid? Yeah, it's Benno Marling. Some copper just rang me up, said we were supposed to get hold of you, something about that shite flick Parmeley did. Don't know what he's on about, but he said it was happening at your place, and we're supposed to be there. So where is this place of yours, and how do I get there, and when? You want to ring me back and give me some gen? (beep)"

"Benno Marling's in." I looked up at Patrick Ormand. "So that's all of Blacklight except for Luke, plus Benno Marling. Hang on, I've got another message."

"(beep) Um, what, this is Harry Johns, who's this, is this JP Kinkaid? So, what's going on, then? Got a message I'm supposed to be somewhere to see a movie or something. Don't know where or when, though. Maybe someone could ring me back, tell me about it. (beep)"

"And that's Harry Johns just checking in, as well." I set the phone down. "I'll ring him back, not that he bothered leaving a number. Lucky for him my phone's smarter than he is."

"So, that's what? A headcount of ten? Are Barb and Cyn coming for this? That's twelve. What about Ian? And has Carla arrived? Is she coming, too?"

Bree was looking tired, and no wonder. That message from Ian had turned things arse over teapot; instead of a quiet day in the sun, swimming and lounging and recuperating from some rough sex, she'd suddenly got stuck with having to play hostess for a lot of people, a couple of whom she didn't know and could probably have done nicely without. And Bree being Bree, she was going to feed them all.

To top it off, there was going to be a long, slow crawl between versions two and three of a movie she hated the sight of, probably with freeze-frames, with everyone watching. I wasn't looking forward to that myself, but for Bree, it was shaping up to be a lot worse.

Patrick had hit his cell phone as soon as I'd relayed the message from Ian. First thing he'd done was to tell me to get on to Mac and see if he still had version two, the clean version, in his possession. Bossy sod, and since my MS was still giving me grief, I wasn't in the mood to take his cheek, you know? I'd punched in Mac's number, handed Patrick my cell, and told him to do his own bloody job, ta. Lucky for him talking was still iffy for me; if it hadn't been, I might have had a few pointed words for the bloke, ordering me about in my own house, you know?

But he'd grinned, and taken the phone, and apologised straight off. Then he'd rung Mac, got his answer, and got the London office on the line, getting Trisha to swing by Mac's and bring along that DVD version, as well. After that, it was on to Pirmin, me getting bored while the pair of them went on and on and back and forth, trying to decide whether they wanted to watch the damned things in sequence or side by side. They finally decided on two of everything, just in case the differences were too small to notice without a side by side.

So, by the time Trisha Ablondi was due at our front door with the two DVDs, there'd be everything and everyone Patrick and Pirmin needed to nail down whatever it was they were after. It wasn't going to be any fun, and I was feeling too limp myself to really come the heavy husband and tell Bree she had to relax; as it was, when Patrick offered to run her down the hill for whatever groceries she wanted, I damned near pushed her into the Ferrari, instead of being pissy about it. It was a hot day, and she didn't need to be slogging up and down the hill on her own, maybe having to dodge paparazzi along the way.

Trisha arrived by taxi at just past five, and by that time, everyone else except Benno Marling and Harry Johns had got there. Ian had rung up to say that Carla was settling in at Luke's villa, with Luke's permission, and unless either of them was needed, he was going to take her out to dinner, and they'd probably be up late, going over things. After all, Carla wasn't just our American ops manager—she was the best PR woman in the business, and this was Cannes. Cedric Parmeley's death had set off a shitstorm of publicity issues, and Dom and Bree being hauled off by the local coppers had just added to the mess, not to mention the little matter of our flat refusal to play Frejus until the mess was sorted out. All things considered, we'd dumped quite a lot on Carla's plate. So we waved them off and told them to have a lovely dinner.

The house smelled wonderful—turned out Cyn Corrigan was a decent cook herself, and offered to act as Bree's sous-chef. I hadn't known that about Cyn, but then, I was beginning to sort out that there were quite a lot of things I hadn't noticed, right under my nose, for a good long time.

We offered Trisha dinner and a bed for the night. You could see she wanted to—the London office staff doesn't get a lot of these particular outings—but she'd got a return ticket for early evening, so we sent her on her way. Meanwhile, a small van had rolled up, driven by a local in front and a flat-screen telly and DVD player in back. Pirmin and Patrick—I had to keep telling myself not to call them the Glimmer Twins—pounced on the bloke, showed credentials, and got things set up.

I've got to hand it to our pet detective: I may not like him much, but there's nothing I'd question about his competence. If there's any smell of weakness, he's there. If there's blood in the water, he's right on it. And something told me the blood he was smelling right now came from an old enemy.

Benno and Harry showed up together, which didn't really surprise me. There'd been a definite whiff of big dog being followed by little dog about the pair of them, back at the cafe in Les Sirènes sur Mer. They were both East Londoners, pure cockneys, similar backgrounds and that sort of stuff.

They were decently well-behaved, which was good, since it saved me from having to bash their teeth in. It did surprise me, though. I was afraid they were going to look at the food and offer up the usual cockney rant about the bleedin' French and their posh cookery, but something about Bree seemed to have them both remembering they'd been taught basic manners, back when the earth was still cooling. They shook hands with her, and accepted plates, and if there was any muttering about not being given sausage and chips, they kept it low enough so that we didn't hear it. Maybe they were just surprised my wife was American, or maybe they believed that all Americans had guns.

If you're curious about details like food and whatnot, I can't help you. No idea what Bree dished up that night, except that there were a lot of different things on plates, a "help yourself" buffet deal. There seemed to be a lot of seafood involved, as well as bread and dipping oils and other mysterious plates and bowls with chopped things in them. I stuck mostly with bread, but

halfway between Benno Marling and Harry Johns arriving together, and Bree telling me that Cyn and Barb and Dom were
doing the after-party chores so would I please just go sit down
and stop offering to help with the washing-up, we slipped off into
the kitchen together and she put together a plate for me, of some
easily digestible stuff for supper.

"Bree, listen." I swallowed some soft cheese, feeling a few re-
sidual stabs in the jaw. "You don't need to sit there and watch
this mess. You know that, right? Only thing you might have to
watch is the end of that miserable thing with Jimmy Wonderley."
I saw her shoulders hunch up, and kept my voice quiet. "I'm
sorry, love. We'll take Patrick aside and ask him. But you might
need to identify Len Cullum."

She looked at me, not saying anything, her arms wrapped
round herself. Her eyes were wretched. I pushed my plate aside
and put my own arms round her.

"I know." I was speaking into her hair. "If we can get Patrick to
let you off, we will. But one thing I'm telling you right now: no
damned way are you staying in the room for a rerun of that
nightmare with me and Cilla. No arguments, Bree. I won't allow
it. Understood?"

"Yes." She sounded miserable. "Thank you. I can't watch that
again, especially not in company. Maybe someday, just with you,
so I can deal with it. But not yet. And not with other people. I—
I just can't."

"I know. I really do get it." She leaned against me, and I was
stroking her back, so I had my head up and saw Patrick over her
shoulder. "Patrick, just the man I want to see. Bree, off you go.
Put your feet up, all right?"

I gave her a push, and she went, not meeting Patrick's eye. He
watched her go, and turned back to me.

"Is there a problem?"

"Yeah, there is." I took a deep breath. "Look, Patrick, I've told her and I'm telling you, I'm not having her watching Blacklight's segment in that last version. There's a scene with me and Cilla, snorting coke and getting naked together, about two weeks before I met Bree. It's damned near pornography, and it wasn't in the film we approved—now I think about it, it wasn't in the earliest version, either."

"Jesus!"

"Jesus had nothing to do with it, not so far as I know." I met his eye. "I don't remember it happening—not exactly a surprise, considering I was coked and sozzled most of the time back in those days. Thing is, I didn't know Parmeley put it in, and Bree got hit with it, had to watch it with no warning, with about two hundred people turning to stare at her, the night Parmeley's villa blew up. There's no way in hell we're having a repeat performance. We clear about that?"

"Yes, of course. I'm sorry." There it was, that almost human look he got sometimes, especially when the subject was Bree. "That must have been like something out of her worst nightmares. She strikes me as a very—private person."

"She is." My own voice had gone hard. "And by the way, if you're thinking I'd have let her see that if I'd known it was there, well, you can think again, mate. The girl's most of my life. Even if I happened to be the sort of sadistic bastard who'd put her through—"

"I don't think anything of the kind." His own voice stopped me, dead on. It was totally calm, no feeling at all. "I was simply commenting on how she might have felt, and reacted. That's all. And of course she doesn't need to be in the room when we get to that. I really just want her to take a good look at a freeze-frame of Len Cullum, and see if she can give us a positive ID on him. Ms. Calley tells us she was too busy fighting a two-on-one to give his face a good look, and that she was mostly face to face with the other bodyguard. She said Cullum was mostly behind her.

172

Have you finished eating? Everything's set up and ready."

"Right. Sorry I got shirty. The truth is, that thing with me and Cilla was as much of a surprise to me as it was to Bree. I flipped my shit completely and I'd do it again, if the damned thing stood any chance of being released. Yeah, I'm done with dinner. Let's get on with it, and get it over."

"Certainly. Oh, JP, one question before we head out, if you don't mind. Just wrapping up loose ends."

I stopped in the doorway, and turned. There was something in his voice, familiar, that too-casual thing; I'd heard it before, back in New York nearly a year ago now, when he'd tried to deke us that he didn't know anything about Bree's bust for supplying me with heroin when she was a teenager. I felt my spine tighten up, hard and quick.

*Right, Johnny. He may be a guest and he may want to get into Bree's knickers or he may not, but he's a cop and this is official business. He looks for a weakness. If he finds one, he exploits it. Remember that, and mind what you say.* "Ask away."

"The night Parmeley's villa went up." He was taller than me, not much, maybe an inch or two, and those light eyes of his were as cold as they ever were. How had I thought he looked human, even for a moment? "I understand from Mac that he rang you within minutes of the explosion, and left a message. I take it you and Bree can vouch for each other for the relevant times? You two were here, and together?"

Just like old times: Patrick Ormand and me, those light pale eyes of his, me being thankful mine are dark opaque brown, locked up in a staring match.

I remembered Bree fleeing upstairs, shutting herself in one of the guest bedrooms. I remembered staying up, unwilling to go to bed without her, heading up finally, resting one hand on that guest room door. I remembered total silence, not hearing a sound, no breathing, no crying, nothing.

I remembered waking up to the explosion, remembered going out into the garden, tasting ash on the wind. Bree's light had stayed out; she hadn't come out even when the sirens got loud. I remembered that I hadn't seen her for hours afterward, that when she finally had come down, she'd looked as if she hadn't slept, black circles under her eyes, exhausted....

"JP?"

He was watching me, just waiting. I took a breath, and looked him straight in the eye.

"Of course we were both here," I told him. "Where else would we be?"

The fact that I suspected I'd just committed perjury, and was nervous about it, got buried under the weight of those two versions of *Playing in the Dark*. More than that, I got a pretty good hint that I wasn't the only one watching with ghosts sitting behind my shoulder.

There's something very weird about watching the same flick, two different versions, one after the other in slow motion. The whole thing was surreal, anyway. We had rock and rollers, the rock and rollers' old ladies, two blokes from Interpol, and two more rockers no one actually knew, in a hired villa, watching side by side, bang in the middle of an investigation into the very messy death of the loopy director who'd done both versions of the film we were watching.

And to put the tin cupola on the weirdness factor, my wife—who was sussy for murdering the bloke she nailed in the back with a stiletto heel—was feeding everyone involved. She was on the move, making sure everyone had got what they needed, topping up drinks, picking up plates and heading them off toward the kitchen. It was Bree in her full-on hostess mode, and at the moment, it was about as bizarre as I was willing to get. And of course, there was also the fact that no one knew whether the one

174

we'd been sent by Parmeley was an entirely different cut from the first three.

I got settled in the rocking chair. Some days I feel like JFK with his bad back, but I like rocking chairs, and always have done. There's just enough movement in them to keep me relaxed, but not enough to start up the inner ear rubbish that comes with the MS. Getting seasick in your own front room's no fun at all.

Benno Marling made a beeline for the rocker, but that wasn't on. Bree stepped in front of him and told him that was my chair, sorry mate, reserved, here, pull up one of those high-backed wing chair things. He looked like getting squiffy about it, but she smiled at him and led him off to the food again, and he mellowed out straightaway. Of course, he'd been there to see her nail Len Cullum with her shoe. After that, I couldn't see him fancying a brangle with my old lady. Besides, she was bigger than he was.

"If I can have everyone's attention for a minute or two, please?" Patrick had the remotes to both DVD players on the coffee table in front of him. He'd got settled in with Pirmin on the sofa, just to his left. "Here's the thing; we've got two versions of the film here. You—I'm speaking to the musicians, Mr. Marling and Mr. Johns included—know what's on the first version. That's the one Cedric Parmeley's distributors sent for your approval, earlier this year. It's also the one he submitted to the festival, for official inclusion; Interpol has done some checking. The other version was sent out by Cedric Parmeley personally, without prior notification or explanation. It arrived at Blacklight's London offices yesterday. With the exception of attending the unofficial screening you all went to at the Theatre deVille, in Cannes, that may have been the last thing Cedric Parmeley did before he was killed."

He stopped, and looked around. He's a good speaker, I'll give him that. Effective as hell. No one said anything, but everyone watched him.

"So," he went on, "we're going to have a look at both, for comparison's sake. We'll watch the approved version first; after that, we'll check the new version. If the changes are small, we'll watch them side by side. If the new version is obviously different, we won't need the comparison."

No one said anything. He looked around the room, and just for a second, there, I had the feeling that somehow, he could see all of us once.

"What I want to know, specifically, is whether any of you can identify anyone who is not a part of your usual circle, either then or now." Same flat, calm voice. "We already know, for instance, that a former employee of Mr. Marling's band, the Isle of Dogs, ended up working as a bodyguard for Cedric Parmeley. His name was Len Cullum, he appears in the version of the film you all saw the other night, and he is, at present, in a drawer in the police mortuary in Marseilles with a bruise on his jaw and a cut throat, awaiting final autopsy results and the appropriate disposal of his remains."

The quiet in the room seemed different, suddenly. It was weighted, as if people were holding their breath. Even Dom looked more concentrated than usual, and I didn't know that was possible. The only exception was Bree; she was standing in the doorway, doing a headcount, scanning the food, seeing what needed topping up. Once a caterer, always a caterer.

I caught her eye and jerked my head, and she came and perched on a floor cushion next to me. She didn't look very happy about it, but she stayed. I rested one hand on her shoulder. It was an old signal between us: *stay put.*

Patrick picked up one of the two remotes, pointed it at the wide-screen TV that had just been hooked up, and brought up the approved version of *Playing in the Dark.*

This time, I watched the entire thing, and I kept Bree with me.

176

Patrick had asked us to, and I owed him that—after all, he'd come to help, at my request. But I had another motive, as well. I wanted Bree to see it, wanted her to see the film I'd told her was okay enough to approve for commercial release. I wanted her to know that, when I'd told her the segments with Cilla weren't anything, really, just street shots mostly, I hadn't been blowing smoke. That little surprise we'd been handed at the Cannes theatre had led to a very bad night for both of us, and I wanted her to see that what I'd approved without asking her really was a reasonably good little film for what it was, a documentary about a touch of popular culture at that moment in time.

And it was, so she should have been relaxing next to me, but she wasn't. I felt her under my hand, not moving, tense as hell. When I looked down at her, I could see her shoulders were hunched up, hard as stone, rigid. She looked like someone expecting bad news, like someone thinking that any moment, she might have to look for a place to hide. And it wasn't needed, that vibe. This was her house, there was nothing coming at her, and anyway, I was right there.

I touched her cheek. That got her attention; I lifted one eyebrow in a question mark, and she met my eyes for a second, and looked away. What she didn't do was relax under my touch. I didn't like it, but there wasn't any way for me to say so, not right then.

I took my attention off my wife when we got to Typhoid Harry's segment in the approved version. It was really bizarre, watching that. Cedric Parmeley had seen the three bands as the past, present and future of rock, yeah? That's what the film was all about, that timeline. That meant he'd thought Typhoid Harry would be around long after Blacklight was gone. And bloody hell, if he'd honestly believed that, based on what he'd seen of the bands he'd tapped to follow, he either had no sense of music, or else he'd been as stupid as mud. The bottom line was, Typhoid

177

Harry as a band, once you got past Harry's stage presence? Just rubbish, really.

Don't get me wrong, I quite like punk. The anger behind most of it was valid, for what was happening at the time. When they sang about being stuck on the dole because there were no jobs out there for anyone, they meant it—they were singing from experience. There were some really solid punk acts out there, back when it was happening, the Clash, Ultravox, the Sex Pistols. Some of those people could really write, and a lot of them could really play. And the entire deal, all that three-chord short stuff that punk was about, that was a nice little balancing act to some of the long, droning, pompous prog-rock stuff that came just before.

So yeah, some damned good punk stuff out there, stuff that's stood the test, but Typhoid Harry wasn't one of them. This was the first time I'd actually sat back and watched them, and the truth is, they were garbage.

So my attention went elsewhere, thinking about that. They'd had two songs hit the charts, one reasonably high up. They'd got a lot of airplay. They'd done one tour of America, and then they'd come back to the UK and headed off to play the Continent. Two weeks in, their drummer had got hold of some seriously bad junk and died of it in a Berlin motel room, and that was it, Bob's your uncle, end of story, or at least, end of that band.

And they were crap, that band. Harry had just managed to tap into something, that moment in time when the unemployment levels were soaring and people were thoroughly fed up with the world they'd somehow got stuck in. So those people, who were listening to Radio One and the BBC and hanging about in odd corners of UK cities, could really get into the rage, the strutting all over the place, the screaming and yelling and destructiveness, all that bullshit that passed as nihilism. The songs were forgettable, and the live act wasn't anywhere near what really good bands like the Clash could put out there.

All Typhoid Harry had as a band were lucky timing and Harry's own ability to grab the eye with his act. And in the end, that just hadn't been enough. They'd been mediocre to start with. They were through.

The DVD ended, no surprises, nothing but credits, and clicked off. Patrick caught Pirmin's eye, some kind of silent cop signal or something, and they both nodded.

"Thank you," Patrick told us. "My associate needs to check a few things with his office, and anyway, I think we could all use a good stretch before we start on the second DVD."

I offered to help Bree carry things between rooms, but she ordered me off her patch; Cyn and Barb were there to provide backup, and I was in the way. She made a pot of coffee, offered tea, wine, beer. I wandered out into the garden, and found myself standing next to Cal and Stu.

It's a weird thing about Blacklight's rhythm section—they don't really look alike at all, but in a way, they do. I mean, Cal's a long lanky bloke, wears his hair cropped short and started doing that back before Charlie Watts made it fashionable for ageing rockers. Barb always used to tease him about his colouring—if he'd been a chick instead of a bloke, he'd have been a pure English Rose, pale and blonde and pink. Stu, on the other hand, is Black Irish, a solid little bloke, right about my height. The only reason he wasn't burned bright red every time he walked outdoors in the South of France is because Cyn won't let him out in the sun without enough sunscreen to protect the County Antrim village Stu's ancestors came from.

But long years of playing together—Cal and Stu had their own band, the Light Brigade, back when Luke and Mac had been playing club gigs as Blackpool Southern—had done what some people say marriage does. They'd been hanging out so long, they moved in similar ways, the way old married couples do.

"Bloody hell." Cal had a beer in one hand. He was looking about as relaxed as I'd hoped Bree would be feeling; he saw Mac moving about indoors, and lifted his bottle in a salute. "Hey, JP. Is it just me, then? Or was Typhoid Harry a complete waste of time?"

I shook my head. "Not just you. You read my mind. I think I've got a song lyric forming somewhere about it, but I'm not pushing it. No talent at all, that lot. All they did was strut, shout, and smash things. Just in the right place at the right time, is my guess. You both get enough to eat, then?"

"Yeah, that's what I think, too—about their band, I mean." Stu stifled a burp. "Enough to eat? I ate enough for three people. Great food. Does Bree cook like this all the time? If she does, why don't you weigh more?"

I grinned at him. "Yeah, she does. Just not in this quantity. This is her party thing, what she trained to do all those years ago. It's her chef's face, her hostess face, you know? I think she looks at her kitchen and sees it as a place she can escape to. Cooking's something she can do when she needs a place to hide."

I heard my own voice say it, and I stopped cold.

Serious insight moment, there, or maybe what Bree herself might call a clue-stick moment. Because I was right, I could feel it, and it nailed me, that I'd never thought about it before. Those early times, when I'd gone back to London because Cilla'd needed me, Bree had disappeared into the kitchen, cooking, planning menus, losing herself in food. I remembered a white-faced, silent, desolate teenager, surrounding herself with tools of her trade, leaving me to pack my own stuff, the only times she'd ever done that. I remembered her trembling as she cooked, stopping to steady her hands with the big chef's knife held too hard and moving too fast for safety. I remembered thinking that it was good, she could be busy, keep herself distracted while I got on

180

with it. Right then, remembering what I'd thought, I could have kicked myself.

"JP?" They were both staring at me. Cal nodded at one of the garden chairs. "You want to sit, mate? You've gone shaky."

"Good idea." I sat down, hard. I wasn't about to tell them that I was writhing inside. I wasn't ready to tell anyone that but Bree herself, and not until I'd sorted it out.

Christ. How many years had she used the thing she loved second-best in the world as a way to keep her heart from breaking, because the man who was permanently pegged in the number one spot on her personal pop charts had hurt her? How many times had I forced her into it? And how had I missed it, all these years?

"JP! Okay, sit for a minute. Do you need anything?" Stu was poised to head indoors. I must have looked like absolute shit. "Should I get Bree?"

"No. I'm fine." I got up. Fucking memory, landmines all over the place. What else had I not noticed? Even worse, what had I noticed but not bothered to process? What else had she protected me from? "Patrick's waving at us. I think it's showtime."

We'd all got settled before Pirmin came in from the garden. He caught Patrick's eye, and there was that non-verbal cop moment again, a signal they obviously both got. Patrick looked around, made sure we were all there, and spoke up.

"All right. We're going to open this DVD, the one sent to Blacklight's offices. I have no more idea than any of you what's in this thing. So I'd like everyone to watch it closely. Mrs. Kinkaid, I won't need you in here for the middle segment—your husband and the other members of the group can answer any questions I may have about it. All right?"

"Yes. Thank you." Her voice was barely audible. She was back on the cushion at my side; I leaned down and brushed my lips against her hair. She looked up at me, not smiling.

181

"Mr. Marling, Mr. Johns—what I said earlier applies even more to this new version. What I want from you, from both of you, is any information about the non-band personnel: hangers-on, friends you haven't seen since, that kind of thing."

Benno settled back in his chair. "Right. And by the way, you blokes are coppers, right? When we're done with this, maybe you can tell me who I'd talk to about finding out where my guitar player's scampered off to. Because we've been playing together forty years, and I'd like to know where he's got himself off to."

"Yes, Mr. Marling, we can discuss that later." There it was, another of those signals between Pirmin and Patrick. I got the feeling they weren't surprised by Benno's question. "Right now, the immediate agenda is this copy of *Playing in the Dark*. So let's do it."

He leaned forward, and picked up the remote.

## Chapter Ten

I suppose, really, I'd been expecting the same version of *Playing in the Dark* we'd been surprised with at that damned screening. Parmeley had been really invested in his pet project, for some reason. I knew that. But still, four versions seemed a bit much, even for Cedric Parmeley.

He'd written "final cut" on the DVD's wrapper, and also on the label. Less than two minutes in, I realised that what he should have written was "director's cut."

This was nothing like the other ones we'd seen, not at first. It opened with a voiceover, Parmeley himself talking over a choppy dark view of the Isle of Dogs arriving for a gig at the Hammer-smith Odeon, back in London. I loved the place, and I'd always fancied playing there, but by the time I'd stopped doing strictly sessions work and joined Blacklight, they'd already gone on to play stadiums. Ham Odeon's a lot smaller, and wouldn't have accommodated the demand for Blacklight tickets. I still wouldn't mind playing one of those intermediate capacity venues, but that was likely going to stay on the what-if list. Those smaller venues, there's fewer of them around every year.

Hearing Parmeley's voice made me jump. I wasn't the only one, either; Bree was taut, her shoulders hunched hard up against whatever she thought might be coming next, and I could see the same sort of reaction I was having myself. I mean, he'd been completely demented, senile would be my guess, and the last thing he'd ever said to me was an insult to my wife. Now he was dead, blown to nothing inside his own house and his two racist bodyguards along with him. Hearing that finicky squeak of his really brought that home. But it was more than that. He sounded lucid, clear. What in hell…?

"…Marling and Wonderley's band, made up of four former teddy boys, reached their peak around the time of the Beatles and Stones. They just missed being a first tier band, probably because of the timing: Isle of Dogs hit just after the first wave of what was called the British invasion, and for whatever reason, somehow never made it across the Atlantic as part of that. They used to play much larger venues, but despite their longevity, they now play rarely and to far smaller audiences…."

It was bizarre, you know? Seriously creepy shit. He sounded focused, on top of it, right there: squeaky, but not barmy. I wondered how fast whatever had caught up to him had hit him. If he'd done this cut recently, the last thing he'd done with film, then maybe the dementia had been intermittent, coming and going.

"…Isle of Dogs had mostly faded by the mid-seventies, lost in the wake of acid and glam rock. But they enjoyed a small renaissance in the late seventies and early eighties, an upsurge of fresh popularity, due in no small part to their East London skinhead sensibilities. Those sensibilities gave them some street cred in the age of punk nihilism, high unemployment, and the general dissatisfaction of England's white working class, especially in the big cities...."

And there they were, Isle of Dogs, waiting in the wings before the show. It was a moment out of history, familiar enough. They were smoking like stacks, Benno Marling looking impatient, Wonderley looking cautious. Then Wonderley turned his head to greet someone coming up beside him, and the picture froze right where it was.

"There." Patrick's voice had gone distant, remote, and every trigger I had jumped to high alert. This was the hunter in full view, feral and bloody dangerous. "On the back of Jimmy Wonderley's neck. Does everyone see that tattoo?"

"What, you mean the horseshoe thing?" Benno Marling sounded bored. "Yeah, I see it. Jimmy had it done along with some mates of his, right around the last gig we played in Glasgow—1978, I think. What about it? Tats illegal where you come from, mate?"

Patrick turned his head, and looked at Benno. I couldn't see Patrick's face, but I could see Benno's, and I could see it change colour. He shut up fast. He must have got his first look at what I'd first seen back in New York, and it wasn't the sort of look you wanted to get cheeky with, not if you had half a brain, or anything to hide.

"Illegal? No. What it represents is illegal, though." Patrick looked around the room. "Does anyone here recognise it? Anyone else seen it before?"

Everyone was quiet. I opened my mouth, caught Mac's eye, and shut it again. Patrick wasn't talking to me, or to anyone with Blacklight. This was all aimed straight at Benno Marling and Harry Johns; we were here as backup, witnesses, maybe for something I hadn't sorted out yet. But I'd caught that tiny shake of

185

Mac's head, got the point, and belted up; this time out, I was in the audience.

Next to me, Bree suddenly reached up a hand and slid it into mine. Damn—her fingers were chilly again. I held hard, warming her, pulling her fingers up and kissing them, letting her know I was there and it was okay.

"Mr. Marling. You said, about this tattoo, that Mr. Wonderley had done this with some of his friends." Pirmin had got into the act. "If you please, can you be more specific? Can you name any of these friends you spoke of?"

"I don't know about that." Benno suddenly sounded uneasy, twitchy. Maybe it had finally got through his head that this was serious shit going on, that whatever he answered would have consequences. "I mean, I knew them, maybe a couple of them, but Jimmy ran with some blokes I didn't dig at all. There was Len Cullum, but you knew that, right? I mean, you've got him in a drawer in cold storage, you must have seen his tat. And another roadie of ours, Jimmy's guitar tech actually, Bryan—shit, can't remember his other name. Burns, Barron, something with a B. Anyway, he got his tat done the same time Len and Jimmy did. A few other blokes, a couple of birds as well, but they weren't mates of mine. Len was a right yob, never liked him much, and didn't miss him when he quit the band."

"Thank you." Pirmin looked at Patrick. "Glasgow, 1978. That is very interesting. The timing, I mean."

"Isn't it, though?" Patrick looked over at Benno. "If the names of any of the other people wearing that tattoo suddenly come back to you, Mr. Marling, I suggest you let us know, as soon as possible. In the meantime, let's move on with the rest of the film."

The scene in the alley, Len Cullum and the other roadie jumping the Pakistani kid with Wonderley egging them on or maybe even ordering it in the first place—that was there, all right, just the way it had been in the theatre. No voice-over added to it,

186

either. It hardly needed it.

"Hang on a moment." Benno was leaning forward. His face was furrowed up. "Right—stop it there a mo, will you?"

Patrick clicked the pause button. "What is it?"

"That other bloke, the one with Len—that's Bryan, Jimmy's guitar tech." He snapped his fingers suddenly. "Right, Benno, you fucking clot, where's your memory gone, then? Bryan Blunden, that was it. A Geordie bloke, he was, came from Newcastle. Mean as hell. So yeah, there's that positive ID you wanted. Bryan's the other bloke in the alley, the one putting the boot in. They were thick with Jimmy, those two were."

"Blunden. Is that Bryan with a y or an I? Good. Thanks. We'll have Interpol on that as soon as we take a break."

Back to the film. Isle of Dogs, back in the club, the music, uninterrupted. There was Jimmy Wonderley, smiling, totally into the music, making exquisite shimmering sounds off his old National guitar, swapping it out for a beat-up old Telecaster, just playing killer stuff.

I swallowed hard. What had happened to him? How could he possibly send his goons out to leave a kid half-dead in an alley for no better reason than the kid not being white, and then go back indoors and play blues, Delta stuff, old Robert Johnson licks, touches of what I recognised as Bulldog Moody played brilliantly, music that had first come out of the black players in the Mississippi delta and the south side of Chicago? I couldn't parse it. There was no sense to it.

Next to me, Bree moved and made a soft noise under her breath. I realised I'd closed my fingers hard around hers, and eased up my grip. It took me a moment to realise that Patrick had paused the DVD again, and was looking at my wife.

"I'm sorry," she told him. She seemed to be having trouble controlling her breathing. "Did you want me to answer some questions?"

"Only one." His voice was neutral, same voice he'd been using all along, but he smiled at her, a really warm smile. Friendly, you know? Damned near intimate. For a moment, a really bad moment, I had a mental picture of just choking him until he stopped breathing himself; it was so strong, I had to close my eyes against it. Stupid, really. This wasn't about that, and this wasn't the moment for me to get pissy about it. I swallowed it down, gave it a moment, and opened my eyes again. "Can you identify either of the men in the scene we just watched, Mrs. Kinkaid? Specifically, either of the attackers in the alley?"

"Yes." Her voice was low, but clear. "The dark-haired one. He was the man I hit in the back with my shoe in the casino the other night, when he pulled a gun on Domitra. The one you called Len Cullum."

"Are you certain of that, Mrs. Kinkaid?" Pirmin didn't sound as if he doubted her, but hell, he was Swiss. Typical Swiss pedantry, dotting every "i," crossing every "t." "Many years have passed between this film and the events of the other night. Is it possible that you are mistaken?"

"No, I'm certain." She was, too. It was there, in her voice, in her face. "For one thing, he had a very weird nose, like a prize-fighter; it looked like he'd been in a lot of fights, like it had been broken more than once. That's not surprising—I can't be the only person to have ever wanted to deck him. And the shape of his shoulders, the way his neck was set. Remember, I saw him from the back, at the casino, when I nailed him, and then the next night I saw him from the front, at the theatre. We had a staring match. It was the same little asshole who beat that kid in the film. Do you want me to sign something? Because I will."

"Yes, we will. But not until later." Patrick was smiling at her again, and I told myself to unclench my fists. *Right, Johnny, he's doing his job, just let him get on with it, he's here because you brought him here....* "And now, I think we're moving on to the next segment, which is Blacklight. If you'd like to give this section a pass, Mrs. Kinkaid, that's fine. I don't think you're needed for this."

"He's right, Bree." I bent over and kissed her. "Off you go. Leave the dishes—I'll help with the washing-up after, I promise. Go have a cup of tea, or something. Okay?"

She nodded, and got to her feet, and I got a surprise, because Barb Wilson and Cyn Corrigan both got up immediately, and followed her out. I wasn't sure what the story was, there—I mean, it's not as if they knew Bree well, or anything. But they were right there with her, and there was a definite smell of Girls All Together, or something, going on.

And here was the squeaky voiceover again, still steady, still not sounding remotely out of it. I probably sounded a complete berk for wanting to smack Patrick Ormand, because with the other half of my brain, I wanted to kiss him, for letting Bree off.

I looked around at my mates, and saw that Mac was leaning forward. Stu and Cal had both inched their chairs closer to the screen.

"...Blacklight got its name blending the names of the first bands of its original four members: founders Malcolm Sharpe and Luke Hedley's first band, Blackpool Southern, had broken up at right around the same time as rhythm players extraordinaire Calvin Wilson and Stu Corrigan broke up their band, the Light Brigade...."

Actually, technically, Parmeley had that wrong. Blackpool Southern, Mac and Luke's duo, had never broken up; they'd just added the Light Brigade's rhythm section and combined the name, as well as the personnel. I'd actually played a few festival gigs where Blackpool Southern had also been on the bill, which was how Luke and I had come across each other in the first place, back in the early seventies.

At first, watching, I couldn't see any differences from the one we'd seen in the theatre. It was choppy, strange, cuts that made no sense. But I began to get it: there *were* differences, just really subtle ones. Camera angles that seemed longer or shorter than what I remembered. And when it got to Cilla, the camera lingered. What had Parmeley called her, back in the Les Sirènes lockup? My pretty little blonde wife?

Music, in the studio, out the door, Viv alive and vital. I thought, for a couple of minutes, that the new version was going to give that night in Dallas a miss, but no such luck. Not only was it there, he'd actually expanded it.

Even with everyone there having seen the first one, except for Patrick and Pirmin, I felt myself wanting to crawl off into a corner somewhere. This time, the camera hadn't stopped or cut away. If I'd forgotten what coked-up sex with Cilla had been like, I had a brilliant opportunity to refresh my memory. Problem was, there wasn't much in the world I wanted less. The camera bloke had had himself a right old porno moment, with the camera aimed squarely at us, full body.

It was a complete nightmare. None of my mates were meeting my eye, and I decided not to lock eyes with Patrick Ormand until I had to. I was just thankful he'd let Bree off. If she'd had to watch this—no, I wasn't going there. No damned way.

"All right." Patrick actually sounded shaken, and I had a moment wondering, crikey, had he actually heard any of the noise from down the hall last night? "That's all for Blacklight's set, which is the middle segment. Is there anything there that anyone thinks might be useful?"

"Useful for what?" Harry made a lewd little smacking noise with his lips. I turned around to look at him, and so did the rest of the band. He shut up fast.

"No," I told Patrick. I sounded fairly curt, myself. "Though I ought to tell you, this one's different from the first three. The bit we just saw, there was—more of it in this one."

"I see." He did, too. We caught each other's eye for a moment, and damned if I didn't find myself liking him again. Because he got it, you know? He knew just how narked I was about it, and he knew just how hard even a shortened version of that must have hit Bree, not knowing it was coming. "If there's nothing there, I'd like to move on to the final section, Typhoid Harry's part."

This time, I watched it all. I could do it, even as intense as having watched myself actually shagging my late wife onscreen in front of a room full of people had been, even as gobsmacked as I was that I could have been stoned enough to invite a camera into our bedroom, and too stoned to remember any of it.

"…the punk movement, from the three-chord exuberance of the Ramones to the doomed posturing of the Sex Pistols and political epiphanies of genuine working-class bands like the Clash…."

Funny thing—this was actually the dullest of the three segments. Isle of Dogs had been chilling and ironic, ours had been scattered and energetic, but here was the stuff that was supposed to be the real thing, all that raw punk energy, and it was boring as watching paint dry.

The backstage and offstage moments started off tamely enough. There was a lot of swearing, a lot of cigs hanging off peoples' lower lips as they sneered into the camera, a lot of wanting a bit too obviously to be Sid Vicious. There was show footage, and I had to remind myself that Harry had actually put on a pretty good show, considering that the band itself was nothing to write home about.

There was a club gig in Manchester, a lot of choppy action in the mosh pit, a lot of Mohawks and safety pins. The camera followed the band into the small smoky backstage area; there was a collection of people, hangers-on in the typical Kings Road Vivienne Westwood gear of the day, except for one bloke who looked different, black sweater, black jeans, similar to what I usually wore. There was something about him, something that set him apart—he looked like he'd been dropped into the middle of this lot from a UFO, or something.

He had a girl with him, small, blonde, curvy. The camera caught her face nearly full on and I saw her smile up at the bloke in black, a nervous smile that sent long dimples curving up in her cheeks. She was as out of place in the middle of all the twenty-something punk rockers as the bloke she seemed to be attached to.

And there was something about the look the bloke was giving. It was careful, somehow, the look of a man who doesn't want to have to answer any questions later on.

"Patrick?" Pirmin had turned in his seat. "What is it?"

The DVD had stopped. Patrick had clicked the remote, the pause button, stopping it, freezing it. The bloke in black, the small curvy blonde with the long dimples—there they were, caught looking into the camera, stopped in time.

"Oi! Patrick!" It was Mac, peering around Dom. "What in hell's wrong with you, mate?"

Patrick turned his head, and Mac shut up. I bit back words of my own. This was a new look for Patrick—he was bleached. All the colour had shifted in his face. His lips were a line; you couldn't tell upper from lower, they were clamped together so tight.

I felt something in my stomach lock down. If I thought I'd seen the predator look before, I hadn't known the half of it. This was beyond predator, and straight into feral.

"Who is that?"

He was looking at Harry, and Harry was looking puzzled, oblivious to the undercurrents, to everything happening around him. He really was dim, was Harry Johns. "Mr. Johns? Can you identify that man?"

"If he can't, I can."

Everyone's head swiveled. It was Domitra.

"That's the man I put in the hospital the other night, with a cracked cheekbone." Her voice was calm, clear, musical. No drama, no big deal, nice and simple. Maybe that's why it was impossible to doubt her. "Cedric Parmeley's second bodyguard."

"Mr. Johns? Can you put a name to this man?" Patrick's voice was a whip, electricity, just crackling. Out of the corner of my eye I saw Bree, standing in the doorway to the kitchen, staring at him.

"What, the bloke in the black gear?" Harry blinked at us. "Yeah, 'course I can. That's Terry. He used to show up at a lot of our gigs, him and his little American dolly bird. Bloody groupie he was, really, always hanging about. He had some sort of club going, always trying to get us to join, but we weren't having any of that."

Pirmin was on his feet. "What kind of club? And Terry what? What was his surname, Mr. Johns? Do you know?"

"Not really." He'd finally sussed something huge was going down. "We just called him the Goffer."

"Terry Goff." Patrick's voice was soft, cold, hot. The words, the names, sounded like they were being yanked out of him by some invisible dentist in a B movie. "And Louise. *Louise.* Dear God."

There wasn't any colour left in Patrick's face right now, but there was hate there, hate and a few other things. I turned my head, caught Bree's eye, and she came to sit beside me, holding my hand. No one was saying anything.

We all jumped half out of our skins when Pirmin's cell phone began buzzing. Even when he muttered an excuse-me and went outdoors to listen, we stayed quiet. Whatever had hit Patrick Ormand, it had hit him right between the eyes, and maybe in a few deeper places, as well.

There'd been extra pepper in his voice when he'd said the woman's name: *Louise.* I remembered telling Bree last night that I thought there might have been a woman behind Patrick's reaction to that damned tattoo, and I looked to be right on the money. But who in hell was Louise? The little blonde bird, obviously, but beyond that, who had she been?

And then Pirmin had come back inside, and right then, I pushed Patrick Ormand and his little mystery bird to the back of my mind, because Pirmin looked about as stunned as I've ever seen a Swiss bloke look. Like I said, they're pretty stolid.

"We have just received word from London," he told us. "A positive identification based on dental records. The body from Cedric Parmeley's film vault has been officially identified as James Walter Wonderley."

Looking back at it now, I'd say Patrick Ormand kicked himself into an entirely different gear after he'd got that look at Terry and Louise Goff. I hadn't a clue why, not then, but there was no escaping the sense that something had stuck a key into whatever clockwork it was made our pet detective tick, and sent him into overdrive. He did his best to bank it down, but you couldn't miss it. He was on fire.

Right that moment, though, we'd all had our attention pulled off Patrick. The news about Jimmy Wonderley did something to Benno Marling: it broke him.

Why that surprised me, I can't imagine. After all, they'd been mates for forty years at least, played together, written songs together, got stoned and pissed together, picked up birds down the local together, shared hotels and memories and groupies and who only knows what else. I can't even imagine what my own reaction would be, if I'd suddenly had the news that Mac, or Luke, or my mates back in San Francisco, like Tony or Kris, had died, and I hope I never know. Losing Chris Fallow had been hard enough, and we'd been expecting that for years.

But I watched Benno's face lose all its colour, go soft, crumple up, fall apart, and it surprised me. Maybe it was having seen Jimmy Wonderley with that tat on his neck, and finding out how much ugly stuff was represented there. Maybe it was remembering him laughing, as his mates put in the boot when they beat that kid in the alley. Or maybe I felt betrayed, finding out that a musician I'd admired, someone with creativity and chops, had turned out to be what Wonderley had been. I didn't seem to have any sympathy for him left in me, and that made getting why Benno Marling was so shattered over it tricky.

Everyone was looking at Benno, not knowing what to do or say to him. Men don't cry around each other much, and with that eagle's neb of a nose and that bony skull, he didn't really look capable of anything as soft as tears. But they were running down his face all the same, and none of us knew what to do about it. It wasn't just the blokes, either. Cyn and Barb had come back in from the kitchen, and they were as uncomfortable as their old men were. And Dom doesn't usually waste sympathy on strangers.

"Excuse me."

Bree brushed past Pirmin, just moved him out of her way as if he was on wheels. She got round Patrick, left him staring at her. She pulled an empty chair up next to Benno, and draped one arm across his shoulders.

"I'm so sorry." Her voice was gentle, and warm. "I know you'd been friends for a very long time. I'm so very sorry. This must be hard for you. Is there anything we can get you? Anything that would help?"

She meant it. She wasn't making pretty polite talk for the fun of it, or playing off some dusty old convention that says you pet and soothe, and she wasn't doing it because that's what a hostess is supposed to do. She was doing it because she'd seen tears on Benno's face. That was more than enough for her.

Saint bloody Bree. There are times when that streak of hers

195

drives me half off my nut, but then there are times like this one, when she makes me remember that not everyone's cynical and that it's okay not to be. Because it was real, what she was doing. She was honestly sad on Benno's behalf, honestly offering him a shoulder to cry on. Right this moment, she didn't give a toss about the fact that the bloke he was grieving for had been a racist and a criminal and who knows what. She was dealing with Benno's grief, not the reasons for it. I remembered her back in our kitchen at home, realising before I did that I was about to break down, giving me space to grieve for Cilla, the Cilla I'd loved once. This was the real thing.

Benno Marling knew it, too. He turned toward the warmth and the sympathy in her voice like a baby bird looking for its mum. Then he buried his face against her shoulder, and just broke all the way down.

She held on to him, got her other arm fixed so that she had some support under her and murmured at him, crooned at him as if he was five years old and had smashed his favourite toy. No one in the room said a word.

And Patrick, who was too obviously going through a few bad moments of his own, was desperate to get on with things. Like I said, he'd gone up a gear; you could smell the impatience coming off him in waves. He took a step toward them, but Bree lifted her chin, glared at him, and shook her head. There wasn't any mistaking that message: *back off, not yet.* And damned if he didn't step back and shut up, even though he was actually swearing to himself. I could see his lips moving. He was talking to himself, he was so antsy.

After a few minutes, Benno stopped. His shoulders were still shaky, but he'd stopped the waterworks. He lifted his face off Bree's shoulder, realised what he'd been doing, and blushed.

"Ta," he mumbled, and straightened up. "Very kind of you, I'm sure. Didn't agree with Jimmy about much, not recently. He

196

knew people I didn't know, and didn't much want to. Thing is, we went to Junior School in Mile End together. That's fifty years, I knew Jimmy Wonderley. It's a loss."

"I know. Losing someone, it's really hard. Even thinking you've lost someone can be just a killer." She patted him on the shoulder, very light, and got up to come back over to me. When she'd got close enough, I pulled her down straight onto my knee, so fast that she squeaked. Then I kissed her, good and long, nice and open, for the entire room to see.

"You're a wonder," I told her. "You know that, yeah?"

She turned pale—I don't know whether it was at the kiss or at the compliment. Then she ducked her head, but I caught a faint smile. When she lifted her face, though, she wasn't smiling anymore.

"I don't want to poke my nose into official business." It took me a second to realise she was talking to Patrick. "But it's not as if I'm not concerned. I've been asked not to leave the jurisdiction. So has Dom. And the guy in charge of things down in Les Sirènes couldn't wait to put us in cells, even though he knew damned well we weren't involved. He knew something, and he wasn't even bothering to hide it. So what in hell is going on here?"

"Bree's right." Dom had got up, and she was stretching. It was amazing—she stood on one foot and lifted one leg to the side, so high it was damned near parallel her shoulder, and flexed the ankle. I don't think I've ever been anything near that limber. "Doesn't make much sense. Santini got us behind bars right away. Fucker couldn't wait to turn the key—he was grinning while he did it. And then four hours later he let us out, without laying a charge, without a fight. Oh, and without an explanation, either. Bree wants to know why, and so do I. I want to know what Santini was doing. I really want to know why he got a stiffy just at the thought of locking us up, but he let us out without thinking twice."

197

"That's a damned good point, angel. You're so right." Mac cocked his head. "There's a few other things I'd like to know, myself. For one thing, what was Jimmy Wonderley doing in Cedric Parmeley's film vault in the first place? Because there was a dead bloke in the bushes, and he used to work for Isle of Dogs. This entire thing has a major reek of fish about it. Was Parmeley down in the vault when it went up? Because I don't get it. I thought it was his house that had been bombed."

"That is not entirely accurate, Mr. Sharpe." Pirmin spoke up, but one eye was on Domitra. He looked fascinated. She was just standing there, stretching the other leg, like an Olympic gymnast, or something. "The first findings have been sent to my office. We are some days yet from making anything public, and of course, there is the question of the local police investigation. But I can tell you that all traces of the accelerant used—the chemical analysis has confirmed that it was C4, a professional terrorist's choice—were in the film vault itself. That was a small separate building, approximately ten metres from the main villa."

"I don't think I follow." Cal had got up to get himself a refill. "When you say accelerant, you're talking about the explosive, whatever it was that was used, right? The C4? Because if the only thing that was supposed to get blown up was the vault, then I really don't understand. What happened to the villa? It couldn't have blown up on its own, and if I get you, there was no explosive in the house. And what about the other dead bloke, Len Cullum? How does he come into it?"

"About the villa, we are not yet certain enough to say," Pirmin told him. "The damage was extensive, and there is still much work to be done by the forensic experts. But they have identified the remnants of a very large propane tank, on the southern side of what remained of the villa. They are working—for now—on the theory that the prime and possibly only target was the vault, but that the fire from the explosion may have ignited the propane and set off the explosion that destroyed the villa. It is probable that the villa's destruction—and Cedric Parmeley's death—were incidental. An accident."

"What?" Cyn Corrigan blinked at him. "Why would the houses here need that much propane? It can't be heating, for heaven's sake—this is the Riviera, not downtown Paris."

Pirmin smiled at her. "It may not be Paris, but we have cold winters here, too. Sometimes the Mistral starts blowing in December and continues all the way into March. Many local houses use propane for winter heating; there is one on the wall outside of this room, in fact. I noticed it when I first arrived."

Bree was still sitting on my knee. A bony seat, I know, but I'd got one arm round her waist, to keep her there. For some reason, right then, I wanted some touch between us. Maybe it was all the talk of people being locked away and blown up, but I needed comfort.

"If no one minds, I'd like to get back to the question of Terry Goff." It was Patrick, damned near grinding his choppers together. Bloody hell, I'd forgot about him, listening to Pirmin and getting the news about the villa not being the target. He sounded very edgy. "Mr. Johns. How well did you know him? And were you acquainted with his wife?"

Bree suddenly stirred on my lap. Looking up, I saw that her shoulders had hunched up. *Wife?* Oh, bloody hell. Yeah, there'd been a woman in it, all right: someone else's wife. No wonder Bree'd gone stiff against me—this was looking like Patrick might have been the Other Man. And there'd been a tiny pause, so short you wouldn't have known it was there unless you had reason to be paying attention, just before Patrick said the word *wife.*

"What, those two?" Harry shook his head, and glared down into his empty glass. His lower lip was stuck out like a baby's. "Sorry, mate, but no joy. Hardly knew them, and didn't much like them, either. That little armful, what was her name—"

"Louise." I don't think I can get across the way Patrick said it, and I won't bother trying. "Her name was Louise."

"Yeah, well, nearest I ever got to knowing those two, the little blonde dolly-bird, Louise, she snuggled up to me." Harry sounded resentful. "Turned out all she wanted was me coming along to her old man's little do, club meeting or something, secret hand-shakes, the lot. Pity, really. I could have fancied her. But I wasn't having any of that Goffer. Some of the shit I heard him talk about doing, well, he creeped me. No, I wasn't going along to anything he was in with, you know? Not that stupid, thank you very much."

"What sort of things did you hear him talk about doing?" Patrick had spots of colour on his face. I peered round Bree, watching him, and it hit me: he resented Louise Goff being called what Harry was calling her. Bree got it, as well. It was one of those moments—if you haven't been one half a couple for twenty-odd years, you probably won't get it or believe it, but I knew she'd caught it.

I leaned forward, and put my lips up against her ear. "It's okay, baby." There was no way anyone could have heard it but her; I wasn't even sure anyone else knew I'd spoken. "This can't touch either of us. It's nothing to do with us; it's Patrick's little issue. Just breathe, love. I'm right here. It's okay."

She relaxed, and leaned back. I caught a tiny nod.

"What the Goffer talked about...." Harry stopped, screwing up his face, trying to remember. "I think...."

"Go on, please." Patrick was stone-faced.

"Well—it was about the blacks, mostly. He really had a thing about the coloureds, you know? Pakis, Indians, Africans, that lot. Talked about how we needed to get them to go back where they'd come from, maybe killing off the ones who wouldn't go." He looked up, and over at Dom. "Sorry," her told her, and meant it. "But the copper here wanted to know."

200

Dom wasn't bothered, apparently. "No worries. But I think Patrick, here, wants to know more."

"Not much more to tell, really." Harry turned to Benno. "Your mate Jimmy used to come by sometimes. You not know that? He and the Goffer's blonde bint, they used to whisper and snicker together in corners. They were thick, those two."

"Her name was—she had a name." The words came out too distinct, and most of the heads in the room turned to stare at Patrick. He went red. "Mr. Marling. Can you corroborate any of this?"

"Afraid I can't, sorry. Like I said, I didn't like some of the rubbish Jimmy went in for, and I didn't like some of his mates. We stopped playing as a band back in the early eighties, and I didn't see him so much anymore."

The room was quiet. Bree stirred on my knee, and got up.

"If everyone's finished, I'm going to start clearing up. Patrick, I have a question for you, by the way."

He didn't say anything, just watched her. She picked up a couple of stray glasses, set them back down again, and turned to face him. Her voice was very clear, pitched so that everyone would hear it and pay attention.

"There were three dead people at the Les Sirènes villa. Cedric Parmeley, in the villa itself. Len Cullum, who Dom and I supposedly killed and by the way, in case anyone's wondering, we didn't. And there was Jimmy Wonderley, who was inside the vault when it went up. Three dead people. Is that right?"

"Yes. That's right." He was watching her, and suddenly, I got where she was headed. It was a wonder no one had thought to ask it before.

"Simple math." Mac had followed her, as well. "Four people to be accounted for, and only three bodies. If Jimmy Wonderley was the bloke in the vault, then where's Terry Goff?"

# Chapter Eleven

If you ever want a moment when everything seems just the other side of weird, realising that the local head of Interpol is arranging armed protection for you because he thinks your wife and your lead singer's bodyguard are in danger of being murdered by a fugitive white supremacist, would do it.

I'm still amazed we could have been so dim. I mean, if I'd stopped to think about it at the time, I'd have been demanding police protection, armed guards, the lot. But I didn't. I don't live in the reality or the headspace where the idea of people trying to shoot me comes to mind. Lucky for us, Pirmin had a grip on it.

Mac hadn't even finished asking his question about Terry Goff before Pirmin was flipping his cell phone open, and punching in numbers at warp speed. Not speaking French, all I got was a rapid-fire string of language, sounding sharp and hard-edged.

The first hint of what Pirmin was up to, I got from Mac's reaction.

"Hang on a moment." Mac had got up, and was exchanging a good long look with Dom. She was at school in Paris, so she knows the local jabber quite well herself. "Official police protection from Marseilles? You seriously think we're in that much danger? Pirmin! Oi, mate, talk to us, please?"

Pirmin ignored him, except for holding up a hand. Bree was holding on to me, her face ashy, her eyes huge. The penny had dropped for her, and right then, just about the time Pirmin rang off, it dropped for me, as well.

Bree and Dom were maybe the only two people still alive who'd gone face to face with Terry Goff. Either or both of them could identify him, especially Dom, and he knew it. What he couldn't have known was that trying to take out either of them was useless—he couldn't know about this director's cut Parmeley had sent out, and I couldn't think of any way he could know we'd all seen it, including the cops, unless he was outside the villa, peering through the windows.

"Gordon BENNETT!" I was on my feet, staring at Patrick. "Bree and Dom—they can identify him, and he knows it. He went face to face with both of them, and he hates their guts anyway. Son of a bitch!"

"John, listen—"

"I want Bree out of here." My nerves were jangling. "I want her somewhere he can't get at her."

"John, if you'd just wait a—"

"Sod that." I turned, glaring her down, and she went quiet. "Don't you bloody start with me, Bree. The bloke's a murderer and a nutter and if he had anything to do with Parmeley's villa going up the other night, then he knows how to get his hands on some really fancy explosives. We've got a propane tank just like the one at Parmeley's, right out there on the other side of that wall—you fancy that sort of fireworks? Because I don't. I want you safe out of here, and we're not going to argue about it or discuss it and I'm not going to wait a minute, either. Patrick! Pirmin! Talk to me, mates. I need a word, here."

"If you will calm down, Mr. Kinkaid, please? I have just requested round-the-clock protection, both for Mrs. Kinkaid and Ms. Calley." No fool, was our local Interpol bloke. "Since we do not know where this Terry Goff may be now, or who may be helping him, I agree with you. Until we flush him out of hiding, it is better that we take no chances."

"You think he has someone helping him?" Barb Wilson had been quiet, but she spoke up, finally. "Someone local? Because my money's on that slimy policeman, down at Les Sirènes."

"As is mine." Pirmin's voice was very hard. "And as soon as backup arrives from Marseilles, and we have established some protective presence here and for Mr. Sharpe and Ms. Calley, I am going to go into Les Sirènes Sur Mer, and have a conversation with Mr. Santini."

"What's on your mind, Pirmin?" Patrick was eyeing him.

"I think he never had any intention of formally charging either Ms. Calley or Mrs. Kinkaid with involvement in Leonard Cullum's death. I think he brought them in for another reason entirely." He saw my eyebrow go up. "On the face of it, that move—bringing the women in, locking them up, then letting them go without a charge made—looks pointless. But perhaps not; it gained him time, four hours, to be precise. And four hours is a decent window during which someone might disappear."

"You think Santini's in contact with Goff?" Patrick didn't sound too surprised. "Or that he was?"

"Either, or both. There are too many officials in the south who are supporters of Le Pen and the Front National. We have long suspected that many members of extreme groups who have been in hiding have taken refuge here. They would find the politics of the coast congenial to them."

Pirmin had that same chilly predator look going, the one I can't stand when I see it on Patrick. Made me wonder if they teach it to new coppers: *right, everyone line up, grab your mirrors, come along, I want some serious mean face-making here!* Or maybe the look's already there when they decide to be cops, some sort of admissions requirement.

"As to Santini," Pirmin said, "There are questions he must answer. That interview is overdue. But I think, perhaps, we should have a contingency plan in place. Unless he is a fool, he will know enough to wriggle and lie. And I doubt he is a fool."

It was right about then that I got it, sussed it out—the bastard already knew exactly what he wanted to do. Because, see, he was talking to Patrick, but he was looking at us. I opened my mouth, shut it again, and waited.

"This DVD." He jerked his head at the telly. "I would like to take it with me, if none of you object."

"Right," Mac said, but it came out just as I was saying "Not until you tell us why." So we had a confused moment that would have been funny under different circs. Not as things were, though. My nerves were far too tight to laugh.

Anyway, Mac decided my answer was better than his, so he backed me up. That left Pirmin clearing his throat and having to come out with it. By the time he'd finished explaining what he wanted to do, pretty much every hair on my body was standing straight up, and I wasn't the only one reacting that way.

"Wait a minute." Stu was slack-jawed with disbelief. I couldn't blame him—I was damned near speechless, myself. "Am I getting this? Are you saying you want to get the Cannes judges and jury to show that damned film? The version we've just seen? That you want our permission to show it? Because that would be a huge fucking hell-no, mate. Not enough no in the world to cover that.

Sorry, but I'm not putting JP through that—I'm not putting any of us through that."

"No, I am not suggesting that. For one thing, I doubt Mr. Kinkaid would allow that, and he is certainly the person with the most cause to object. But you have not understood me. That is not my intention."

"Then maybe you'd better clue us in," Cal told him.

"What I want is for the Festival officials to announce that they have received this DVD—the director's cut, if you like—and that they plan to show it. What they will actually show, however, is the DVD they already have—the version originally submitted to them, that you all approved. It is what I think Patrick would call a bait and switch."

I got a look sideways. Patrick was pretty poker-faced, he's good at that, but I had the feeling he'd sussed it out well before any of us. I also got the vibe that he approved of it.

"That is not generally accepted procedure in the Palme d'Or judging, by the way." Pirmin was rabbiting on, nice and careful, making sure we all got it. Good thing, too, because if I was going to tell him to get stuffed, I wanted all the details first. "They usually allow no deviation from the original submission. I will propose that they publicly agree to make an exception, and announce it as such—deference to Sir Cedric's memory, an exception made for an exceptional director who has died tragically. If they agree, they will announce a different version to the one they would actually show."

Pirmin was looking straight at me now. I had my arm round Bree, and I wasn't letting her go. At some point, she was going to ask me how bad that segment with Cilla had been in the final version, and I wanted to put that one off as long as I possibly could. I was still feeling sick at my stomach over it, and the idea of telling her that what she and Cyn and Barb had blessedly missed—and which Patrick, not to mention Dom, had stayed

206

and watched—had included footage of me actually rogering my first wife, made me even sicker.

So I had that running through my head and I didn't get it straight off. But Benno, of all people, did get it.

"Oh, right," he said. "You want to use it to sucker that Goff wanker out of the shadows. You want to use the Blacklight people to get him. It's a booby trap. Right?"

"Exactly."

Another penny dropped right about then, something else I hadn't thought about at all: Interpol must have been running all of us, our backgrounds, lives, associates, every detail they could find, through a really fine sieve, ever since I'd rung up Patrick, and maybe before. If Harry and Benno, or any of us, had been suspects, this entire conversation would be taking place behind closed doors, one on one. And it wasn't. Benno and Harry were in the clear. We all were.

Patrick was doing the talking, now. "Yes, Mr. Marling, that's correct. It's like this: if Terry Goff can't say for sure whether he's there and identifiable on that film, he may feel he has to take action. And since Santini hasn't seen this version, he can't offer any assurances—"

"Patrick? Half a mo, will you?" I cleared my throat. I sounded really calm, damned near conversational. Not how I was feeling, if what he was suggesting what I thought he was. "You said, take action. What sort of action are we talking about, here? And by the way, mate, most traps have bait in them. Want to say something reassuring? Maybe some sugar, to keep me from choking you to death? Because it sounds as if you're about to suggest that the two people he'd be trying to kill get dressed up in their priciest gear and hit the red carpet. And since that's Dom and Bree, well, obviously, you aren't suggesting that. Are you?"

He grinned at me, out of nowhere, a real live grin, genuine. Behind him, Pirmin wasn't grinning. I thought about smashing Patrick with something hard and sharp and really heavy, and waited.

"Yes, that's exactly what I'm suggesting," he told me. "JP, just relax, okay? You'd all be covered. Every second person in sight would be one of ours. There would be more official eyes in that crowd than anything else. Once Goff was spotted, there would be two dozen highly trained marksmen with his skull in their cross-hairs. You'd be surrounded by bodyguards. All you'd need to do is walk down the red carpet, up the stairs, and into the Palais des Festivals. The rest would be up to us."

"I don't fucking believe this." I must have been holding Bree too tight, because she suddenly winced. "You're actually standing there and asking Bree and Dom to be bait."

He opened his mouth. God knows what he thought he was going to say. Didn't matter, because I wasn't giving him a chance.

"You're a piece of work, Patrick, you know that? A bloody wonder. I mean, seriously, it's almost funny. You're a guest in our house, you came because we asked you to help, and you're asking Bree to be bait for a terrorist and a murderer. Want her to paint a red circle between her eyes, while she's at it? Or maybe she can wear a backless formal and paint it on her neck, instead of a tattoo. And by the way, I'd suggest you not having the cheek to tell me to relax. There's something really fucking insulting about you doing that. Just, don't, all right? Much better not to."

My voice had gone all the way into the red zone. Everyone else was quiet. Right now, it was just me and Patrick, me and the bloke who'd supposedly come to help. My mum used to have a saying she liked, about how a leopard can't change its spots, and she'd been dead on. It could have been designed for Patrick Ormand, that saying.

"This is a game for you, yeah?" We might as well have been alone in the place, me and him. He wasn't smiling. Neither was I. "A nice old-fashioned board game. What's it called, Patrick? 'Let's Play God Today'? Move the people around, be in control of

208

it, nothing can go wrong. That it? Problem is, that's bullshit, and you know it. This isn't a damned game, it's people and their lives, our lives, you're messing about with. You haven't got any control. You can put Bree out there on the red carpet. Hell, you could have the entire police force dressed as waiters or paparazzi or whatever, ten deep at the back of the line. All Terry Goff would need is one second, one clear line of sight, and he'd put a bullet in her head. You know it, I know it. So don't tell me to relax."

Those damned light eyes of his, dirty ice, were locked up with mine. It wasn't like New York; this was different. That had been the pair of us, trying for the advantage. This time, he wasn't saying anything. He was just listening.

"I'm not speaking for Dom," I told him. "Got no right to do that. But get this through your skull, Patrick: You're not using my wife as bait."

"John?"

I looked at her. If my stomach had been doing twisty little cartwheels before, things were about to get much worse—I could tell. Her face was set. I knew what was coming; I didn't even bother aiming the thought at her, *no, don't do it.* It wouldn't do any good.

"I think we should do it. Let's get it over with." She wasn't meeting my eye. She didn't dare, not just then. "Honestly, if this guy decides he wants to take me out, he can find me just as easily in San Francisco, or London, or in the wings at a Blacklight show. At least this way, we'll have a lot of cops with guns and walkie-talkies as backup."

"No." I turned her all the way round in my arms, so that we were face to face. I had her by the shoulders, maybe holding too hard. "Don't even go there, Bree. I'm not having it."

"It's my choice, not yours." Her voice was very calm, but that was bollocks; I could see her mouth trembling, and the beginnings of tears. "I want this guy caught, John. I think he's evil and a waste of space and I won't feel safe until he's been taken in or taken down, period. The sooner, the better. Let's just do it."

I'd forgotten about Patrick Ormand, about Pirmin, about anyone else in the room. It was just me and Bree, Bree suggesting we do something really stupid, something really dangerous, something that could get her killed, me holding on to her, knowing I was supposed to try and talk her out of it, and knowing that wasn't going to happen.

We looked at each other. I remembered crying into her lap, how tough she could be, how tender, how stubborn, how many times she'd done that for my benefit, how rarely she'd done anything for her own benefit. And I gave up. There was no point having a row about this one; she'd made up her mind, and she wasn't changing it.

"Okay." I moved my hands up, and cupped her face. "If it's got to be that way, I'm not wasting my breath arguing. There's one thing, though."

I turned toward Patrick. "Just want you to know something," I told him. Everyone was listening. Good; I wanted witnesses. "If anything goes wrong with this little game of yours, and anything happens to her? I'll kill you. Just wanted to let you know that. Don't want you saying you weren't warned."

Pirmin stirred, and took a step forward. But Patrick held up one hand. He was actually smiling. This was one I hadn't seen before—dark as sin.

"If anything happens to either of them, you won't have to kill me. I'll save you the trouble." I suddenly remembered his loyalty thing, how much he respected it. Might be the only damned thing he did respect. "You're right about one thing, JP—I'm not going to tell you to relax. I'm not relaxing, myself, not until this over. I have a much better idea of what Terry Goff is capable of than most people. But it's okay. Nothing will go wrong."

Once Bree dropped her little "it's my call, not yours" bomb, Dom weighed in. Short and simple version is, she backed Bree up. Dom's motives were different: she'd sent Terry Goff to hospital once, and she was itching to do it again.

So her backing Bree up, that didn't surprise me. What did surprise me was the fact that Mac, of all people, went ballistic over it. He literally went nonlinear. He told Dom there was no way in hell he was allowing his bodyguard to turn herself into a walking rifle range for Terry Goff or anyone else, was she out of her tiny little mind, and a whole lot more of the same, and he was shouting at the top of his voice.

I couldn't help feeling that using the word *allow* was a piss-poor idea, considering who he was talking to, and I wasn't wrong. Dom took severe exception to it, and it got overheated, the two of them yelling into each other's faces and Dom getting progressively more dangerous-looking, until Stu decided he'd had enough of it.

"Cor stone the bloody crows! Dom, Mac, shut the fuck up! Will you both just put a sock in it?" Stu's a Londoner, born and bred, but right then, he had his Irish on. He rarely gets pissy about anything, but his nerves were as messed up as the rest of ours. "Patrick, look. Before we agree to anything at all, we need Ian here. He's the band's manager, and what you and Pirmin want to do with the film, permissions and rights, that's Ian's job. Anyway, you can't do any of it unless we get Luke Hedley's permission, and Luke had the good sense to grab his daughter and get the hell out of France. And right now, I'm wishing I'd done the same. But we want Ian."

Cal was nodding. "Not just Ian, Stu. We're going to want Carla, as well. If there's going to be media stuff that wants handling, she needs to be here. I personally wouldn't take a step without her. Let's ring them up, and get them over here. Nothing's going to happen without either of them."

Of course they were right. We'd got hold of Ian and Carla, and got them over to the villa. The conference had gone on into the small hours. Bree'd started looking frazzled, and I started hoping she was having second thoughts, but it turned out she was actually worried about getting dinner for everyone, because there wasn't enough left over from the pre-screening feed-up to go round. And since Santini knew where we were, odds were Terry Goff knew as well. So I wasn't about to let her trot merrily off down the hill to buy a couple of chickens and some veg, not with Goff maybe hiding in the bushes with a rifle.

Poor Ian was in quite a bind, one way and another. Of course he was horrified by the whole thing, and the last thing in the world he wanted was to let any of us out there until he got to personally view Terry Goff in a jail cell, or maybe a shot at gobbing on Goff's headstone. Bree and Dom putting themselves in harm's way was bad enough, but me and Mac refusing to let them do it by themselves meant we'd be out there as well. That had him sounding shrill.

Carla calmed him down, basically by telling him that there was fuck-all he could do about it. He thought about arguing, but Carla has a nice nasty clear way of looking at things, and she laid it out for him.

"Ian, you're not thinking." She patted his hand. "Look at it, will you? Even if JP or Mac happened to be willing to let it go down without them, it wouldn't fly. The whole thing's useless if we can't sell it. It has to look real, and that means we're all in for this one. The entire band needs to be out there. No, don't give me any grief, please. I know you don't like it. I don't like it either. It sucks rocks. But can you look me in the eye and tell me I'm wrong?"

"Shit!" He was damned near grinding his teeth. "No. No, you're not wrong, Carla, and you know it. God! I hate this."

I sat back at that point. We were going to end up doing what

Patrick and Pirmin wanted; I'd accepted it. It was obvious that Bree wasn't going to budge—she'd decided it was her contribution to society this week, getting the big bad nasty scary racist his just deserts, and qualifying herself for some kind of bullshit citizenship award or whatever at the same time. I really could have thumped her.

It was also pretty obvious that Patrick had a major jones to nail Terry Goff, and it was something personal. My money was on the little blonde wife, the one whose name he kept tripping over, the mysterious Louise. He didn't know it yet, but he and I had a conversation about that coming up. He was damned well going to come clean before he risked my wife's life on his pet vendetta.

So, between Bree acting like a Girl Scout looking to earn her merit badge in self-sacrifice, and Patrick acting like a heat-seeking missile, I'd sussed that arguing about it was worse than useless. For a few moments, I seriously thought about faking an MS relapse. That was the only thing likely to get my wife to back the hell down, but for some reason, the idea struck me as really bad karma. Besides, if anything actually did happen, I was probably going to have a heart attack anyway.

We ended up with a full house for what was left of the night. Pirmin headed out, saying he had things to get done. Bree offered him a bed—it was nearly two in the morning by then—but he shook his head.

"It is very kind, Mrs. Kinkaid, but I think I will be more useful at my desk. There is much work to be done, and little time in which to do it. Your protection has been arranged, however, and in fact they are here. So I can leave you with a quiet mind."

Cyn Corrigan was staring at him. "What protection? They're here? Where?"

"Outside." Pirmin stepped to the door. He called something, very soft-voiced, and then I damned near did have a heart attack, because out of nowhere, there was a big bloke in dark clothing, stepping out of the shadows. He was armed to the teeth—I'm not a gun bloke, so I couldn't tell you what he had in the way of weaponry, except that it scared the shit out of me.

What scared me even worse was that I'd had no idea the bloke was there. That really brought it home to me, about Terry Goff, and how nasty this whole mess was. If Goff had blown up Parmeley's film vault, he had access to some dangerous stuff. And if he was used to doing this sort of thing, I wanted a damned platoon of Pirmin's people out there in the bushes. Our villa suddenly seemed really isolated, and that was fine if we were talking about ducking the paparazzi. It was less pleasant if we were talking about ducking an assassin.

Pirmin and his quiet friend had a few soft words. Then the bloke faded out again.

"Right." I must have sounded shaky, because Bree was there, looking worried, one hand on my arm. I shook my head at her. "Pirmin, look, mate—if you don't mind me asking, how many of your people are out there, anyway?"

"This particular group is from our counter-terrorism unit, and they are a standard six. The man I just spoke to is in charge—if you need anything, or see anything suspicious, he is there. Tell him at once. Your villa is protected. There is also hillside surveillance, closer to the main road. About anything from the air, I have not had time to arrange protection. But I doubt Terry Goff has the means to arrange for that either, not at such short notice." Pirmin nodded at us. "I must go back to work. I shall be in touch tomorrow, with final details."

I never would have believed that villa could feel crowded, but it did that night. We had four spare bedrooms, and Patrick was already in one of them. Between Benno and Harry, not to mention the Blacklight contingent, we ran out of bedrooms, and Bree reached the edge of her nerves over it. Fortunately, Ian and Carla, who'd taken over Luke's place in St. Tropez, opted to drive home and then come back in the morning. So we just about managed, and still ran short of blankets. Damned good thing it was warm.

I wish I could tell you about the planning sessions over the next two days, but truth is, I didn't pay much attention; I was too busy being scared half out of my mind about the entire situation. And it's not as if I had any chance to get away from it, not with six armed experts rustling out there behind the orange trees and mimosa, changing shifts every six hours to keep them all fresh and perky.

The only hope I had was that the Festival officials would dig their heels in and refuse to go against tradition. That hope went west in a hurry; they agreed to go along with Pirmin, down to the last detail. Patrick gave us that news, since Pirmin himself was apparently having a right old rave-up back in Marseilles, nailing Lucien Santini to a fucking wall. Seems the Interpol people had taken a quiet butcher's at Santini's bank accounts and tax records, and found a flow of large contributions, larger than French law allowed, and all of them were to Le Peniste candidates. So they had him on money laundering charges, which gave them something to use against him as leverage straight off. And of course, there was that missing copy of *Playing in the Dark*.

So, the bloke in charge of the Les Sirènes cop shop was in deep shit, with some serious explaining to do, and looking at hefty jail time if he didn't roll pretty damned quickly. I saw Bree's mouth curl up, and her eyes go nice and green, when Patrick told us that. The girl had really taken a scunner on Lucien Santini, and I didn't blame her. I was just sorry I couldn't be there to watch. I wasn't likely to forget that he'd threatened to put handcuffs on my wife.

The official screening of the approved version of *Playing in the Dark* was set for the following night, Friday, fourth night of the festival. I couldn't have named one nominated film for the entire deal, except Parmeley's. We hadn't gone near any of it since the screening, and if I'd been given a vote, I'd have opted to keep it that way.

Carla had been dealing, as well. Hell, the girl had got so much done since start of business Thursday, I wondered if she ever slept. She and Ian showed up together for a late lunch and a confab with the rest of the band, as well as with Patrick. Ian looked completely wasted; Carla looked as if she'd just had a lovely ten-hour kip and maybe a good workout and rollerblading session. She was ready for action.

She'd got hold of Luke, in Italy. I still haven't got a clue how she'd managed to convince him to do what she wanted, but she had. Upshot was, he was leaving Solange with a school friend and the friend's family in Venice, and coming back alone for the main event. She'd booked him a flight into Nice, and he'd be coming down to the screening with Ian and Carla, since they were at his villa.

As mind-boggling as that was, she hadn't stopped there. She'd done up a press release about the screening. It was in every newspaper south of the Midi, and the local non-print media, as she called it, was running it verbatim. The language was clear, and simple, and the information itself was total bullshit. It told the world that the official Palme d'Or committee had received a mysterious director's cut of *Playing in the Dark,* complete with juicy add-ons and narration, including previously cut scenes. Although it deviated from the festival's long tradition, the tragic death of Sir Cedric Parmeley had led the judging panel to the unanimous decision to air it in the memory of a true innovator who would be sorely missed, blah blah on and on, et cetera. As a bright shiny lure to get Terry Goff out of the woodwork, it was brilliant.

A lot of what happened between that morning and the band hitting the red-carpeted stairs up into the Palais in Cannes itself went straight over my head. I was too concentrated on what might be about to happen to Bree or Dom to pay much attention. One thing that did happen, though—I got hold of Patrick and took him off into a corner of the garden for a quiet little talk.

Of course, he came. He didn't want to—he really does have a few issues with not being the one barking out the commands—but he was a guest under my roof and he was planning to possibly get my wife and maybe a few other people I care about killed, and I was in no mood to leave him any wiggle room. He was eating a fast late lunch on Friday afternoon, a couple of hours before the whole mess was due to start. Carla was there, as well; she was just clicking her phone shut when I walked in, nodded to her, and turned to Patrick.

"Right," I told him. "Come along, Patrick—I want a word with you. Out in the garden."

"Now?" He didn't look happy, but I wasn't shedding any tears over that. The way I saw it, the bloke owed me.

"Yes, now. Carla, excuse us for a few, all right?"

"Sure." She looked at Patrick, and said something I couldn't make any sense of. "Norway's a go. Halvard—the attaché—says, eight. It's all set up and ready. They have your number." She caught sight of me, standing there blinking at her, and smiled. "Sorry. Were you guys going outside, or should I wander off and leave you by yourselves?"

"No, you stay where you are." The last thing I wanted was Bree accidentally wandering in for this. This was Patrick and me, period. "Patrick? Finished your lunch? Good, let's go."

He followed me out of doors. There was one nice corner of garden, off the actual terraced areas, with a couple of lawn chairs and a table under an umbrella. It was very quiet and very shady, tucked in under the shadow of the hill; the umbrella was just for show, since there's no real sun to screen off. Not the place most people would likely fetch up, not with the sea in the distance if

217

they went damned near anyone else on the property. But it was perfect for what I wanted, which was a one on one, no interruptions. It was possible Pirmin's invisible chums would hear it, but that was fine with me.

I've got to hand it to Patrick; he didn't waste any time arsing about. We sat down and he went straight to the point.

"What's on your mind, JP?"

"Terry Goff." If it was upfront and blunt he wanted, that was going to save a lot of work and time. "Or, rather, Mrs. Goff. You've got a personal stake in all this, Patrick, and that's lovely, whatever. We've all got our ghosts; hell, you got to watch me having sex with one of mine."

He watched me, not saying a word. Fuck it. He wanted to know what was on my mind, that was exactly what he'd get.

"Thing is, you've got something extra going on over nailing Terry Goff. Yeah, I know you like nailing people, gets you hot, but this one? It's something special. You're licking your lips over it—you can barely hide the spittle. Again, what the hell ever, I don't care. But I can't say, not my business, and let it go at that, can I? Because you're playing Great White Hunter and you're using my wife as bait, and that makes it my business. So let's get it over, it's time you dished. Let's have it. What the hell is there between you and Terry Goff?"

You know the colour snow gets in a big city? Where people walk on it, leave dirt and grit and city trash in it, and then a hard freeze hits and it's ice in the morning, hurting people, just waiting there for them to slip and fall and damage themselves on their way to work? His eyes were that colour. So was his voice.

"You really want to know? Seriously?"

It was tricky holding the stare, but I did it. Like I've said, there are times I'm glad my own eyes are as dark as they are; makes them hard to read, unless you're Bree. She's got the knack for it. "Not particularly. But I've got about as much choice as you have, and that's none at all. Equal footing, Patrick. Bree's dangling on the end of your hook. What's between you and Terry Goff?"

"Two dead bodies." It was nice and flat, that statement, no drama in it. He wasn't showing off or making it fancier than it was. But something went down my back. He went on, in that same flat voice, with a hard unpleasant edge at the back of it. "One was his wife, Louise Royalton Goff. The other was a very sweet guy called Pete Fernandez. He was my partner at DEA Miami. That answer your question, JP?"

"Not really, no." I was watching him, trying to get a read on his face. It was tricky. He was used to this sort of game; I knew that much, from back when he'd been in charge of the Perry Dillon investigation. I wasn't used to it at all. But this was my turf, not his. It was my wife he was putting in harm's way. So far as I was concerned, that gave me all the edge I needed. "You saying Terry Goff killed them?"

The eyes weren't quite as dead all of a sudden, and his voice had movement in it, as well. "Yes. One bullet to the brain, each of them. Pete had been tortured first. Louise was probably forced to watch—knowing what I know about her husband, he probably wanted her to know what was coming. He left them on my doorstep, dumped them there like garbage, and disappeared, probably with Louise's money to grease the wheels. It was my fault it happened—I made a mistake, Pete ran with it, and it got both of them killed. I underestimated Goff, didn't get enough information about him before I set things up, didn't spend enough time planning it out, figuring out who he was, figuring out how to anticipate what he might do. And that's all I'm going to tell you, because the rest is irrelevant."

"Okay." We'd locked up stares, and I was almost shocked at the hate I saw in his face. "I don't care about the rest of it, Patrick. I just wanted you to know how obvious it was, that you had a personal thing about this Goff nutter."

"Fine. I know. You made your point. So that's that." He got to his feet. "In case you're wondering, I haven't made that mistake since, and I don't intend to ever make it again. Bree will be covered. So will Dom. Shall we head back? You guys are due on the red carpet in a couple of hours, and I have some things I need to take care of between now and then."

"Okay." I got up as well. "Patrick? One more thing."

He stopped, a few steps ahead of me, and turned back, not saying anything. I was pretty sure he knew what I was going to say, and I said it.

"I invited you here," I told him. "I rang you up, got you the resources, asked for your help. All of that was on Bree's behalf. I asked you to come to help her. That's the only reason. I wouldn't have done it for anyone else."

"I know."

"Do you? Good. Because here's the thing: I get that you want to nail Terry Goff. I want the bastard nailed myself, believe me. But you've got a streak half a mile wide, a thing that comes out when you smell blood. I don't like it much, you know? I didn't like it when you were after Bree—you jerked us around, played innocent when you weren't, all that rubbish. And now that you're supposed to be looking out for her interests, I like it even less. So I wanted you to know—anything happens to her, I'll use everything I've got to bring you down myself. As it happens, I've got quite a lot. Just want to be clear."

"So do I." His lips were a line. "I also meant what I said: if that happened, I'd save you the trouble and bring myself down. After Louise—after Pete—I couldn't live with it. But it won't happen. Bree and Dom are going to be completely covered. And if we're both nice and clear, let's head back. I've got work to do."

# *Chapter Twelve*

It wasn't until I was buttoning Bree into a really eye-catching green velvet dress that I finally got it: the girl was having serious second thoughts.

We'd got dressed in total silence. I was so edgy that I was about to do up the back of the dress she'd got back in London for what we thought, then, would be the Frejus show, before I realised that her shoulders weren't tight, they were shaking.

"Oi!" I rested my hand on the small of her back. Bree's chilly to the touch too often for my peace of mind, but the small of her back is like a furnace, always warm. Just then, it was nearly cold. I suddenly understood the shaking shoulders, and the chill. I got both hands on her arms and turned her around, fast.

"Bree? Baby, are you okay?"

"Oh, *fuck*." Her face was a mess. She'd done her makeup

first—she always does, so she won't muck up her dress. But she was in tears, and her lash goop was all down her cheeks. Both hands came up, patting at it, getting her hands mucky as well. "I'm an idiot. I'm sorry. It's just—"

She started to shake, serious shudders, and the rest of the words got lost. It took me a moment, I was so freaked, but she was sagging at the knees. *She's going to faint, she can't faint, she never faints....*

"Gordon *Bennett!*" I got her over to the edge of our bed and she sat, right around the same time her knees gave way entirely. I sat next to her, rubbing her arms, trying to sort it out. I'd never seen her like this. "Bree—"

"I'm sorry. I didn't mean to be such a damned baby."

She focused on me, through smeared makeup and everything else. Her lips were shaking, as well. And yeah, so maybe I was preoccupied, but I got it, finally, right between the eyes: the girl was scared shitless. She was scared out of her mind.

Twenty-seven years, and this was the first time I'd ever seen her actually crack under the weight of being scared. Yeah, she'd had a moment back in London, jabbing herself with Cilla's old works, but this felt different.

"Right," I told her, and started to get up. "That's it. You're not going out of doors in this state. I'm not having it. I'll tell Patrick it's not happening. He can go catch his bad guy without you as bait—shit, come to think of it, we're all bait. We're not doing this. I'm going to tell him."

"No!" She got hold of herself—the effort was visible. I watched her do it. She dug her nails into her palms; she closed her eyes, you could practically hear her chanting under her breath.... And then I realised, that was exactly what I was hearing. She was deep-breathing, and there were words in it: *not scared, not scared, not scared.*

"Bree." I kept my voice gentle, damned if I know how. All I

222

really wanted was to thump her over the head, knock her out, tie her up and keep her safe until they'd got Terry Goff in a cell or a body bag or something. That wasn't an option, more's the pity. "Look at me, love. Listen to me. You listening?"

She nodded, hiccoughed once, and knuckled her eyes like a little girl. It nearly broke me, her doing that. In some ways, I'm always going to see her as the fierce teenager I met at the Hurricane Felina benefit, all those years ago.

"Okay. Good." I got both my arms round her. "Here's the thing. You don't owe Patrick Ormand a fucking thing. All he cares about right now is getting Terry Goff, because Goff killed a couple of people and left them on Patrick's doorstep. So yeah, I get that Goff needs to be taken down. That doesn't mean you've got to play, Bree."

"I know that." Her voice was as messed as her makeup, just all over the place. "I don't care about Patrick's reasons. This isn't about him. I'm just—"

She stopped. I waited. And out of nowhere, she was talking, the words coming out in a rush.

"It's knowing that he's out there, John. It's knowing he could have as many people helping him as Patrick and Pirmin have got helping us. Because we don't know. How can we know?"

I stared at her. She was staring right back at me, and her eyes were enormous.

"So they got Santini, and they're going to lock him up." I'd got hold of her hands now, and they were curling tight under my grip. "So what? Big deal. What the hell good is that going to do? How many others are there? Cops, local town officials, drinking buddies—you said the South had all these racist crazies. Pirmin was talking to one of his people on the phone, he was going over it. I heard him say that Goff and Cullum, the guy I hit with my shoe, they've been Parmeley's bodyguards for years and years."

"Right." I must have been a lot more rattled than I thought, because I sat there, waiting for the rest of it, not thinking. She saw it, too.

"John, don't you get it? It means they have friends down here. Not just fellow assholes—real live friends. They've had years to make friends, people who like them, who wouldn't think twice about a casual lie to cover for their pals. People *knew* them. And...." She swallowed hard. "And they knew people. Who? How many? So Santini rats a bunch of people out—he can't tell the cops what he doesn't know, can he?"

"No. Christ." I heard myself, whispering it. My own skin was cold and crawling.

She was right. Patrick had told me he wasn't going to make the mistake of not thinking it out twice, but that was just what he'd done. He hadn't thought it out, not all the way. Santini could cut a deal or whatever they called it, he could sing like a fucking nightingale on crack, and he could be telling the absolute truth, so far as he knew it. The chances were, Goff and Cullum had associates, mates, whatever, that Santini didn't know a damned thing about.

I looked up, and met Bree's eyes. "Goff got that explosive from someone, didn't he?" Her voice was quiet. "Who?"

"Hello? I'm sorry, but I've been knocking...."

We both jumped about a mile. Neither of us had heard Patrick at the bedroom door. Bree made a noise under her breath. She was in a bind—what with her dress not being done up, she didn't want to turn her back towards Patrick, but her face was a wreck. I solved it for her by jerking my head at Patrick, a clear signal to wait outside.

I'll give the bloke this, he's not dim. He took a fast look at Bree's face, at her hands in her lap, streaked with mascara, nodded at me, and stepped back outside.

"Here, let's have your back." I did up her buttons in a hurry. "Right. We need to have this out with him, Bree. We're supposed

224

to be leaving in less than an hour. You're not setting foot out of doors right now, not until we've got this sorted out. Let's have him in, all right?"

She nodded. I got my arm back around her, and raised my voice. "Patrick! All decent. You can come back in. We need a word with you, anyway."

When he came back in, he had his mask on, the Ormand Patented Professional Mask: game face. He knew damned well something was up, and he was ready to do his chain-jerking thing. But this time, I was ready, as well.

"Bree." I was talking to her, but I caught Patrick's eye, and made him look at me. It's really all about knowing how manners are likely to work, this game, you know? I'm the one speaking, so all the social training says he has to look at me, or else he's a rude berk. "Tell Patrick what you've been thinking, will you, love?"

She looked at me. I could see it, she didn't want to tell Patrick she'd had second thoughts. But I nodded at her, and she told him.

She started out carefully, talking as much to clear it in her own head as to tell him. Once she got started, though, it came out in a flood of words. She let him know just why she thought he hadn't thought it through; she parsed it, clear and calm, from the understanding that Goff and Cullum would have friends Interpol or even Santini couldn't know about, all the way through her own understanding, that Goff was a bad one, and needed to be brought down. And when she got to the end of her list of reasons, she got her courage up and met his eye and told him that she believed his reasons for wanting to nail Goff, whatever they were, might be too big for him to see around with any clarity. I was really proud of her.

He didn't take it the way I'd thought he would. He listened—I mean, really listened, you know? He heard her out, he even nodded in a few places, as if she was bringing up points he hadn't thought about before, and was happy to hear. He didn't interrupt, either, not one damned word; he stayed quiet until she'd finished. And then, being Patrick Ormand, he took all the wind out of our sails.

"That's good clear thinking." He was actually smiling. "As it happens, though, I was coming in to give you an update, from Interpol headquarters. I have some news that ties in to what Bree was worrying about—Pirmin just called, to fill me in. Want to hear it?"

"Sure." Absolute bullshit, that was; what I wanted was for him to fuck off and not be able to talk Bree into hanging a bulls-eye round her neck. I'd caught that past-tense thing, that "Bree was worrying" line. Subtle bastard. I had a sinking feeling he was about to get his way, yet again.

Patrick's big news was that Pirmin had broken Santini. During the past couple of hours, with help from a couple of big agencies and some of the police in the local municipalities, something like twenty people had been brought in for questioning as being associates of a man wanted for terrorist activities. That's one thing about law enforcement in a post 9/11 world: you say that word, *terrorism,* and everything ratchets up a notch. The Interpol staff was pretty busy right now, and the people they were talking to weren't getting out of the cop shop or Interpol headquarters for quite a while yet.

He also shared a hint at what Pirmin had set up. No details, of course, not really, but there enough to make us both get that this wasn't just the Patrick and Pirmin Show. It wasn't going to be the intimate little do I'd mentally been classing it as. This one was big, a major operation of some kind, with all sorts of people called in to help.

"…so the bulk of the peripheral threat, those associates of Goff's or Cullum's, have been removed from the equation." He was slipping into the sort of language you hear on American telly, cop shows. Any minute, he was going to start using words like "perp". I could have cheerfully killed him. "And while there's obviously no way to guarantee that the sweep caught everyone involved, we both feel that any threat has been significantly lessened. JP, you're rolling your eyes. Why?"

"Well, you do sound a bit like Central Casting, Patrick." I shook my head at him. "But you know, I'm still not in love with the odds—what, Bree?"

Next to me, Bree wasn't shaking any more. She got up and said something about her face, and headed off into the bathroom. I looked at Patrick.

"She's just changed her bloody mind back again." Why in hell had I asked Patrick Ormand for help in the first place? I was talking too fast. "She's going to redo her makeup, and she's going to want to go do it, take the walk down the red carpet. She's scared half out of her wits, it's the last thing on earth she wants to do and just about the last thing she ought to do, but you've talked her back into it. Ta, mate. Cheers. Brilliant fucking job. You couldn't have found another way to nail Terry Goff, could you? No, of course you couldn't."

I heard my own voice, and was blown away by how bitter I sounded. Patrick heard it, as well.

"I'm sorry, JP." He probably was, too. That didn't make it any better. "All I can tell you is that this is the best shot we have at getting him, and that there won't be anyone within a thousand feet of you people, including in any of the hotel windows along La Croisette, who isn't in our sights."

"Lovely." I heard water running in the bathroom; Bree washing her face, most likely. That meant she was going to redo her makeup, and that meant we were going to end up doing what Patrick wanted. "Not making me feel any better about this, Patrick."

"I know. I'm sorry."

That was the second time he'd said that; this time, I didn't believe it. Like hell he was sorry. The fucker was taking it for granted he'd be getting his way—he hadn't once believed he wasn't pulling all the strings.

I didn't know if he'd deliberately played on Bree's conscience, and it didn't matter. What mattered was, I'd brought him here to help, and he seemed to think that gave him the right to do anything he wanted. And there was something all the way wrong here. Maybe it was tunnel vision, maybe he was obsessed. Whatever was doing it, he was listening to himself, and not letting anything else in.

He was still talking. "By the way, Pirmin was right, about those arrests Santini made, about why he detained Bree and Ms. Calley. Santini doesn't know where Goff's hiding out, but he did tell us that Goff called him twice after Parmeley's villa went up, ordering Santini to stage something in the way of a diversion to let him get under cover. He had no way of knowing how fast we'd identify Jimmy Wonderley as the man inside the film vault—after all, there wasn't much left to identify. But these days, we don't need much. The technology is stellar."

"Fuck the technology." The water had stopped running. Five more minutes, I thought, and she'd be stepping out of the bathroom with a new makeup job, her very own mask, scared out of her wits and refusing to act like an adult woman with half a functional brain. "And fuck you too. You might as well belt up, yeah? Because it's all bullshit, and you know it, Patrick. And it's really making me want to fucking strangle you before you get my wife killed."

"I'm not—"

"I said, belt up!" Three minutes. She'd be redoing her lipstick.... "You want upfront, here it is: even if nothing happens, forgiving you for putting us through it is going to be iffy, as far as

228

I'm concerned. I'm curious, Patrick. When people ask you for help, is this the way you usually handle it? Shove them in front of the bad guys and bullshit them into holding up a placard that says *Target, Please Aim At Me But Don't Kill Me Unless You Have To?* And yeah, that's what you're doing."

"JP, we're taking every precaution to ensure—"

"Oh, for fuck's sake! You aren't dim. You're much too good at your job to be dim. You know exactly what you're doing, so stop trying to bullshit me, or yourself, or whoever, because it won't fly. I've sussed you out." A buzz from behind the bathroom door— the hair dryer, being switched on. *Shit.* "In just about two minutes, Bree's going to walk through the door with her hair all done up, and nice fresh lipstick, and some powder to hide the fact that she was sobbing in terror just before you walked in. She's going to smile, and say, let's do it. I'll ask her if she's really okay with it, and she'll say yeah, of course she is. And she won't mean it—but she'll do it anyway. But you knew that, didn't you, Patrick? Like I said, you're a bloody wonder, playing control games, dropping assurances you can't possibly live up to."

The buzz of the dryer stopped. I took a deep breath and looked straight into Patrick Ormand's face.

"But you aren't the only one who knows people, Patrick. I've got ten years on you easy, and I've had some time to find my way around. Besides, I know my wife. And what I've sussed out about you is, you'll do whatever it is you think will get you what wants doing the fastest. Doesn't matter in the end who gets hurt over it, does it? We're all game pieces on your personal chess board. Yeah, you'd be sorry if anything happened to Bree, or Dom. You'd regret it. But that wouldn't stop you doing it, because you don't have enough conscience to tell yourself to not. You've got blinders on for this one and it's not convenient to take the damned things off, is it, you heartless manipulative son of a bitch?"

I'd hit home; I could see it. He opened his mouth to say something, but he never got the chance. Behind me, the bathroom door swung open.

Bree's hair was done, part up, part down, showing off her neck and throat. She'd washed all the telltale streaks of mascara off her hands, and redone her face. There was extra colour on her lips, to hide how pale she was.

"Ready." She took my arm, and managed a smile. "Let's do it."

I've been a touring musician for a good long time. I'm a member of a band that regularly plays to packed arenas—we've done some stadium shows in our time as well, sixty thousand screaming fans. Crikey, we did Live Aid, the Wembley Stadium show, a hundred thousand people. But that walk down the red carpet, and up toward the stairs of the Palais, was the first time in my life I've ever been spooked by a crowd.

I hadn't even bothered trying to talk Bree out of going through with it; there'd have been no point. If she'd noticed the spots of colour in Patrick's face, seen how furious he was, wondered what we'd been saying to each other before she came back out of the bathroom all nice and ready to martyr herself for the good of humanity or whatever the hell she was up to, she didn't say so. She was so damned scared that the only way she could get through it was to kick everything aside and focus on not losing it. Like I said, I know my wife.

We climbed into a waiting limo, with Patrick and two of the commando types Pirmin had left hanging about in the shrubbery. On the way down the hill and all the way into Cannes, Patrick went on about the set-up for that walk up the red carpet. He had a lot of time to go on about it; the traffic at festival time is always bad, but this particular event had got a lot of press, and that meant a lot of onlookers. I could have done nicely without either the stop and start traffic making me queasy, or without Christ only knows how many extra bodies complicating things, but I wasn't getting a choice.

Patrick kept on about it, and after a while, I started feeling like one of those dancers in Broadway musical number: step here, smile there, stand next to this one, remember that that one's right behind you and slightly to the left, be aware of this, leave that bit to the professionals. If things hadn't been so tense, it would have been almost funny, you know? He didn't want to talk to me, not after that scene back at the villa. He would far rather have wrung my neck.

Thing is, he couldn't not include me, not the way things were. So he'd tell Bree something, looking at her, and then I'd lift the one eyebrow, he'd catch it and remember that I was just as involved as she was, and move his head to include me. The whole time he was doing that, he didn't meet my eyes, not once. That was fine with me. I may have been ready to break his neck for him, but we were about to walk into potential trouble and he didn't need to be distracted by being forced into a pissing contest with me.

"I want to make sure I do this right." Bree was fighting to show her voice who was boss—I could tell, because all the music was missing from it. "We're supposed to get out of our limos. The band poses for a group shot, to keep the paparazzi happy. Then we head down the red carpet and up the stairs into the Palais. And you said there's a specific order?"

"Very specific." He still wasn't looking at me, so I just tightened my hold on Bree's hand, and listened. "You'll go two couples abreast. There will be two of the Festival organisers, with their wives, leading the way in. Behind them, Benno Marling and Harry Johns. Right behind them, we want a threesome: Ian Hendry, Carla Fanucci, and Luke Hedley. After them, the Corrigans and the Wilsons. You two, with Mac and Ms. Calley, will bring up the rear. Behind you, two of our people. And I'll be right behind you, middle of the aisle."

231

"Why?" I was rubbing Bree's hand—it was icy. "Where do you expect trouble to come from?"

"We don't know yet." He looked at me, finally. "Right now, Pirmin's on the ground, with nearly sixty people circulating. There are helicopters, and ours won't be distinguishable from the Bells the press corps uses—except that ours don't have chatty reporters or gossip columnists, they've got trained marksmen. Every hotel along La Croisette has been swept, and there isn't a high-rise window or a rooftop unaccounted for or left uncovered. Pirmin's getting constant communication—this is a massive operation, and very well coordinated. Believe me, the second Goff's spotted, we'll know. If it happens before we get there, we'll take him, or take him down, and you can just go inside and watch the movie and eat popcorn. If not, where we put you, how we move you, is going to depend on where he is when we pick him out."

"Lovely," I told him. "Good to know. But that's not what I meant. Why put Bree and Dom at the back? If they're first on Terry Goff's list, why are you leaving them out at the back, instead of surrounding them—surrounding us—with people? If you've got all these people, why only two behind us?"

"Because we're bait." Bree leaned back against me suddenly, and her voice wasn't calm anymore. "Any fisherman knows that the worm gets left out, dangling on the end of the hook. Otherwise, what's the point? I'm a worm, John. So is Dom."

I stayed quiet the rest of the ride, just shut my gob, not a word. If I'd opened my mouth, I would have said something even Bree might not have been able to forgive me for. Either that, or I'd have gone for Patrick Ormand's throat. Under the circs, it seemed smarter to just zip it. After all, he was paying the silent types riding along with us, and they had guns. The limo driver, one of Pirmin's people in borrowed livery for the evening, was probably packing something small and unpleasant in the way of firepower, but I didn't give a damn. I'd already come to a deci-

sion, after Bree's comment about the worms: I was going to surround her as much as I could, and if Patrick Ormand didn't like
it, he could fuck off and die, for all of me. Sod him, sod his fancy
operation and sod his personal vendetta, as well. I'm very fond of
Bree's back, and I wasn't about to leave it exposed to Terry Goff.

It didn't help me hang on to my self-control to get there and
find that no one else was any happier about it than I was. From
the minute I got out of the car, I was so tense that every nerve
felt exposed to the air.

I don't know how we got the limo through the crowd, but we
did. Bree'd gone completely silent, and very patchy under all the
face paint; I don't think she'd understood quite how dense the
crowds were likely to be, and she doesn't love crowds much to
begin with. At a Blacklight show, she'd be protected from it—in
and out, backstage all the way, all-access, and we get some control of the situation. But this wasn't Blacklight, and if you want
the truth, I didn't think anyone had control. The scene outside
the Palais was a fucking mob zone.

We were the last ones to arrive, which was actually a help, as it
turned out. It meant I could get out of the limo first, help Bree
out, and immediately strong-arm her into the middle of the
group. Patrick opened his mouth to say something, but I was ig-
noring him just then. I didn't give a rat's arse whether he approved or not.

It was a madhouse, a complete zoo. My heart was stuttering,
ramping up high and then down hard. If Patrick believed sixty
people gave him control, he was off his nut entirely. No one had
any sort of control of this mess. It wasn't physically possible.

"Right." My eyes wanted to check everything at once, but of
course, not a chance in hell—there were thousands of people,
just a solid wall of them. Bree was wincing at the noise—even
though we were outdoors, the sound levels were insane. I had a
moment of being glad Blacklight doesn't do stadium shows any-

more. There were helicopters circling, adding to it; there's really nothing that can push the noise quotient through the ceiling faster than a helicopter close by. "Dom, you look amazing. First time I've ever seen you in a dress."

She was in black, slit up both sides, less of a dress than a second skin, showing all her muscles. Barb and Cyn had gone all out for the evening, sequins and spangles and glittery flashes of brilliant colour—Barb had a gorgeous spangled shawl on, matching her dress. Carla was wearing something very short and slinky, and getting away with it, too. She's got the great legs and bum women seem to get when they do the skating thing; living in LA, she rollerbladed to the office, most mornings.

"God." Bree was shivering, and wincing, and I heard the panic in her voice. "Too loud. Too many people. Who are all these people? Why are they all here? Don't any of these people have jobs?"

"It's okay, love." Two of Pirmin's people behind us, check. Luke off to Bree's right, in his favourite tux, not smiling. Me on her left, one arm around her. Right, okay. There was nothing I could do about the mob directly in front of us, behind and around the photographers. "Let's get it done."

We posed for a group picture, then a second, then a third one. The entire time, my heart was popping and stuttering along with the flashbulbs. Every time a bulb went off, I thought it might be a shot being fired.

Right then, I came to a decision: this was the last time I was coming anywhere near the Cannes Film Festival. If Bree still wanted a place down here for holidays, fine, we'd have one, but I wasn't coming near the place during the Festival.

"All right." Patrick had come up behind us. He was having trouble pitching his voice over the crowd noise. "Line up, people, would you please? And remember, you're supposed to be walking up the steps to enjoy your movie. Act naturally. Smiling and waving is a good idea. Let's go."

Right. Showtime.

Looking back, I think we did it wrong. We should have staggered it: me, Bree, Mac and Dom. Instead, Mac and I were on the outside, and the two women together in the middle. At the time, we did it that way so that Pirmin's blokes, behind us, could stay together and at least pretend to provide some sort of cover for the women. I did, anyway. And of course, Patrick, with his earpiece in place and those dirty light eyes cycling between us and the crowds in a kind of rhythm, had tucked himself in between Dom and Bree, just at the back.

I took Bree's left hand. She was cold, freezing really, and that was nuts, because it was hot out there, but she was scared as hell.

Up the red carpet, toward the stairs. Patrick had said something about acting naturally, acting normal, waving to the crowd, smiling, but he must have been off his nut to think that was even possible.

I must have looked deranged, because my eyes wouldn't stay still. I kept looking, trying to spot the trouble, seeing if Terry Goff was somewhere out there, wondering if I'd even recognise him in that crush of faces and bodies if he was there. Looking in the sky, at the choppers. Looking at the crowd on Mac's side. Looking just off to my own left, to the crowd to the east. The last thing I had to spare was any attention for smiling and waving.

The festival organisers had got in safely. I saw Harry and Benno, their backs at least, disappear through the big doors.

We were halfway down the red carpet, almost to the steps ourselves. The doors to the Palais were surrounded by people. It was very weird: the people looked larger than the doors. Took me a moment to figure out that it was because the doors seemed so far away.

But we were almost there, the entire group in the order Patrick had got us in, and so far, not a damned thing. I saw Pirmin, waiting at the top of the steps. He had a wireless headset on, and I saw his lips moving, and then out of nowhere, I saw him tense up, one hand waving high and wide and then he began to move and right then, all hell broke loose.

In the movies or on the telly, when someone gets shot, you hear the bang of the gun first. Turns out that's bullshit. You don't hear the gun at all, or at least I didn't. I was looking where Pirmin had been looking, off to the east, and a lot of things seemed to happen all at once.

There were very clear, distinct screams, two different voices. They came from the other side of the red carpet, and I jerked my head around in time to see a photographer, one of the paparazzi, go down hard, holding his leg, his pricey camera gear hitting the ground. Pretty much simultaneously, I heard a genuinely sickening noise, a sort of pop-thud thing of a bullet hitting a bone. Yeah, right, I know—that shouldn't have been possible, not with all the crowd noise. But I heard it, believe me. I wish I hadn't.

There was blood all over the place, and the photographer was clutching his leg and screaming, and everyone around him was screaming right along. That was the moment I realised I'd heard a second scream, not an echo of the photographer's yell. Someone else had got hit.

What happened for a few minutes after that, I don't know. I mean, I've been told all about it, but I can't vouch for whether it's accurate or not, because all I've got are fragments. I didn't actually see anything, because about two seconds after that second scream, I went down hard, face first, with Bree on my back.

I really thought I was about to have a heart attack, because, for one very bad moment, I thought she'd been hit. She was on my back, and she felt like a dead weight. And she'd never been on my back this way before. There just aren't any sexual positions I know of where her lying facedown on my back would show either of us a good time, you know?

So my heart was doing a fucking samba, I couldn't breathe

properly, people were screaming in this huge suffocating wall of noise, and all I could see was the red carpet, because my face was pressed into it. The thing about that level of noise, that much sound coming from that many bodies at the same time, is that it literally comes in waves, washing over you and messing with your perception of what you're really hearing. I know something about how sound works. There's nothing quite like crowd noise.

So what I did was, I added to the noise: I started yelling Bree's name, over and over, hoping she could hear me, hoping she was okay.

"John, I'm fine, it's okay, I'm okay, are you okay, please tell me you're okay...." Her voice was right in my ear. She sounded fine, just scared half out of her wits. Not even going to try to tell you how relieved I was, because I can't. No one's invented the words yet.

"Jesus! I thought you'd got shot." I was absolutely pinned, and it was really uncomfortable. As I've said, she's not a skinny little thing. "Bree, get off me, love. I need to get up."

"No." She'd got her hands out, and got hold of my wrists. I had a mad moment, remembering that rough sex a couple of nights ago. This was a reversal, and I wasn't liking it at all. "Stay down. There's a firefight."

"I said, let me up!" Bloody hell, was she joking? I tried to heave her off. That wasn't on—she seemed to weigh about half a ton. I wasn't getting enough air to really put any threat behind my voice. "Bree, if you don't get off me—this isn't a bloody cop show. What in sweet hell do you think you're doing?"

"Covering you. Keep your head down, damn it!" Her own voice sounded short and breathless. "I can't get off you until Patrick gets off me first. But I wouldn't, even if I could. Just lie back and enjoy it. Think of England, or something."

I managed to get a mouthful of air into my lungs. Right there, I thought the top of my head was going to blow straight off. "Wait just a damned minute. What do you mean, Patrick has to get off you first?"

"I mean I'm the monkey in the middle." She wriggled, both breasts rubbing hard, and then there was another sort of wriggle, someone on top of Bree....

Oh, fuck no. No way. Not possible.

The picture came into my head, in full colour: a sandwich. Me at the bottom, kissing the red carpet. Bree pressed down hard against me, in the middle. And that meant that Patrick Ormand had his sensitive bits pressed up against my wife's bottom.

I was stuck, right where I was. Noise, way too damned much noise, but suddenly I remembered that second scream.

"Bree—who got hit? Did you see?"

"No. But it was close to me, very close."

She wriggled again, and I managed to twist my head slightly. I still couldn't see her—what I could see was one of Patrick's hands, the left one. It was resting on Bree's wrist, probably leaving bruises on top of the ones I'd left.

"You know what I feel like?" It was very peculiar. Bree's voice had gone almost conversational—it was as if she'd either decided that she might as well take her own advice and relax, or that she'd had too much bubbly and was having a corker of a drunken dream. "I feel like the middle of a cookie. A sandwich cookie, I mean. A man-sandwich cookie. I'm the creamy white filling in a man-cookie. How did *that* happen?"

I opened my mouth to say something, God knows what. But I never got it out because there was yelling suddenly, seemed like about twelve different languages, all jumbled up. A voice cut through, Patrick's voice, just about six inches behind my head: *target spotted east northeast four shots fired from exit to underground parking Norway covering.*

The words made no sense to me—I didn't know why everyone kept rabbiting on about Norway, and just then, I didn't care. I

238

couldn't see a damned thing, because Bree had shifted her weight and I now had my cheek sideways, with what seemed to be her left breast keeping it there. I was tasting red carpet, other peoples' shoes, and Bree was up against my back, and she wasn't cold anymore. If it turned out she was nice and warm from Patrick Ormand's private parts being up against her, I was likely going to shed some blood, myself. And I was worried as hell, on top of it, my heart racing up and down through a couple of octaves. I hadn't forgotten that second scream. What had Bree said? *Close to me, very close....*

I had no visual references, none at all. I had smells of perfume and cookery in the air, with the smell of the sea mixed in. I had the taste of the carpet. I had that tidal wave of crowd noise. I had Bree's body and breath and heartbeat against my spine, and finally, when everything was hurting like hell and I really didn't think I could take it anymore, the weight eased up and she rolled off me, onto her knees. Then I was up myself, trying to get the feeling in my legs back, trying to stand, looking for Dom and finding her.

She was on her knees, as well. The black dress was hiked up to her thighs. She had someone in her arms, cradling them.

It was Mac.

I don't know that I've ever moved that fast. I was up, vaulting past Bree, reaching them. My heart was slamming against my insides. I was yelling, trying to make myself heard, God only knows why. Words wouldn't fix this. All I had was one clear thought: Patrick Ormand was going to pay for this.

There was blood, a different shade from the red of the carpet, and it had poured out of the wound in Mac's right arm. His tux jacket was sodden with it. Barb Wilson, in the circle of Cal's right arm, had lost her pretty sparkly shawl; she was just finishing tying it tight above Mac's right elbow as a tourniquet, trying to staunch the bleeding. Dom was talking to Mac, a ridiculous stream of words.

"…get up son of a *bitch* I don't believe this shit you die on me I'll kick your sorry ass oh man come on motherfucker don't even think about dying on me you're making me look bad no way are you dying you're okay not bleeding anymore ambulance is almost here it's fine it's cool dude wake up and for fuck's sake *talk to me*…."

Sirens, the crowd being shunted aside, medics, a stretcher. We'd formed a protective circle round Mac and Dom; as the ambulance people lifted him onto the stretcher, he opened his eyes for a moment, and they were clear.

"Good evening, Cannes," he told us, and blacked out again.

Bree slipped her hand into mine; my eyes were wet. Luke had already climbed into the ambulance, along with Dom. We watched it scream off into the evening.

Behind us on the red carpet, I heard Pirmin's voice, clear and detached, speaking into his headset.

"Suspect down, at the Cinema de la Plage," he told it. "Repeat, suspect is down. All units to coordinate."

I turned around, and looked at him. He nodded at me.

"You are safe," he told us. "Terry Goff is dead."

# Chapter Thirteen

"*(beep) JP? Jesus wept, will you pick up your fucking phone, man? It's Tony—we just saw the news from Cannes, it's on every channel, but no one has any details. Is Mac going to be okay? Are you okay? Is everyone okay...? Oh, man, look, call me, I don't give a shit what time it is, just call! (beep)*"

"Another one?" Bree had been busy reassuring her mum that we were alive, and her voice was starting to sound shrill. "Who was it this time? Tony? Kris? I've already had Katia on the phone; she says she's going to let everyone know what went on."

"Good." I clicked the phone off. "Because that was Tony, and if I don't have to ring anyone else right now, good."

I looked around the front room of the villa, at our guests. We had the same collection of people we'd had for the screening, but the vibe was different, to say the least. For one thing, Patrick

Ormand didn't seem to have a clue what to do with himself, how to meet anyone's eye, what to say. Unusual, for him.

Everyone had been busy on their own phones—for awhile there, we'd looked like some sort of sick telly ad for a cell phone provider service, or something. Carla had disappeared for awhile, and come back to tell us that the official press release was written and out with the media. Luke had spent ten minutes on the phone with a hysterical Solange, trying to convince her everything was fine, that no one was dead, that her godfather wasn't lying on a slab somewhere. She hadn't believed him, or calmed down at all, until Luke had got Mac on the phone with her. She's a good kid, our Solange is.

"Tony rang up? How is the adorable Katia?"

Mac, pumped full of painkillers and with his arm in a soft cast, was stoned off his head, or at least, I was assuming he was. I mean, he'd never been a druggie to start with, and I was pretty sure the last time he'd had anything worth mentioning was right around the same time as me. So he couldn't possibly have had any tolerance for the stuff; he had to be whacked. You wouldn't have known it, though—he sounded very much as usual, just a touch wired. "How much of it made the news, back in the States?"

"No idea, but I'm guessing it's all over the place." I was keeping close to Bree, not wanting to let her out of my sight. Hopefully that wouldn't last long, because it would drive her nuts after a while. "Tony's message said it was on all the networks, so I'm guessing those helicopters up there had a live news feed going. At least they probably pre-empted the bitchy people who stand about and say rude things about peoples' outfits. Bree, what do you want to do about dinner? I could fancy something to eat."

"Have they got a decent Indian carryout place anywhere between here and Paris?" Barb Wilson sounded exhausted. No surprise, really—it was just after midnight. She'd surprised most of us, I think; after Ian had got back to us with the news that Mac was going to be okay, she'd had a sobbing fit all over Cal. Stress, probably, but I'd always thought Barb was pretty hard to ruffle up. "Because if they do, I'd vote for that. Brec doesn't need to cope, does she?"

"You're damned right she doesn't," I said, and blew Barb a kiss. That surprised a laugh out of Bree, but the truth was, she was as wrung out as everyone else, and there was no way I was having her worrying about cooking.

"Are people hungry? I can take care of it." Of course, that was Carla. Once she'd made sure that no one in the Blacklight contingent was dead or irreparably damaged, she'd gone into a corner with Pirmin and Patrick, and come out looking smug. I couldn't imagine why—there didn't seem to be anything to congratulate herself about, not with our lead singer being shot. "Give me ten minutes on the phone—what's the nearest hotel to here? Ian...?"

"Great. Thanks, Carla." Bree leaned back against me, and closed her eyes. She was looking every minute of her age, and fragile with it. I got an arm round her, and rubbed my lips against her cheek.

"You're getting some kip, lady, once we've had food." I caught Mac's eye. "Oi, mate, those French doctors give you any instructions about eating, when they glued your arm back together? Anything you can't have? And I'm talking about supper, not pornography."

"Don't be cheeky," he told me, but he was grinning. "You're not the one who took a bullet from—bloody hell, what *did* Goff shoot at us with?"

"A Heckler and Koch." Pirmin had spent most of the evening out in the garden on his cell phone. He'd been out there so long, I'd almost forgotten he was still here. "A precision rifle. An extremely powerful gun, in fact—the Germans developed it after

243

the Munich Olympics fiasco, when their own people had not enough firepower capability to keep the terrorists from killing all the hostages. We use it extensively, here in Europe; it's a favourite of NATO's special forces people. Very well-made, with a good long range. Expensive, as well. It is a favourite among the elite sniper units. The gun is highly prized for its accuracy. We found it where Goff dropped it. It was completely undamaged, fortunately."

I've said it before: the Swiss are peculiar, you know? He sounded about as enthusiastic as I'd ever heard him, blithering on about the damned gun.

"So, I got a thumbnail-sized chunk of my humerus torn off by, what? A sniper's wet dream? Charming." Mac shifted his shoulder, and I saw his brows come together for a moment. "Damn. Hurts. Why didn't I agree to stay in hospital, the way they wanted me to? Hooked up to a Demerol drip, surrounded by pretty nurses with smashing bums and adorable pouts, all catering to my every whim?"

"You're alive, dude. Stop whingeing." Dom had been mostly silent since we'd got back. There was a nasty byplay going on between her and Patrick, though, and it was really getting on my nerves: every once in a while, they'd lock eyes, and his would drop first, every time. Then there'd be this tense little silence. Something was going down between those two. I just hoped no one would expect Bree to clean the blood off the walls when it did.

I was edgy as hell, myself. I couldn't sort out my own feelings about the entire mess. I was furious with Patrick, but I'd asked him to come, asked him to deal, asked him for help. And he'd done it; he just hadn't done it all that well, and he hadn't done it in a way I could approve of. He'd accomplished what I'd wanted—Bree was alive, unhurt, safe, and so was Dom, and Goff was dead. Mac was going to be okay. So I couldn't justify nailing Patrick, no matter how much I wanted to.

At least I'd managed to sort out my reactions to the whole man-sandwich thing. Right, I know, but Bree's phrase had got jammed in my head and it was stone perfect, that phrase, and now I couldn't picture it any other way. But I still had to parse it out in my head, cope with that picture. Turned out it was actually pretty easy: yeah, he'd had his bits and pieces up against Bree, but he'd knocked us both down and covered us and kept her from getting shot. I decided to do my best to forget that comment she'd made, about being the creamy white filling, or at least to file it away in some deep dark hole in my memory, at least for now.

Poor Bree was in a trickier situation than I was. Patrick was a guest under her roof, and that's not a small thing in Bree's world. But he'd repaid her hospitality by using her as bait, putting her at risk. I wasn't likely to forget the misery in her voice when she'd described herself as a worm on Patrick's hook, not anytime soon.

"Right. No more whingeing." Mac's voice jerked me out of it. He suddenly looked wide awake and very alert. "Pirmin, Patrick, talk to us. I want to know what in hell just happened. I want to know why I got shot at all. That photographer, is he okay? Why would Goff shoot him, aside from him being a member of the paparazzi, that is?"

"The photographer—he's an Australian—is going to be fine. He left the hospital long before you did." It was the first thing Patrick had said, and he wasn't meeting Mac's eye. "Goff didn't shoot at him—the photographer's got a cracked tibia, from the same bullet that hit you. It went through your arm, glanced off the bone—that's how the bone broke—and deflected out and into this guy's leg, hard enough to break it. Goff only took one shot, and he missed badly."

"Define 'missed.'" Mac shifted his arm. "Ouch, damn it."

"Why did he miss?" Ian was keeping one eye on the door; Carla had got off the phone and whispered something into his ear. As capable as they both are, I was assuming the food had been taken care of. "The bloke was a terrorist, right? Big-time white supremacist? You saying he was a crap marksman? Because that's a big stretch. I thought all those types fancied guns."

"It does not follow, not as night follows day," Pirmin told him. "But there is a mystery to this, that I suspect we must wait to unravel until the forensic people verify things for us. Our suspicion, our belief, is that this gun was unfamiliar to him, and that he underestimated the strength of its recoil. There is physical evidence on Goff's face to support that theory."

Harry Johns snickered. "If you're talking about Goffer's face, he was already pretty banged up. Mac's bodyguard, here, she put a big, big hurt on him, back at the casino. His eye, you know? Bet that fucked him up, good and proper."

"What physical evidence?" Luke was feeling around in his pockets. "Carla, do you need a credit card for dinner? No? Good, because I don't think I've got one with me. Everything's in Italy, with Solange—Christ, I may be bankrupt by tomorrow. I hope she leaves me enough to pay the bill at the Cipriani. What physical evidence? What's this about Goff's face?"

"His right eye." Patrick managed genuine eye contact of his own this time, looking at Luke. "There was a fresh contusion, and possibly a cracked orbital bone, too. Also, his right shoulder appeared to be separated, and I don't think he could have held and fired that HK rifle if his shoulder had already been screwed up. The inference is that he didn't know how to use the gun, or was unfamiliar with it. It has an enormously powerful recoil."

"Wait a minute. His right eye? And right shoulder?" Dom stared at Patrick. There was no challenge in her voice, just concentration. "You saying he was looking through the scope with his right eye, and bracing with his right shoulder?"

There it was again; he met her eye, his dropped. "Yes. Why? Why is that relevant?"

246

"Guy was a lefty, that's what." She smiled suddenly, a nasty little grin. "I fought him, hand to hand, remember? When I fucked his shit up at the casino, he pulled a knife—that was in his left hand. He used his left leg to kick, too. And when I kicked him, I went for his dominant side. Trained, you know? I do that by instinct. Trust me, he was a lefty."

"So the half of his body he'd normally have used wasn't working." Cyn Corrigan had been curled up in a chair since we'd got back. She looked limp. "And he wasn't, what, coordinated enough with his right hand and eye to do it right?"

"That would explain certain things." Pirmin turned to Mac. "There is your answer, Mr. Sharpe, and Mr. Hendry's as well: however proficient Terry Goff may have been with guns, he was incapable of handling this one with any accuracy. It is a mercy he didn't realise it—it is an even greater mercy that no one was killed. But the injury to his natural side, that is the reason you were hit. It is also why Ms. Calley and Mrs. Kinkaid are alive."

"I'll take that trade-off any time." Mac reached out with his good hand, and patted Dom on the shoulder. "It'll heal, brat. Just a broken arm."

"I want to know what happened at Parmeley's villa. I still don't understand."

Bree was beginning to fade out on me; it sounded like an effort just to keep her voice audible. I got up and headed into the kitchen, grabbed a clean plate, and rummaged in the fridge. Cheese, a cold ripe pear, some leftover pâté: that ought to hold her until dinner got here. I headed back, balancing the plate and a glass of juice and bumping the kitchen door open with one hip, and realised they'd waited for me. I walked into silence.

"Here you go," I told her, and set the food down. "Room service. You eat something, lady."

Pirmin waited for me to sit back down. "About the villa, we do know a few things—Goff and James Wonderley both spoke with

247

Santini, and gave him orders. Santini is not nearly fool enough to admit to supplying his fellow members of White Omega with contraband explosives, or weaponry, but that is likely where both things came from. We will conduct a full inventory of the Les Sirènes evidence locker, be sure. Ah—I believe the food has arrived."

Carla had got the staff of one of the local hotel kitchens to work overtime. Three employees carried in dinner, in steam trays and on covered platters—they'd even brought china, and cutlery. I made a mental note to send Carla a nice thank-you present, for sparing Bree the cooking and washing up. We settled down to eat, listening to Pirmin, who was filling us in between mouthfuls. Even Interpol experts get hungry.

"I think we will never know the full sequence of events that led to the firebombing, but our best guess is that Parmeley may have said something to his bodyguards, after the fracas at the casino. If he told them that there was a fourth, expanded version of the film in the vault, Goff at least would have seen the threat. Parmeley was on the fast road to dementia; he had moments of lucidity, but they were erratic, according to the local shopkeepers he dealt with."

"What, you chatted up all the locals already?" Benno Marling was getting through quite a lot of food. "Fast, you lot are. So it was Goff who ordered the bombing? What was Jimmy doing there, then?"

Patrick didn't seem to be hungry. "He was doing what his boss told him to do. Goff had access to the house, and to the vault; since the target was the vault, according to forensics, Goff probably felt killing Parmeley would raise more hell than it was worth. After all, unstable, well into his eighties, he wasn't likely to live long anyway, so why risk killing him? Goff probably asked his old lieutenant Wonderley to handle planting the C4. If things had gone the way Goff planned it, Parmeley could babble about his final version until hell froze over, but that's all it would be: babble. No evidence."

"But why did Terry Goff kill his friend?" Bree asked. She suddenly sounded ragged, not really in control. "Look, I'm sorry—I just want to be able to make some sense out of this, okay? I mean, I injured Len Cullum. I'm the one who made his right arm useless. I don't regret it, he was planning on shooting Dom, but it meant he couldn't defend himself, doesn't it?"

"Bree—"

"No, John, I want to know. I want to know why he would have needed to defend himself. Against who? Why? I don't understand."

"Oi!" I got hold of her hands; they were shaking. "That's it, you want sleep, is what. We're going to finish this up. Patrick, Pirmin, someone, answer the girl's question, yeah? Then we can finish eating and crash for about ten hours."

"I may have an answer for Mrs. Kinkaid's question." Pirmin suddenly looked, I don't know, formidable. Maybe austere would be a better word? Everything on his face went detached, remote, as if he was about to pass sentence on someone. There was a definite "may God have mercy on your soul" thing going on, there. "We asked our associates in Manchester to run a check on any incident reports that might have matched the beating of that boy in the alley, by Len Cullum. They were able to track it down, and the result of that incident, as well."

"The boy died." Mac's voice was quiet; next to me, I heard Bree's breath catch in her throat. "Didn't he?"

"Yes, the boy died. There were head injuries, and massive internal bleeding."

Mac shifted his arm. He suddenly looked as tired as Bree did. "Damn. Right, okay. So there it was, basis for a jail term and maybe a special circs murder charge, put up on film in competition for a fucking Palme d'Or. Plus, his best chum was a wanted terrorist, and the last thing either of them would have wanted was that kind of official attention. They'd been hiding out down here, all comfy and invisible, damned near forever. No wonder everything went nuts so fast—it was the screening of the third version that did it. Who got windy, do you think? Goff or Cullum?"

"As Patrick has said, we will probably never know. But you are correct, about that screening; it showed a criminal assault that ended in a death. That, alone, would have panicked Cullum. If Parmeley had mentioned an expanded director's cut—and Santini's testimony makes that a reasonable supposition—Goff would have wanted to bury the film as deep as he could."

"I wonder if Cullum got spooked enough to make Goff decide he couldn't be trusted not to lose it." Luke had polished off a lot of food in a very short time. He sounded drowsy. "I'm curious about something. I was told that there were two people wanted for killing Cullum. Isn't that why they nicked Dom and Bree? What's the story with that?"

"That was before the full medical examiner's report came in." Patrick was moving around the room, restless, picking things up, putting them down again. He was really getting on my nerves. "The results are inconclusive. Cullum may have been kicked unconscious, dragged into the bush, and had his throat cut well after he was knocked out. There's nothing to suggest a simultaneous action, requiring two people."

"So Goff maybe kicked Cullum, and slashed his throat later. Good. Works for me."

Something was happening to Dom's voice. Whatever it was, it did something to the base of my spinal cord, the kind of feeling a Neanderthal might have got if he heard something big and hungry, outside in the bushes. "And if we're done talking about it, that's good too. Because there's something I want to get off my chest. See, I need to vent."

I didn't even see her move. The girl's so fast, she's scary. But there she was, sitting next to Mac, and then she wasn't, because she was on her feet and there was a blur of motion that was her right arm moving. Then there was some very confused noise, and a crash.

I started to say something, but never got it out. Patrick Ormand was on his arse on the floor, about three feet from where he'd been standing. He was holding a hand over his left eye, staring up at Dom with the one she hadn't aimed for.

"You made me look bad." Her voice was dry ice, matter of fact, dangerous as hell, maybe because she sounded so rational. "You damaged my boss. I told you I thought you weren't using your head, and you blew me off. You had this coming, dude. You want to discuss it, go get some ice for your eye and we'll take it outside. I don't want to mess up Bree's furniture."

He stayed where he was. It was a really awkward moment. No one was saying anything, not a word; Pirmin's mouth was open, but it was shock, not language. I was still processing what Dom had said, about having told Patrick the same thing Bree had.

And then someone laughed, a nice easy chuckle. It was Mac.

"Dom, angel, give the man room to get up." He was looking at Patrick, and he'd laughed, but he didn't look amused. "You know, you ought to be thanking all your gods that all you got was a right cross to the eye. Dom's right. You had that coming, and a lot worse. She's got her professional pride to deal with, but really, she's not half as narked with you as I am. Christ, Patrick, what the fuck were you thinking? Dom told you. From the look on Johnny's face, I'm guessing he and Bree told you, as well. But you went screaming in anyway. Not exactly a moment for your professional highlight reel."

Patrick was on his feet. He squinted at Mac out of his one good eye, and then turned to face me, and Bree.

"I'm not arguing," he told us. He looked sick. "Mac is right. So was Ms. Calley. And so were you, Bree. You told me what you thought I was missing, and I heard it, but I didn't really *hear* it. You asked me to come, you asked me for help, you made all the resources available. I let my own personal stuff get in the way of getting it done in a way that might have prevented the shooting."

He stopped, and swallowed hard. Apologising couldn't be easy for someone as used to being on top of it as he was.

"I'm sorry." He looked around the room at the rest of us, finally. "I got it done, but I got it done the wrong way, and I endangered people in the process. That's not acceptable to me. I'm a professional."

There was a long uncomfortable silence. Carla broke it.

"Well," she told him, "It could have been a lot worse. Let's just be thankful for Norway."

That broke the tension, all right. Pirmin grinned suddenly, and so did Patrick.

"Right, that's absolutely it." I got to my feet, and yanked Bree upright. "I need meds, and some kip, and Bree's asleep on her feet. What in hell did Norway have to do with anything? Why does everyone keep going on and on about Norway?"

"That favour I called in, to the Norwegian ambassador." Carla stretched her legs, and I heard ankle bones crack. I had the feeling that the first thing she'd be doing when she got back LA was a nice long rollerblading session in the Hollywood hills. "I got diplomatic credentials for Patrick, remember? When Interpol got involved after the villa blew up, one of the Embassy attaches called Patrick, and offered some backup. Turns out their local staff of special forces all have Olympic medals for sharp-shooting, or something like that."

"It was one of the Norwegian marksmen who took out Goff." Patrick took his hand away from his left eye, finally, and my stomach did a nasty little dance. Dom had nailed him, all right; I saw a trip to the casualty ward in his immediate future, if it was half as bad as it looked. His eye was a mess, purple and yellow surrounding it, the eye itself completely bloodshot. "A single shot from about a hundred yards, straight to the base of the neck. Killed him instantly. So Goff's face wasn't damaged, and we were able to see clear evidence of his mishandling of the gun."

He yawned suddenly, a huge, deep yawn. I felt my own jaws wanting to do the same. There's something contagious about yawning. "If no one minds, I'm feeling a little dizzy, so I'm going to wrap this up and head to bed. But first I'm taking Ms. Calley's suggestion, and getting some ice for my eye."

*"Bon soir, Frejus!"*

It was an absolutely gorgeous evening. We were just a couple of days away from May becoming June, and the weather was fantastic. Out in the amphitheatre, eleven thousand or so people had parked themselves on the stone benches. The days were long, and the gig, which was supposed to begin as soon as the skinny French bloke from the Department of Tourism finished introducing us in two or three languages, was starting off in daylight, even though it was half past eight.

Luke had his Strat tuned and ready. "Nice night we picked for it. Ought to be a good show. I'd have liked more rehearsal of the seventies stuff with Benno and Harry, but c'est la vie, right? Where in hell is my daughter—oh, good, she's with Bree. That's all right, then. You know, JP, this is the first time I've ever seen Bree looking completely relaxed. You're doing something right, mate."

"I hope so." I was running my fingers up and down Little Queenie's neck, loosening up, playing some runs. I had the set list in my head, but there were notes on the amps, as well. Stu had come up behind me, rattling a pair of drumsticks. Cal was talking to Barb; they both looked nice and mellow. I watched Bree coming toward us, Solange in tow. "She's had a pretty dodgy honeymoon, you know? What with one thing and another."

253

*"It is a great privilege to be able to present this free concert, given by Blacklight, with special guests, to raise awareness of the ugly presence of racism in the midst of…."*

"Honeymoon?" Luke was giving me a long, straight look. Suddenly, my shoulders were prickling; I could see him deciding to say what was on his mind. "She's had a pretty dodgy twenty-five or so years, JP. Cilla, your immigration situation, the multiple sclerosis, a few other little things. Not that it's any of my business, and not that I think she'd trade a minute of it. But when I said this was the first time I've ever seen her relaxed, I meant it. The key word is 'ever.'"

"Right." I was giving him back look for look. I love the bloke, he's one of my closest friends, but I was damned if I was going to let him think I was completely oblivious. "Thanks, mate, I'm aware of it. Just curious—do you think I don't know? Or that I don't know that she keeps me alive?"

"I just wondered whether you forget it occasionally, that's all. Taking it for granted is much too easy. I do wonder sometimes, whether you get that she does a lot more than keeping you alive. She makes it possible for you to be who you are." He turned his face away, and something happened to his voice for a moment. "Take it from someone who lost the other half of the puzzle way too soon, JP. What you've got, it's unique."

"I know." I rested both hands against the guitar, Bree's wedding gift to me, my favourite stage axe. "Believe me, I know."

"God, what a gorgeous night. Everyone ready, then?" Mac was dancing in place, his usual pre-gig warm-up. The dance wasn't as energetic as it might have been, not with his right arm in the cast and sling. Dom was a few feet away, scanning the crowd, looking for trouble to prevent. Her gig was a lot trickier in an outdoor arena than it would be indoors. "You both happy with the encore stuff, with Harry and Benno? With the order of songs, I mean?"

Luke and I shared a grin. We hardly ever do covers of other

people' stuff; not much need for that, not with thirty years of Blacklight's material to choose from, plus the stuff Luke and Mac had done together, back when they were doing the small theatre and festival circuit as Blackpool Southern. "Of course. Nice little triad of Clash songs, there. I'm glad to see Jas got my Paul set up—I'm damned if I want to thrash away at Queenie for a bunch of three-chord punk wonders. Bree, love, hello. Solange, you've gone all tan and golden."

"Hi, Uncle John. I'm glad it looks better than it feels." Now that I looked at her, she was a bit too golden, actually. She didn't seem comfortable; she kept twitching her shoulders. "I fell asleep by the pool at the Cipriani, back in Venice. Not enough sunscreen. Ouch."

"Poor Solange. Remember to keep it moisturised—when it starts peeling, it's hell." Bree leaned in and kissed me. The crowd noise was beginning to rise, the crowd smelling music in the wings. "Oh, swell, now it's German. How many languages does this emcee guy intend to introduce you in?"

"Not a clue, but I think he's about done." I jerked my head sideways; something across the stage had caught my attention. "Crikey, is that Patrick Ormand? With a *date?*"

Bree grinned. "Isn't she adorable? An agent or something at Interpol—her name is something incredibly French. Monique, or Dominique, or Genevieve, or something. Tiny little thing, but she's got dimples for miles. She looked impressed by the Ferrari—I saw them pull up. Of course, she was also eyeing Mac, so poor Patrick may be getting his heart broken—John, stop laughing, damn it, that's just mean!"

*"And so, ladies and gentlemen, mesdames et messieurs, signore e signori, damen und herren...."*

"Do a good gig, baby." She reached out for me, got up close, and got a hand between us, and between my thighs for a quick hard squeeze. "Mine."

255

It had become a tradition recently, her sending me out onstage with a full erection, but I hadn't thought about whether she'd do it under the sky. But she had, and Solange had seen. She was pink round the edges, and her eyes were wide.

And Bree knew it. She turned round and gave Solange this look—hard to describe it, maybe because I'm male, but it was conspiratorial and amused and sort of knowing, as if she was sharing something with a baby sister.

"It's a perk," she said clearly. "Of being married. It's mine. I get to say so, loud and clear. Mine."

"BLACKLIGHT!"

It was a really superb show. Considering the last-minute nature of it, the rush our production and sound design people had had to put on, we gave that crowd a night to remember. Nial Laybourne, our production designer, had been cranky about the lack of staging, but he was too chuffed at getting to work at Frejus to stay shirty about it. And our sound genius, Ronan Greene, was basically salivating. The setting was gorgeous to begin with, but it had been awhile since he'd had a shot at doing the band's sound in an outdoor setting, and Frejus, well, that's got its own romance to it.

We took the stage for a shorter show than usual—right around ninety minutes, plus a planned encore with Harry Johns and Benno Marling. The first thing Mac did when he hit the stage was, he slipped his cast out of the sling, and turned it out to face the audience. Of course the big video screens showed the close-up; it was covered with peace symbols and logos from the various humanist organisations he worked with. That set the tone for the rest of the gig; the crowd went bonkers.

I think I spent the entire show grinning, loving the crowd, loving my mates in the band, loving being alive. Nothing hurt, nothing at all. It was as if I'd left the MS, the dodgy heart, back at the villa, or along the road. Just for now, I seemed free of it.

I looked off into the wings, and there was Bree, dancing, shaking her hips, always visible. Once or twice I looked across the stage, and there was Patrick, dancing with his date. And Dom was out on the prowl, doing her rounds, doing her job, making sure there was nothing and nobody out there looking to give Mac something to worry about. But there was nothing. The crowd knew what this gig was for, and they were with us, all the way.

Eighty minutes, ninety. We closed the set, took a breather in the wings just offstage, and came back out for the encore.

"Right." Mac had the mic in his left hand, and really, I was so used to him doing it the other way, the visual actually threw me off. "Thank you, *mesdames et messieurs*, ladies and gents. We're going to try something tonight we've never done before, and we haven't had a lot of time to really get it down, so if we mess up, please remember that I've only got the one good arm right now, and don't throw things, all right? Because I can't catch them and throw them back."

Hoots, catcalls, cheers. Luke and I nodded at each other, and I caught Cal grinning, as well. This was going to be good.

"...Harry Johns, of Typhoid Harry, and Benno Marling, of Isle of Dogs!"

We did a Dogs number first, one of their hits from the sixties, "No More Roses". It was a typical Isle of Dogs piece, medium length for its time period, at about four minutes. I had a guitar solo in the middle of it, about forty-five seconds of vicious little cascading slide guitar on the Les Paul, and I was playing what had been Jimmy Wonderley's part.

About twenty seconds into it, something very strange happened: a song lyric popped into my head. Not a fragment, either—a complete verse. I had to pull my concentration away, and back to the solo. But the verse stayed right where it was.

I finished the solo. Benno was singing, but I wasn't hearing him. I kept seeing Jimmy Wonderley's face in my head, and the song lyric I couldn't seem to stop hearing had parked itself, and wasn't moving:

*You there, with the black tattoo? I know exactly what you do.*

Cal was playing a bass line, a wicked little grinder of a run, snarling and booming, twisting itself as far down the bass range as it could go. I heard it, but only with part of my mind. There it was, more of the lyric:

*You were good, you had no reason/you twisted up that gift so bad/talent marries hate, I call that treason/to all the music you once had.*

Song was over, and Benno stepped back, letting Mac take centre stage again.

*I don't know how you found that hole/I don't know how you lost your soul....*

"...Harry Johns!"

*But I can't deny it's true: we will remember you.*

We did Typhoid Harry's one big hit, "Piss Off". That was a three-chord wonder, about three minutes, typical anthem of the punk era. It was all about the rage of the period, and what spooked me was, even if the song was simplistic, the anger wasn't dated. It hadn't aged. Christ, that's why we were here, wasn't it? That was why Mac had his arm in a sling. That was why we were out under the stars, playing this show.

*You there, with the smashed guitar? I know exactly who you are.*

258

Cal was ramming the bass, business as usual for the Bunker Brothers, in a perfectly synced lockup with Stu. Luke and I were playing straight rhythm, until Luke took a fast solo. The original version hadn't had that.

*You had your fifteen minutes/To strut and fret your stuff on-stage/The time was right, you were right there in it/audience was ready for some noisy rage.*

Harry was all over the stage, doing what he'd done back when Cedric Parmeley'd thought Typhoid Harry was the future of rock and roll.

*But now that's past, it's time to go/you did your bit, you're off the show/maybe it'll help to know….*

"And now, we're going to say goodnight, with a medley of songs that came out of London, back when the National Front in the UK was spreading their dirt, and a lot of rockers spent a lot of time out there fighting against racism and hate. This one's for the Clash!"

*…we will remember you.*

We launched into the medley we'd rehearsed, Mac and Harry and Benno all trading off lead vocals. First up was *White Man in the Hammersmith Palais*, followed by *Career Opportunities*. We finished up with *Know Your Rights*.

I looked into the wings. Bree was there, not dancing, just watching. As I watched, she reached out and took Solange's hand. And there they were, Solange looking like Viv, just like Viv.

Christ. So much history, so much memory, so much there I'd just taken for granted. I remembered what Luke had said, just before we'd gone onstage, about how he'd lost it too soon.

*We never know just what might happen/we never know how high to fly/Maybe we get to keep each other/or lose it all in the blink of an eye....*

"JP?" Luke was right next to me. "You okay? You look like you're seeing ghosts."
"Right. I'm fine."

*And now I lay me down to sleep/you're everything I want to keep....*

"Just writing a song in my head, that's all."
Stage lights up, bathing the entire band in the Blacklight logo, moon against an inky sky. Arms round each other's waists, bowing. There was a lot of champagne lying about, but tonight, Mac held off from spraying the audience with it. After all, this wasn't your usual Blacklight gig, and he only had the one useful hand. Besides, that's not what you're supposed to do with champagne in France. You're meant to drink it.

*If you should wake and find me gone/feel free to live, and carry on/so much to do, so much to see/I only ask one thing: Remember me.*

"Goodnight!" Mac gave one last wave. The houselights came up, and we headed offstage, back to our lives, our wives, our lovers, our families and friends, and, tomorrow, back to London.

# *Epilogue*

"Here you go, mate. 18, Howard Crescent."

It was a beautiful sunny day in Camden, NW1, just like the last time I'd been here, the last time Bree had been here. There were people out on the Crescent, just like last time; the elderly bloke with the pug didn't seem to be out, but there was a couple walking a pair of matched bulldogs. The same gardener who'd been trimming roses down near the north end of the Crescent was out again today. A nanny went past us, smiling and nodding a greeting, pushing a pram with a sleeping baby in it.

It was our last day in London for the next ten days at least. We were due to head down to Kent tomorrow, to Luke's farm and studio at Draycote; I'd written four complete songs, and Mac and Luke had half a dozen of their own. Between us, we had enough to lay down the basic tracks for the next Blacklight CD. It was interesting, the shift in the lyrics; all of a sudden, Mac and Luke were writing about being adults. And so was I. I'd played the song that had come into my head during the Frejus show, and they'd got goosebumps over it, so we'd recorded me doing it on a single guitar, Mac singing it.

I'd also had a conversation with Bree about the money sitting in the London house account. She'd seen where I was going with it, and agreed; if we could spare that much without ever noticing that it was gone, there was no reason not to do something useful with it. So Blacklight Corporate had been handed a continuing power of attorney, and the money that had gone into Cilla's maintenance would be going to a variety of things, starting with funding an addiction recovery clinic in her name.

We'd got a lot accomplished. There was an errand we still needed to do at Howard Crescent, though, and I wasn't looking forward to it.

I paid the taxi driver, and got the keys out. Ghosts, so many damned ghosts; I was honestly expecting a replay of that odd moment of disassociation I'd gone through last time, seeing my younger self walking out the front door, Cilla up in the window, waving me off. The last time we'd been in this house, Bree had ended up going through two of the worst days of her life, and I'd been blaming myself for it, then and now.

"John?"

"Right." I reached for her hand. "Let's have a look at the damage, yeah? See what the company we hired did about cleaning the place out."

I don't what I was expecting. Maybe complete emptiness, you know? I mean, we'd hired this firm through the local police, paid them to clear the house out. We'd told them to ship all the clothes in the upstairs bedroom to Blacklight's offices, for sorting out; some of that flash gear from the seventies was going to the Hall of Fame in Cleveland, when the band went to the opening of the Blacklight exhibit the museum was planning.

I walked in ahead of Bree. First thing I did was look up, then down, checking out the walls. I let my breath out; the walls were mostly bare, just a few spots of photo backing paper and glue that hadn't wanted to come off without a fight. Behind me, I heard Bree sigh, a soft exhale of relief, and I realised, she had to have been holding her breath, as well.

But they hadn't known what to do with all the stuff they'd taken down. It was all here still, stacked up, tidy little piles on the floor of the front room: photographs in one stack, with the largest at bottom and the smallest at the top. Clippings and articles were another pile. The gold records had been sent to Blacklight's offices.

I must have looked at that first pile for just a moment too long. The photo on top of the stack was an eight by ten: me and Cilla, Cilla on my arm, wearing a tube top, her hand in its black lace glove tucked into my arm. She was smiling up at me, and I was smiling back down at her. You could see the love there, both ways—no way to miss it, you know? It was just the sort of photo to bring a tear to the eye, if the eye in question happened to belong to someone really sentimental. It wasn't a posed shot, either. It had been snapped, God only knows by who, as we came out of a hotel doorway....

Like I said, I looked a second too long. Bree reached past me, and picked the photo up.

The silence seemed to stretch out forever. The house was quiet, visibly dusty. There was no life in it—it was just an empty house, with a beautiful garden. We still had an errand to do, out of doors. But right now, I wasn't moving. I was silently praying to whatever might be listening: *don't let her ask when the picture was taken, don't let her ask, it'll break her heart, she doesn't need to know, don't let her ask, oh Christ if she asks I'll have to tell her the truth, don't let her ask....*

"Wow." She looked up at me, finally, and smiled. It was a real smile, a genuine smile. "You two look so happy."

I couldn't say anything. I could hardly swallow. I knew which hotel Cilla and I had been coming out of; we'd only ever been there once. I knew exactly when the photo had been taken. *Don't let her ask....*

"And young." She stared down at it again, then back to me. The smile was gone, but her face was soft, somehow. "You know what? I'm glad about that. I honestly am. I'm glad you've had women in your life who could make you happy. You deserve that."

Something was happening in my chest, constriction. Took me a moment to realise there were tears in there. I managed to smile at her.

She looked at the photo, one more time, and of course, she blew me apart and asked the question. "What hotel was this? When was it taken?"

I opened my mouth, and closed it again. Why in hell did she have to ask? Why couldn't the girl just leave well enough alone?

"John...?"

I looked her straight in the eye. "Do you really need to know, Bree? I'll tell you, if you insist on it. But I'd rather not. You won't like the answer."

"I think I want to know." Her shoulders were tight suddenly, as tight as I'd ever seen them. "Yes. I do want to know. Where? And when?"

"Going to dinner just before the Hollywood Bowl gig." My throat was dry. "The night before the Hurricane Felina benefit."

She went limp. It was really strange, watching her sag, and I suddenly got it, that tension: she'd thought my not wanting to tell her meant that I'd cheated on her, been with Cilla after Bree and I had got together.

But the relief wasn't going to last, not with her conscience.

Any moment, she was going to connect the timing in her head….

"Damn." And, bang on the money: there she went. There were tears in her eyes, spilling over. "Oh, damn. If you two were that tight—and I leaned over and kissed you, what was I thinking, it's not as if I didn't know you were married, what was I doing—"

"*Stop it.*"

I snapped it out, much harder, much more harshly than I'd meant to. But this was what I'd been worried about, that bloody martyr thing she gets. I watched her face, reacting to my tone.

"Enough, Bree. Just, enough, okay? I told you this back in New York, when she did herself in: you didn't break us up. Get that through your skull, will you please? Yeah, we had a couple of very good years, me and Cilla. Yeah, she made me happy for awhile. But by the time that photo was taken we were on the way out, whether you believe it or not. That miserable film Patrick let you off watching? That said it all. Cilla couldn't get any interest up in sex without a gram of cocaine to start her up, and I was so fucking stoned I let a camera crew in to watch me shagging my wife. You call that happiness, do you? *Do you?*"

"I don't know." She whispered it. "No. I don't."

"Good. Glad to hear it." Now I'd started, I couldn't seem to turn it off. We stood there in that empty house, and I just let it come. "Miranda told me about you and the tequila and my pain pills, back when I was taking care of Cilla. You think Cilla was making me happy, Bree? You think me waking up drunk six mornings out of seven was me being happy? Bloody hell, you can't possibly be that stupid. This house, her in it, that was something I escaped from. If I hadn't had the band to keep me sane, I couldn't have stood it. Christ, I played the same songs over and over, take after take, anything at all to not have to come back here. And there were a few times, I didn't come back here. I

265

woke up drunk in a tube station one morning. Never told you that, did I?"

She was listening to me, not saying a word, just listening, the way she does when it's me talking. I thought about what Luke had said, just before we'd gone onstage at Frejus, about how Bree made it possible for me to be me.

Maybe—maybe not. Maybe that balance was about something else. It didn't matter. All that mattered was that here we were, we'd come this far, and I was sick of her blaming herself for the few things in my life she hadn't been able to make perfect or whole.

I reached out, and took her face between my hands.

"Listen to me," I told her. "If I hadn't had you back there in San Francisco, I'd have died. Sounds like night-time telly, right, but it's true. I was with Cilla for a few years. I've been with you ever since. Never been anyone else, anything else. There's just been you. Let it go, Bree. Please? Cilla, all that, it's ancient history. It's what you saved me from."

I kissed her, long and deep. I felt the tension go out of her, move through me like a memory of something I'd let go a long time ago and never needed to think about again. When I stepped back, she was smiling at me.

"The ring." She knuckled her eyes. "We should bury Cilla's ring."

We found the perfect spot together, under the apple tree at the eastern end of the garden. The tree was an old one, with a welter of roses growing under it; it was shady there, quiet. Even when the weather got bad, the creepers and roses and thorns would keep the ring safe and dry.

I got down on my knees and got busy, with a small trowel from the garden shed. We buried it deep, the ornate gold ring in its hand-made coffin, sprinkling dirt on top, packing it down, protecting it.

266

"Right." Outside, in the distance, I heard a car horn, children's voices, a radio. Tomorrow, we'd head down to the south coast. I hoped Bree wouldn't be too bored, while I was locked in the studio ten hours a day. "Ready? Let's head home, then."

"Do you want to say anything?" Bree asked. So she'd felt it as well, that sense of cutting something off, putting something where it belonged.

"Not really." I turned back for a moment, looking at the roses, the apple tree, the sun and the shadows. "Well—only goodbye."

Photo by Nic Grabien

Deborah Grabien can claim a long personal acquaintance with the fleshpots—and quiet little towns—of Europe. She has lived and worked and hung out, from London to Geneva to Paris to Florence, with a few stops in between.

But home is where the heart is. Since her first look at the Bay Area, as a teenager during the peak of the City's Haight-Ashbury years, she's always come home to San Francisco, and in 1981, after spending some years in Europe, she came back to Northern California to stay.

Deborah was involved in the Bay Area music scene from the end of the Haight-Ashbury heyday until the mid-1970s. Her friends have been trying to get her to write about those years—fictionalised, of course!—and, now that she's comfortable with it, she's doing just that. After publishing four novels between 1989 and 1993, she took a decade away from writing, to really learn how to cook. That done, she picked up where she'd left off, seeing the publication of seven novels between 2003 and 2010.

Deborah and her husband, San Francisco bassist Nicholas Grabien, share a passion for rescuing cats and finding them homes, and are both active members of local feral cat rescue organisations. Deborah has a grown daughter, Joanna, who lives in LA.

These days, in between cat rescues and cookery, Deborah can generally be found listening to music, playing music on one of eleven guitars, hanging out with her musician friends, or writing fiction that deals with music, insofar as multiple sclerosis—she was diagnosed in 2002—will allow.

Visit her website at www.deborahgrabien.com

Manufactured By:     RR Donnelley
                     Momence, IL  USA
                     July , 2010